D0514063

Against the Tide

THERESA TOMLINSON

Against the Tide

CORGI BOOKS

AGAINST THE TIDE
A CORGI BOOK 0 552 55279 8

Beneath Burning Mountain first published in Great Britain by Red Fox 2001
The Flither Pickers first published in Great Britain by the Littlewood Press 1987;
Walker Books edition 1992
The Herring Girls first published in Great Britain by Julia MacRae 1994;
Red Fox edition 1996

This collection first published by Corgi 2005

Copyright © Theresa Tomlinson, 2001, 1987, 1994, 2005

1 3 5 7 9 10 8 6 4 2

Set in Caslon Old Face
Corgi Books are published by Random House Children's Books,
61–63 Uxbridge Road, London W5 5SA,
a division of The Random House Group Ltd,
in Australia by Random House Australia (Pty) Ltd,
20 Alfred Street, Milsons Point, Sydney, NSW 2061, Australia,
in New Zealand by Random House New Zealand Ltd,
18 Poland Road, Glenfield, Auckland 10, New Zealand,
and in South Africa by Random House (Pty) Ltd,
Endulini, 5A Jubilee Road, Parktown 2193, South Africa.

THE RANDOM HOUSE GROUP Limited Reg. No. 954009
www.kidsatrandomhouse.co.uk

A CIP catalogue record for this book is available from the British Library.

Printed and bound in Great Britain by
Cox & Wyman Ltd, Reading, Berkshire

CONTENTS

Part One: *Beneath Burning Mountain*　　　1

Part Two: *The Flither Pickers*　　　159

Part Three: *The Herring Girls*　　　251

PART ONE

Beneath Burning Mountain

For Tom

Chapter One

FISH-FACES

The fifth of July was a hot afternoon. I crouched down beside the bushes of plump bilberries, picking steadily while my fingers grew sticky. I stopped every now and then to lick up the sweet juice, but still my apron gathered new stains of deep red and purple. The waves lapped gently far below us, making me sleepy, while my brother and sister lolled in the springy heather, just creeping into flower.

'Get picking . . . yer lazy beggars!' I grumbled. 'This is my birthday and it's supposed to be my day off, not yours!'

They both ignored me — they always ignored me. Joseph, who's the oldest, lay there scratching his fleabites while he chewed a tough stem of grass. I didn't really

3

mind him so much, for I knew how he hated his stinking job, going round with the mule, picking up jugs of urine from folks' doorsteps and fetching it back to the alum works in barrels on the beast's back. A day away from that was bliss for him. Polly and me were grateful for a day away from helping Mam with her spinning, scouring and cooking. We were usually sent seaweed gathering in the afternoon.

Polly, who's our youngest, simply gazed out over the sea, gently wafting flies away from her face. 'One of these days,' she muttered, looking far down onto the little dock cut into the rocky shore, beneath the alum works, 'one of these days I'm going to sail away from here and never come back again.'

I stopped picking and sighed, rubbing my back and looking northwards towards the fine house that stood on the cliff edge. 'I'd never want to sail away from Burning Mountain,' I told them. 'But I'd like to live at Whingate Hall instead of Alum Row, and I'd like to wear fine clothes, instead o' patches.'

The both exploded with laughter.

'Lady Nan!' Polly teased.

'Some chance of that!' said Joseph.

I returned to my picking. It wasn't fair – they always left the hard work to me. 'I'm telling Mam,' I complained. 'You've done nowt to help . . . neither of you.'

'Stop bleating Nanny Goat!' said Polly.

I gave up then and ignored them. My name is Anne and I don't mind being called Nan, but I hate it when they call me Nanny Goat. My shoulders ached from the picking, but I'd nearly filled our second best pudding basin. It would be all right, I told myself. Mam had promised me a honeyed bilberry pudding for my birthday supper, and she would know who'd done all the work; she only had to glance at the bright stains on my hands and clothes.

'Come on,' I told them at last. 'We're going back, there's still Mam's tea leaves to fetch.'

'Come on then, Lady Nan,' Joseph got up from the heather. 'Take my arm and I'll lead thee down to Whingate Hall.'

I didn't take his arm, I slapped him hard instead, but all he did was laugh.

Sir Rupert the Alum Master lived at Whingate Hall. He owned Burning Mountain where we worked and lived, as he owned all the land and sheep around us. But even though he was so very rich, he did not own the secret of alum making, and needed folk like my father and his brother Robert who'd been brought up knowing the mysteries of the work.

Whingate Hall was a beautiful stone built house with a fine south-facing walled garden. We strode through the heather towards it, but as we drew near we had to take the side path that led round to the kitchen door. None of the alum workers would ever dare to go knocking on the front door, but we were regular visitors to the back. Dame Bunting, the sharp-witted cook, did a nice bit of business selling used tea leaves. They were dried on the stove and sold on to us for a few pence.

As we walked around the side of the house we heard lovely music and turned to look at the ballroom windows. The place blazed with lights, even though it was only mid-afternoon, and we could see young ladies in bright new gowns, dancing with fashionably dressed young men. I couldn't help but stand and stare; it looked so beautiful in there.

'Get on Lady Nanny Goat,' said Polly grabbing my arm. 'No dancing for thee.'

'Mam says have yer got a twist o' tea leaves?' I asked politely when Dame Bunting opened the back kitchen door to us.

'I have that Miss Purple-Fingers,' she said. 'Just bide there while I fetch them, and don't touch anything. I'd have thought you'd all be working so early in t'afternoon.'

'It's Nanny Goat's birthday,' Polly told her mercilessly. 'So Mam's given us the afternoon off.'

'Bless thee lass,' said Dame Bunting pressing a small packet of tea into my hand. 'There's another fine birthday party going on *here* – Sir Rupert's youngest daughter, she's thirteen today.'

'Exactly the same as me,' I cried.

We left Whingate and set off home to Burning Mountain; I'd tea leaves in one hand and the bowl of berries in the other, but I couldn't help glancing back at the ballroom windows with longing. Then, as I turned round at last, something sharp shot through the air and caught me a stinging blow on the cheek. I gasped with shock and staggered, catching sight of an arm lashing fast as a whip, shaking the bushes down below us on the sloping cliff-side.

'Stones! Duck down!' Joseph shouted.

We ducked. Hoots of laughter came from the bushes, then a second stone grazed my hand. Mam's pudding bowl slipped from my grasp and crashed down at my feet. Joseph and Polly rose up from the grass, furious now.

'Damned Fish-faces!' Polly snarled. 'I bet it's them.'

I still clutched the tea leaves, though my wounded hand throbbed and a wave of sickness lurched up through my belly. Mam's bowl had broken into three pieces, spilling the precious berries everywhere.

'Stinking Fish-faces!' Joseph yelled as three big lads from Sandwick Bay shot up from the bushes, laughing fit to bust.

It was just too much; I couldn't keep back tears. Joseph shouted and waved his fist, but it was Polly who snatched up stones from the ground and marched fearlessly towards them. They smirked when they saw her coming, but as she went determinedly on, they began to back off. She pelted them, then bent to snatch up more.

'I'll show tha . . . I'll show tha,' she bellowed. 'We know yer Tommy Welford and we know yer mam.'

The lads turned and walked away whistling as though they were simply out for a pleasant stroll. But they kept on going, moving away from us, skidding a little as they went back down the steep cliff-side towards Sandwick Bay, their tiny fishing village that clung to the cliffs north-west of the alum works.

Our Polly still followed them, screaming abuse at the top of her voice till Tommy Welford turned and stood his ground for a moment. 'Raggy Piss-pourers!' he shouted, then he made a rude sign and ran to catch up with his mates.

'Tha's no right calling us names,' Polly howled. 'Yer mam leaves a jug of piss out on your doorstep each morning. You want yer penny don't yer? Piss-sellers you are!'

She came back to us, red faced and angry. We three stood looking down at the broken bowl and spilled berries, mashed into the rocky ground.

'Best pick it up,' said Joseph. 'Mam might be able to fix it with a bit o' fishbone glue.'

I bent to gather the pieces, swallowing hard. I scraped together some of the berries but it was hopeless, the soft fruit was squashed and caked with dirt. All my hard work for nothing.

'Well,' Polly spoke with disgust, folding her arms. 'No birthday supper for thee, Nanny Goat.'

We marched eastwards through sprawls of golden-flowered, sweet-smelling gorse that we call whins, then set off downhill, skirting the quarry that's cut from the cliff-side in the shape of a crescent moon. At mid-afternoon it was full of pick-men busy cutting and shovelling up the grey alum shale. We walked past three burning clamps that stood like giant charcoal stacks, forty feet high on a bit of level ground close by, so that the workers didn't have too far to go with their barrows. The barrow-men ran back and forth, feeding the smallest smoking clamp with oily fresh-mined alum shale, that turned dark red as it began to burn. The great piles burned away for three months at a time while clouds of sulphurous smoke rose from the top of the heaps, giving the place its name – Burning Mountain. We all believed that it was the foulness in that smoke that constantly turned our clothes to rags, so that our mothers sat by the fireside patching every night and we were known for our rag-tag clothes.

Chapter Two

RUN LIKE THE WIND

Heavy with disappointment we continued our way down, treading carefully around the edge of the shallow steeping-pits where burnt shale lay soaking, turning the water red; it wouldn't do to go slithering into that. We went on, skidding down the cliff-side again, alongside the wooden channel that carried the steeped alum liquor downhill to the works. We passed more flowering whins and the manager's house standing at the head of Alum Row.

As the smell of stale urine grew, Polly pulled a face and wrinkled her nose. 'No wonder they call us foul names,' she complained.

'The less yer fuss, the less it bothers yer,' I told her. 'Well that's what Father says, anyway.'

'Not true!' she replied. 'Not when you've been away up there, breathing decent air for a while.'

The smell was strongest by the warehouse, where large barrels of urine were kept; the staler it was, the better it worked. The stinking stuff would be poured into the boiled alum liquor and then boiled again to make the precious crystals form. Those crystals would fix dyes and soften leather so that woollen mills and tanneries paid good prices for them. Mam often complained that the money rarely reached the workers, but despite the terrible smells she insisted that it was a healthy place to live. 'Perched up here like eagles on the cliffs,' she'd say. Though we hated the sulphurous smoke that rose from the clamps and drifted down on to our cottages, fisher-wives from Sandwick Bay would bring their coughing children up to breathe the fumes. 'That smoke kills everything,' Mam said. 'It even kills whooping cough!'

Thomas Langtoft, our father, had the important job of watching the boiling pans and judging when the urine should be added. Father's skills were greatly respected even by the manager. His brother, Uncle Robert, had been invited to do the same job at Peak so that he and Aunt Margaret, who had no children and fussed us as though we were their own, had had to go over to Ravenscar to live. We missed them very much.

Our cottage on Alum Row was small, built on a wide cliff ledge above the ship dock and the cold North Sea. Us lasses longed for a cosy cottage like the ones by Sandsend Beck, all sheltered by Mulgrave Woods.

I stopped for a moment, looking back towards the smoking clamps above us. 'What a place to live!' I sighed. 'No wonder they call it Burning Mountain! No wonder they say that we're cursed!'

I'd feared Mam's anger when she saw the smashed bowl, but I needn't have worried about that. As we neared Alum Row we saw that something was wrong – something much worse than broken pots. There were no cries or shouting, but the coopers, the housemen, and the liquormen all started to run out of the work sheds and scramble up the steep cliff-side. The hens squawked and goats scattered in all directions as workers rushed through them like the wind.

Joseph grabbed both us lasses by the arm. 'What is it?' he whispered.

The three of us watched open-mouthed as women hurried from their cottages in quiet panic, waving their arms and signalling to each other. I saw Father tear out of the boiler house and kiss Mam; then he climbed a little way up the steep bank. As we watched, he dived into one of the brick-built culverts which protect the channel that carries the alum liquor. Even Mr Douthwaite the manager ran out of the counting house and followed Father into the dark tunnel-like culvert.

Still nobody shouted or called and the strange quietness made me feel even more scared than if they'd been screaming at each other. Mam turned and saw us. She beckoned wildly and we started running down the path to meet her.

'What is it, Mam?' Polly gasped, her voice shaking.

Mam hushed us, putting her finger to her lips, then took my arm. 'Come and see,' she whispered. She pulled me along with her, the other two following fast, heading for the ledge that overlooked the sloping cliffs to the east. We looked where she pointed and saw a great gang of burly men swarming over the rocks towards our small ship dock, pistols and cudgels in their hands.

Joseph pulled me sharply back from the edge. 'The press-gang!' he hissed.

'Aye,' Mam whispered. 'Lyddy Welford told me they'd set themselves up in Grape Lane in Whitby. They've taken over that public house we call "The Grapes" and they call it their rendezvous. Lyddy says there's a big ship and tender on the sea roads, hovering there out of sight, ready to take the men they capture down to the Thames.'

A sudden rush of sickness lurched again, deep inside my stomach. The press-gang were more feared up on our cold stretch of coastline than constables or even pirates. Last time they'd come our way they'd carried Bess Tippet's dad off and her older brother too, taking them away to man the king's ships. Bess's family had never seen their menfolk again since the day the press-gang came. They'd had a terrible struggle to survive without them.

'What can we do?' I cried, really frightened now. I couldn't bear to have my father taken.

Mam shook her head, looking lost and scared herself. We followed her back towards the cottages and just as we got there our old neighbour Annie Knaggs stumbled out from her doorway dragging a heavy spade.

'Eeeh Annie – what're y' doing wi' that?' Mam asked.

Annie hauled the spade up on to her shoulder. 'I'll give 'em a good thumping with it,' she said. 'I'll thump 'em hard if they come near any o' my lads!'

I didn't know whether to laugh or cry but Annie seemed to make Mam's mind up. 'Ey Annie – tha's got the right idea!' she said, suddenly brave again. She rushed into our shack and snatched up her broomstick. 'Nay!' she cried, 'not that,' flinging it on to the floor. Then she went to lift down from its nail, the sharp hand-scythe that Father used for cutting brushwood. 'That's better!'

'What're yer going to do?' Joseph asked.

'Whatever we can,' Mam was steely-eyed now. Then suddenly she looked thoughtful. 'But I doubt it's our men they're really after,' she said. 'Our men know little o' seafaring ways!'

'Sandwick!' Joseph understood what she meant. 'They're after the Sandwick men.'

Polly was still angry with our attackers. 'Smelly Fish-faces!' she cried.

We all knew that since the fighting with France had started up again, the press-gang were not too fussy who they took, but fishermen were a real prize for them; that way they'd get men already skilled with boats and weather

14

and sailing winds. The press-gang would make a lot of effort to get a fisherman.

Polly folded her arms. 'Tommy Welford and his mates have stoned our Nan and smashed our bowl. Let the press-gang take 'em smelly Fish-faces – take the lot!'

Mam looked puzzled for a moment. Then she saw the shards of pot that I still clasped in my hands. 'They stoned y' Nan?'

I nodded miserably. 'Aye. That big lad, Tommy, Lyddy's boy.'

Mam was not deterred. 'I'll speak to his mam about that I promise I will, but would you want his father carted off, taken away and never seen again? Would you want that?'

I hesitated, my cheek and hand still stinging.

'Nay,' said Joseph firmly. 'I'd not want that.'

'Then run like the wind and warn 'em,' said Mam. 'Go to, Lyddy – tell her we'll hold the gang up as best we can – and you must keep out of sight, our Joseph!'

'What!' I cried. 'They'd not take Joseph! Haven't they got t' be eighteen?'

'They've taken lads before,' Mam insisted. 'They just have to look eighteen . . .' She shrugged her shoulders. 'Now get on your way, all three of yer. One go to Top Green, one to Bottom Green, one to the staithe. Tell any-one – everyone! The first person you see.'

We stared for a moment, miserable at the thought that we must run back almost the way we'd come and further still, but then Joseph snatched my hand and we were off,

15

scrambling along the bankside towards Sandwick Bay.

Polly stumbled after us, still resentful. 'And they called us Piss-pourers!' she growled.

We knew the winding pathway well, but I don't think we'd ever covered the ground so fast. I caught my foot in a rut, but pulled it out and staggered on while sharp stinging gorse prickles slashed my legs. Though I still smarted from the stoning that afternoon, a sense of urgency grew with every step. They didn't deserve us helping them like this – well, Tommy Welford didn't, but Joseph was right; I'd hate to see his father carried off. There'd been many times when the Alum Master had not paid his workers properly and only a good parcel of Sandwick Bay herrings had saved us from hunger.

'Look!' Polly shouted, pointing back to Burning Mountain.

Joseph and I stopped and looked behind. The gang of men had reached our small dock and turned away from the sea, scrambling up towards Alum Row.

'They *are* looking for our men,' I whispered.

'Aye,' said Joseph smiling. 'But see what greets 'em.'

Then I saw what he meant. The rocky ledge that juts out beneath our homes was covered with women waving what looked like weapons but we knew must be spades, scythes, hoes and rakes.

As we watched the numbers grew.

Joseph laughed. 'They're not going to get past that lot easy!'

'No,' I agreed. 'But come on! We've got no time t' waste!'

Joseph ran ahead but then suddenly skidded to a halt, pointing wildly out to sea. I couldn't understand what was wrong for a moment; then I saw what it was that bothered him. As the light began to fade and the sun sank down over the cliffs, there appeared on the seaward horizon a line of small black dots.

I grabbed Polly's arm and pointed. 'The fishing boats,' I cried.

As we stared at them the dots grew bigger, heading fast towards the staithe at Sandwick Bay.

'Coming back with the tide!' Polly said. 'They won't know! We're too late!'

'No,' Joseph cried, breaking into a run again. 'We've got to get there.'

'Run faster,' I gasped at Polly. 'Mam said run like the wind.'

Chapter Three

THE FIRST PERSON YOU SEE

We did run fast, faster than I had ever thought possible. My ankle ached and my throat hurt, but we were determined to get there and we did. Joseph went scrambling up the bank to Top Green, while Polly headed for the staithe. I hobbled up the dirt track that led to Bottom Green.

The first person you see? Mam's words echoed through my head, but all I could see were sleeping cats and a braying tied-up donkey. Then a door opened and Tommy Welford came out dragging an old fishing net behind him. He didn't even notice me, but sat down on his doorstep spreading the net out beside him, looking for holes.

'Oh no . . . it would be him!' I whispered. I drew breath and screamed at him. 'Where's your mam?'

He leapt to his feet, mouth wide open, shocked at seeing me there, of all people.

'I never meant no harm,' he cried. 'It were nowt but larking, lass – just a lark!'

'Nay!' I gasped, finding it hard to get my breath and speak clear. 'Not that! Not that! It's the press-gang. Press-gang coming – tell your mam.'

He stared horrified for just one unbelieving moment, then he vanished inside the cottage, yelling for his mam.

I sat down on the Welfords' doorstep, gasping and rubbing my ankle. My side hurt too now, all of me hurt. But I heard the small tinny sound of a pan being beaten with a spoon, up at the top of the steep hill. Then Lyddy Welford threw open her upstairs window above me, leaning out, banging her kettle with an iron ladle. 'Press-gang! Press-gang!' she screamed.

Quickly she was answered by more clanging, followed by the thudding beat of a drum. The noise grew, windows and doors flew open, until at last a deafening row came from all around.

Tommy dashed past me banging wildly on an iron skillet, carrying the alarm down to the seafront and the little landing staithe. I picked myself up and followed him. The women flooded out of their houses, hammering for all they were worth on kettles, buckets, pans and drums, screaming and howling at the tops of their voices. 'Press-gang! Press-gang! Turn about – turn about!'

The noise they raised was deafening, but we all stared anxiously out to sea. We made a huge row but we didn't know if it would be loud enough to carry warning over the grey rolling waves? The noise subsided while everyone watched, the low sun warm on our backs.

'They're still coming,' said Tommy, a small uncertain catch in his voice.

'Try again!' his mother insisted, and once more the terrible din was raised. It came from the attics, the hilltop, the staithe below, and the banging of drums thundered across the sea. Then suddenly the boats seemed to have slowed their shoreward progress and were coming about.

A great cheer rang out as we saw the boats turning against the tide. The boat-skills of the fishermen were great, no wonder the press-gang wanted them so much. Our warning had clearly been heard and understood.

'Right,' Lyddy cried. 'Now – lads, get thissens up into the woods!'

Everyone headed back up the hill. The boys who'd been too young to be out on the sea with their dads were sent up the bankside, towards the ravine and the thick green shelter of the woods. Baskets with bread and a bit of smoked fish were pushed into their hands, warm jerkins shoved beneath their arms. They'd have to stay out all night to be safe.

When at last the sounds of running feet had died away, Lyddy Welford came and hugged me tight. 'Bless y' honey, for yer warning,' she cried. Her cheeks were pink, her eyes full of tears.

Then she held me gently away, looking carefully at my

face. 'Tha's fair done in. Come inside and sit thissen down, I can see tha's limping! I've a pan o' good fish head stew still bubbling on my fire. Take a sup with me and rest that foot; the press-gang be damned!'

I was glad enough to do as she said, so I hobbled after her and sat down by her fire. I was soon given a bowl of steaming stew and I'd just raised the spoon to my mouth when Polly came knocking on the Welfords' door.

'You're here,' she snapped. 'I can't find Joseph anywhere.'

'Well,' said Lyddy, 'if he's any sense he'll keep well away all through t' night, then creep back over the cliff tops. Here lass, settle down and have a sup, like yer sister.'

Polly didn't need telling twice. I whispered to her under my breath, 'I see tha's not so high and mighty that yer refuse Fish-face's food.'

Polly shrugged her shoulders and smacked her lips. 'Shut tha mouth, Nanny Goat! I'm starving and it smells so good!'

Again we settled to eat, but the cottage door banged open wide and Tommy followed by Joseph rushed inside.

Lyddy flew up from her seat. 'Still here? Why the devil aren't yer up there in t' woods?' she demanded.

'Too late!' Tommy cried. 'They're here, swarming all over the village. We'll have to use our hole!'

'Aye! It's the only thing,' his mother agreed, calmer now. She slammed her own bowl down on the table and flung open the cupboard doors beneath the dresser.

Tommy began hauling out roughly strewn fishing nets and old battered baskets, dumping them down on the cottage floor. The dresser was made of solid oak and built into the wall. Tommy reached in at the back and pulled out a light wooden panel that he handed to his mam.

'Tha's seen nowt o' this!' she spoke fiercely to us.

'No nowt,' we hurried to reassure her. We were awed and silent, knowing that we were being trusted with a big secret. Though everyone knew that most of the fishing families did a bit of smuggling on the side, as did the alum workers, we'd never seen proof before. We never asked about secret hiding places, so the knowledge of how it was done was kept very quiet.

Tommy dived into the bottom of the cupboard and vanished from view.

'Yer must get in too, Joseph,' Lyddy Welford insisted. 'Yer mam'd not forgive me if they took you instead o' our lad!'

Joseph hesitated, but the sounds of banging and shouting out in the narrow yard made him duck his head and scramble quickly into the small dark space after Tommy.

Lyddy Welford pushed the loose panel firmly back into place so that it looked just like the solid back of the cupboard, then we all stooped down with shaking hands to pile the old fishing nets and baskets back in.

A loud crash close by told us that the press-gang had reached the cottage next door.

'What can we do?' I whimpered.

'Sit down and eat as though nowt be wrong!' Lyddy told us.

Chapter Four

NOWT BUT LASSES!

So though we shook with fear, we did as she said. No sooner had we raised our spoons once more than the cottage door was thrust open and two big men swinging cudgels burst in. One of them grabbed me by the shoulders, staring closely at my face. He stank of ale and tobacco and roughly shoved my bonnet back.

'Wench!' he snarled, disappointed.

The other snatched hold of Polly and pulled up her skirt.

Polly's clog came up sharply and kicked his shin. 'I mightn't be a lad, but I'll fight like one,' she growled.

'Damned bitch!' the man groaned, lifting his hand to slap her.

'I'd not do that if I were thee!' Lyddy Welford cried,

taking up the kettle of boiling water from her fire. 'There's nowt but lasses here, so be on yer way!' She was a big angry woman, with powerful arm muscles and she looked as though she'd use that kettle if she had to. I knew that most of the village lads had felt her hand on their ear at one time or another.

The men hesitated for a moment, glaring peevishly around the room. They pushed the settle aside and pulled open the cupboard doors. One of them dragged out an old basket and flung it on the floor. 'Rubbish!' he muttered.

'Nowt in *this* place is rubbish,' Lyddy growled.

The bigger man looked as though he'd a mind to tip the settle right over, but he glanced back at Lyddy again and seemed to change his mind.

'Come on,' said one. 'There's nowt for us here. I want m' dinner. They'll have brought the carts to t' bank-top by now. I'm off back t' rendezvous.'

The other fellow was not so willing to leave, he moved towards the table still rubbing his shin where Polly had kicked him. 'There's some dinner here for thee,' he grinned nastily.

Lyddy put down the kettle and snatched up one of the bowls of stew instead. 'Yer can have it on yer head!' she promised. 'Tha'll not have it in tha belly!'

'Bitches!' the big man spat out, but he backed away towards the door. He could see that nothing would be gained easily. He lashed out with his cudgel and knocked a flower-painted pot from the dresser, so that it smashed on to the floor. Then suddenly they'd gone, and all was quiet. Polly and I sank down on to the wooden settle, hugging each other tightly with relief.

'Damn them, that was my best bit o' china,' said Lyddy. 'Never mind . . . it's nowt to the thought o' losing my Francis or Tommy. That's my brave lasses,' she praised us warmly. 'Tha's both done very well with that.'

'Can't stop shaking,' I gulped.

'A good meal is what's needed, though we've been at a deal o' trouble to get it. Sit down again and I'll ladle out some fresh hot stew.'

She brought steaming bowls to us and scraped the cold food back into her pot. This time we did manage to eat our fill, and the rich fishy gravy warmed and cheered us.

'Mam, Mam,' Tommy called from the cupboard, his voice faint. 'Let us out now? We're cramped an' hungry.'

Lyddy winked at us. 'Just a moment or two, my lads. Just a moment more to make sure those damned fellows've gone right away.'

As soon as it was really dark, with the oil lamp lit and shutters closed, Lyddy let the lads out of their hidey-hole and gave them their supper. They came out grumbling and groaning at their cramped muscles and empty bellies.

'Yer must all stay here till morning,' Lyddy said. 'And don't step outside this door; I don't trust those fellows, not one bit.'

'This bread is dry and the stew's cold,' Tommy complained.

'Better than what your father'll get!' his mother told him sharply.

Tommy hung his head then, understanding that his father and the other fishermen would be out at sea all night, with nothing to eat or drink to warm them. 'Aye,' he nodded.

'Must they stay out all night?' I asked.

Lyddy nodded. 'If they want to be safe they will, and they'll be desperate tired and cold by morning, wi' their catch o' fish starting to waste. Still, better than being carried off by that lot. Now then, you two lasses'd best come and sleep in my big bed wi' me. Joseph, I'll set a mattress down here, so yer can sleep wi' Tommy beside the fire.'

I was expecting Polly to fuss, but she didn't. We stripped down to our petticoats and fell into the Welfords' lumpy bed with relief.

'What a day,' I whispered. 'M' birthday too!' It seemed ages since we were picking bilberries, though my fingers still carried purple stains. I gently touched my cheek where it still smarted from the stone.

'Get to sleep,' murmured Polly. We both slept as though we'd never wake again.

Lyddy had us all up and the shutters open as soon as the first rays of light showed in the east. She made us porridge and while we were eating it she crept out into the quiet streets.

Tommy kept looking at me while I ate, making me feel a bit fussed.

'What's up with thee?' Polly snapped at him. 'Stop staring at our Nan like that!'

Tommy put out his hand and I saw that it shook. He touched my sore cheek awkwardly, but very gently. 'Did I do that?'

'You did,' I nodded.

'And yer called us bad names,' Polly insisted.

He went red in the face and looked down at his bowl for a moment, but then spoke up firmly. 'I'm sorry,' he said. 'It were . . . ignorant, ignorant o' me.'

I looked at him doubtfully, wondering if this was another of his larks, but he turned away still blushing and I saw that perhaps he did really mean it.

'I promise yer this, Nan Langtoft,' he said, his voice low. 'I'll never do ought like it again.'

'Not to anyone?' I asked quietly.

He looked surprised for a moment. Then he answered me. 'Not to anyone.'

All four of us ate on in silence, then suddenly Tommy lent across and kissed my sore cheek. Both Joseph and Polly exploded with laughter. I must have blushed beetroot red then, for I know I went all hot and couldn't think what to do or say.

Just then Lyddy came back in through the door. 'Well, I'm glad you bairns can still laugh after the night we've had. It all seems quiet out there and I see the boats coming back.'

'Will they be safe now?' I asked.

'Aye. We must pray so, lass, and we must see that thee

28

and tha brother and sister get home safely to Burning
Mountain. Tommy! Walk over the sands wi' them, and
make sure that all is well.'

'Aye,' Tommy gave a quick nod.

Chapter Five

BEHIND STARHOLE ROCKS

We set off from Sandwick Bay, walking eastwards along the sands, sparkling waves lapping beside us, the sun warm on our faces. It was a beautiful fresh morning and we could see the fishing boats coming back. The two lads walked in front of us lasses, talking and kicking pebbles, they seemed to be thinking much more kindly of one another since they'd had their frightening wait together, cooped up in the back of the Welfords' cupboard.

Polly kept digging me in the ribs with her elbow. 'He's sweet on thee,' she whispered, nodding at Tommy.

'Hush tha mouth!' I told her. 'He wasn't sweet on me yesterday morning.'

The sand was smooth and fresh where the tide had washed it, but as we wandered on I suddenly saw something that turned me ice cold. A patch of sand ahead of us, close to Starhole Rocks, was patterned with deep footprints. I stopped, trembling as I stood there. I couldn't take another step.

'What is it?' Polly asked.

I nodded my head in the direction of the rocks. 'Footprints,' I hissed. 'Masses of them, coming down from the bankside.'

Polly looked and saw what I meant. Then even worse, I noticed a pair of large booted feet, sticking out from behind Starhole Rocks. Somebody was hiding there and beside them on the sand lay a stack of cudgels and a pair of pistols.

'Joseph!' I called, my voice low and shaking.

He turned and must have seen the fear in my face. 'Summat up!' he told Tommy. They both came back to us fast.

'The gang,' I whispered. 'Behind Starhole Rocks.'

Both lads looked for themselves, and saw what I had seen. Then while we stood in stunned silence, we heard the murmur of voices and a low laugh.

'Waiting for the fleet!' Tommy gulped. 'I must go back! You go on home! They'll not follow yer if they think they can get our men!'

He turned at once and ran back to Sandwick Bay. We three stared at each other for a moment, unsure what to do, then we set off after him, tearing along the beach once more, towards the returning boats. Suddenly all pretence of hiding was done. The press-gang realised what we were up to and came after us, like dogs after a rabbit, cursing and swearing for all they were worth.

Tommy reached the staithe ahead of us and stood there waving his arms frantically, 'Turn about! Turn about!'

We joined him pointing and screaming so that they looked and saw the press-gang streaming after us. The boats were so near that we could see the weariness in the men's faces, but they quickly understood our frantic signals and turned about. One of the fishermen struggled to the stern and looked as though he'd jump out and wade towards us, but his friends dragged him back. I knew then that the man was Francis Welford, Tommy's dad, and my heart sank as I heard the howls of rage behind us. The press-gang, furious that we'd given warning, had snatched Tommy and our Joseph instead of the men that they were really after.

'Damned brats!' they bellowed. 'We'll take thee instead of thy fathers!'

I screamed, 'Yer cannot take them, they're nobbut lads.'

'Big lads these! They look eighteen to us! They'll do for now!' the angry men growled.

'Give him back! Give him back!' Polly shrieked and grabbed Joseph's arm. 'He's only fourteen.'

One of the men swung round and slapped her face hard, grinning with satisfaction. He was the man that she'd kicked yesterday, and it was clear that he'd been longing to do that ever since. 'Oh he'll enjoy his life as a cabin boy, missy! Tha'll not know him when he comes back to thee! If ever, that is!'

Polly fell with a thud amongst the shingle and I crouched down at her side, trying to protect her from the trampling feet. When I glanced up again I saw that the men were forcing open Tommy's tight closed fist. He resisted for all he was worth, but they were so much stronger than him and at last they pressed a dirty shilling coin into his palm.

'Done!' they cried. 'Taken the king's shilling! That's one impressed. Now the other.'

Joseph was given the same treatment and the two boys were hauled off up the bank, jolted and shoved at every step. The commotion brought the old men and fishwives, shocked and bewildered, out from their cottages. When they saw what was happening they began to protest fiercely, but the press-gang were determined that they should take somebody back with them. Anyone who interfered received a swift swing of a cudgel. The boys were dragged off up the hill, followed by angry women hurling abuse at them. Though I wanted to go too, I knew that I must see Polly safe.

She lay there on the pebbles, white-faced, her mouth bleeding and swelling fast, so I went to the fresh water where the beck trickled into the sea and dipped my stained apron into the cleanest part. When I returned to her, Polly was struggling to get up.

'Oh, Nan,' she whispered. 'Have they got our brother?'

'Aye,' I murmured. 'They have.'

*

The Sandwick women found us huddled together on the staithe, when they came back down the hill. Their voices were hushed and gentle now, though their faces were white, shocked at what had happened. Lyddy Welford took us both by the hand and insisted that we go back to her cottage. She made us sit down and have a sip of warm ale with herbs in it. Other women followed after us, crowding into her small home-place.

'Wh . . . what should we do?' I asked.

For once Lyddy had no answer. She shook her head and stroked Polly's hair. I saw that the knuckles on her big strong hand were bruised and the skin torn. One of the press-gang had certainly felt her fist and I was glad at least of that.

We sat there for a while still stunned, the women full of sighs and angry muttering, then at last Lyddy got up. 'I shall take these lasses back to Burning Mountain,' she said. 'Their mother must be told what's happened, and their father, too.' She sighed. 'I hate to do it, but I think I'd best do the telling.'

The women agreed reluctantly and began to wander back to their own homes, arms folded, faces grim.

It was a sad slow walk back home. We spoke little and I still hobbled, while Polly's cut face began to swell. All seemed calm at Burning Mountain; a few seaweed gatherers were down on the beach, for Father was working hard to find a way of using kelp instead of the hated urine, as we knew some other works did. Annie Knaggs was at her usual task burning the stuff in a small kiln, then she'd collect the ashes and carry them up to the works.

When we walked through our cottage door Mam stopped her spinning wheel and jumped up, rushing to hug us.

'What happened? Where've you been? I've been so fearful,' she cried. Then she looked properly at Polly's face. 'What's this?' she cried. 'I feared summat like this!'

We just shook our heads for we could not speak.

Chapter Six

LADY HILDA, HELP US!

When Lyddy followed us inside and stood awkwardly by the door Mam knew that there was something terribly wrong.

'Joseph?' she called, pushing past us to the doorway.

'Mary. I'm terribly sorry,' Lyddy whispered, catching her arm.

'No,' Mam whispered. 'Not my Joseph. They've not taken my lad?'

Lyddy nodded.

Mam was aghast. 'How could yer let them, Lyddy? When I sent my own bairns to give warning?'

Lyddy just stood there sorrowful and silent.

'T'wain't Lyddy's fault,' I whispered. 'She did all she

could t' look after us – and their Tommy's been taken along with our Joseph.'

'What? Tommy, too?'

'Aye,' Lyddy whispered. 'Tha's three brave children Mary,' she went on. 'Without their warning we'd ha' lost all our men. Because o' them none of our fellows is taken, they're all staying out in the sea roads.'

Mam went to Lyddy then full of shared sorrow, flinging her arms around the fisherwoman. They clung together, tears pouring down both their faces. Polly and me crept outside, leaving them be.

The news of the two lads' capture spread fast around the Alum Works. Father stopped his work and came home with many of the workers following him. Henry Knaggs, our neighbour, left his barrow and came down from the spoil heaps to see what was up. They gathered about our cottage door, their voices low with concern. Mr Douthwaite came to ask why work had stopped, and when he was told, even he turned away with no complaints and went quietly back to the counting house.

'They'll be keeping them in the back room at The Grapes,' said Henry. 'My grandmother lives close by and she can hear the poor fellows complaining and banging on the bars they've had put int' windows.'

'Aye,' Bart Little, the smith, agreed. 'They'll be there a day or two mebbe, then they row 'em out to the tender, and that's the last y' see of 'em . . . unless you're very lucky.'

Father looked sharply at the men, beginning to see what they meant. 'So there's a day or two before they carry them off to the Thames?'

'Maybe longer,' Henry told him. 'Depends how fast they can fill up their tender. I hear they're causing a deal o' havoc but I don't believe they're having much success. I'd swear that's why they took your lads, they're getting desperate.'

We were all quiet at the thought of the two boys locked up like that, but we knew that even worse would await them on a man o' war. If the fighting didn't get them, the fever most likely would.

Suddenly Father spoke up firmly. 'I'll go to Whitby. It cannot be right that they take lads o' fourteen.'

'Nay,' Lyddy whispered, 'they're nobbut bairns.'

Henry shook his head. 'All protections 're cancelled,' he told them. 'They're not worth the paper that they're written on. They're calling it an emergency, this threat from the fellow they call Napoleon Buonaparte, and even boatswains and harpooners can be taken off the whaling ships.'

'Tha'll not be going, Thomas,' Mam told Father, pointing a determined finger at him. 'They'd clap you straight into their back room along wi' the lads. No, I shall go instead.'

Father shook his head, looking thoughtful for a moment, then suddenly hopeful. 'That's it,' he cried. 'I shall go and offer myself in return for the two lads.'

'No you *will not*!' Mam bellowed, her upset turned to anger. 'That way I'd be sure to lose thee both.'

'Mary's right,' said Lyddy. 'You cannot do deals with those fellows, Thomas. They'd snap yer up as well as the lads. No, Mary is right enough, and if she goes, I'll go with her. We can put up as good an argument as thee, and at least they'll not want us for their ships.'

Though Father was unhappy about it Mam was determined. She got up early next morning and dressed herself with care. She put on her Sunday gown and bonnet, a spotless apron and her one pair of good boots that she'd polished till they shone. When we saw what she was about, Polly and I quietly started to dress ourselves in our Sunday clothes as well.

'What are you lasses up to?' Mam demanded, when she saw what we did.

'We're coming too,' I told her.

'You'll not,' she insisted. 'Father, tell these lasses they're not to follow me.'

'Nay, Father,' I insisted. 'Tell Mam that we must go, for what if ought should happen to her, who'll come back here and fetch help?'

Father looked bewildered for a moment.

'This is no holiday jaunt,' Mam told us.

'We know that,' said Polly. 'We're not bairns – neither Nan nor me.'

Father heaved a great sigh. 'There is something in what they say, Mary. Will you promise me this, my lasses, that you'll not set foot in that dreadful rendezvous place, but wait safely outside for your mother to come back out again?'

'Aye, we will,' we both agreed.

'Then Mary,' he said. 'I think that they're right. It's true what they say. They didn't act like bairns yesterday, did they? They may be a good help to thee.'

Mam sighed. 'Aye well, remember what you've promised. I cannot bear to have another of my bairns taken from me. Tha'd best come quickly then, for I've promised to meet Lyddy at Bank Top in time for the carrier's cart.

Going to Whitby in the carrier's cart would be a treat on any other day. We set off rattling along the rough coast road, past packhorses laden with seaweed and wagons full of fish. I turned about and saw in the distance behind us the tiny figures of the alum miners, running with heavy barrows from the quarry to the burning clamps, from the burning clamps to the steeping-pits. They looked like ants, running back and forth all over the cliff-face that was cut into terraces and round the bottom of the smoking clamps. I could see the piled-up shale turning red as it burnt and the men opening up one of the great piles that had finished burning, so that we could see its deep red heart torn apart. On any other day I'd be thrilled to be getting away from the stink and hard work, to breathe the fresh clean air of the moors.

Polly sitting beside me looked pale and determined, and I felt a touch of shame that I should be thinking of anything other than our Joseph. What would it have been like for him, to spend the night locked up in that place?

Then I thought of Tommy, and touched the place on my cheek. It was still sore, but I remembered the gentle kiss that had followed and knew that I didn't want Tommy taken away any more than our Joseph.

'All out!' the carrier cried, as we reached Lythe Bank.

Most of the passengers grumbled, but we got down obediently.

Polly stretched her back. 'That's better,' she smiled, but then she caught Mam's solemn face. 'Are you scared Mam?' she asked.

Mam looked as though tears might well up again, she couldn't speak, just shook her head.

'Aye lass,' Lyddy answered for them both. 'We're scared. But we're more scared that we'll fail to bring our lads back, than of ought that those villains might do to us.'

We set off walking down the hill, relieved to stretch our legs. All the carriers made their passengers get out and walk at that point, for many a laden cart had come to grief, so steep was the winding bank at Lythe. Once it was emptied, the man led the strong Cleveland Bays round to the back of the cart and fastened them up again. We could not help but slither a bit as we followed the carrier, walking beside the horses, using their weight as a brake. As we rounded the bend we caught our first glimpse of Whitby in the distance and the beautiful broad sweep of white sands that stretch from Sandsend to Whitby harbour.

'Not far now,' Polly said pointing ahead. 'I can see St Hilda's Abbey in the distance.'

'Lady Hilda help us!' Mam whispered.

'Amen to that,' Lyddy spoke with feeling and we all went quiet again.

Chapter Seven

DOWN GRAPE LANE

I always loved arriving in Whitby. We got out of the cart and walked along the harbour side, breathing in the strong smell of fish, enjoying the bustle and arguments over fish prices. I stared across the harbour up to the ancient abbey ruins that loomed above us now.

Beneath the Abbey Cliffs and church stood Henrietta Street with its gaping spaces where once fine houses had stood. They'd been lost in the terrible landslip that had carried many dwellings down into the harbour a few years ago. Along the north-east coast we had regular slips of land; we all lived with the fear of it, and mostly they were small, but just now and again it would happen quite suddenly and a large lump of cliff would go crashing down into the sea.

Lyddy and Mam looked at each other, suddenly uncertain now that they'd got there.

'What shall we do?' said Lyddy. 'Staring up at the abbey's no good. Shall we go straight to Grape Lane and demand they return our children or round to Frank's cousin, Hester's? She'll give us a bite to eat and a sup o' ale?'

'My stomach's heaving so I couldn't eat or drink. Best get it done wi',' said Mam, her voice shaky. 'I doubt the constable will interfere, I hear the gang have been taking whoever they want. Let's get it done.'

So then we turned about and walked off fast towards the bridge. The Grapes public house, that the press-gang called their rendezvous, had a reputation for dirt and rough behaviour. Men with cudgels and pistols stuck in their belts stood around outside, swigging back drink and smoking their pipes. Two open barrels were set up at the back of the bridge, and as we passed them the stench told us their purpose. This was the Whitby method of urine collection. People brought their chamber pots to empty into the barrels and they weren't always particular whether they spilled it or not.

Polly pinched her nose. 'That stuff'll probably be sent to Uncle Robert at Peak Works,' she said. 'Though Father told me they're beginning to use a lot o' kelp there instead.'

'See him,' I nudged her and nodded her head towards the rendezvous. 'He's the one who knocked yer down.'

'Let me near him!' Polly growled.

'I certainly won't!'

He was lounging against the wall and laughing; I remembered his foul breath in my face. I slowed my steps, fighting the urge to run. I knew that this was no adventure.

Mam turned round, her voice sharp and threatening. 'Right now, lasses, y'd better do as yer promised yer father. Stand over there by Maggie Megginson's fish stall and don't move from her side. Yer can see all who go in and out from there.'

My heart was thumping and a terrible urge to spew grew in my stomach. I was glad enough to go and stand beside the sturdy fishwife, out of the way. Mam and Lyddy gathered themselves together and marched quickly past the men's foul insults, up the steps and into the rendezvous.

I grabbed hold of Polly's hand. The fishwife turned to smile at us. 'Now then, lasses, Mary Langtoft's bairns from Burning Mountain, aren't tha?'

'Aye,' we nodded.

'What brings thee into Whitby Town? Can I sell thee a fresh codling or summat?'

We shook our heads. 'Mam has told us to bide here.'

'If that's all right with you, Maggie?' I added.

'Aye course it is,' Maggie laughed. 'Where is it Mary's gone?'

'She's gone with Lyddy Welford,' I told her. 'Into The Grapes.'

'Eeh now!' Maggie laughed. 'Whatever are they doing in there?'

'They've gone to see about our Joseph and Tommy Welford. They've been taken by the press-gang and they're only fourteen.'

Maggie's laughter fled. 'Eh lasses,' she whispered softly. 'I'm right sorry to hear that.' She frowned at the news and looked worried. 'Here!' she said, 'take these.' She pushed warm boiled crab claws into our hands for us to suck.

I don't think we had to wait very long, but the time seemed to drag. We sucked politely at our crab claws but the more I sucked the sicker I felt. Maggie sold her fish steadily. Respectable Quaker dames came and went, dressed in plain gowns with black scarves about their shoulders. I stared at them, they were so clean and though they'd clearly got money they didn't send their servants out to do the shopping. Farmer's wives with baskets full of vegetables cried their wares all about us. Each woman that came to Maggie's stall was told why we were waiting there.

'Poor bairns!'

'They never have! Fourteen years old – nobbut lads?'

Shocked whispers flew around and we were treated to many sympathetic glances.

'They'll have no hope of getting 'em out o' the rendezvous!' one woman muttered. 'Once they're locked up in that back room,' she shook her head. 'They've set up iron bars at the windows!'

'It's not right,' one customer declared. 'They'll be taking bairns in clouts next.'

Another woman who brought smoked herrings to the stall for Maggie to sell glanced furiously across the street to where the men lounged. 'They make our lives a misery,' she hissed.

'Aye, they do that right enough!' Maggie agreed.

'Our Samuel's hiding away back in t' yard, getting under my feet and making me nattered. He no sooner came back from Greenland and stepped off his whaling boat than the gang arrived and set up over there. Now I daren't let the lad out on t' street for fear they take him. At the slightest hint of trouble I make him shin up our chimney, so I can't get much of a fire going either!'

I looked about me then and saw that what she said was true. Whitby did seem rather quiet and those around were mainly women and old men. Where were all the boat-builders, fishermen and whalers that usually thronged the streets?

Maggie clicked her tongue in disapproval. 'Tha wouldn't mind so much if they'd treat 'em fair and give decent pay, but they say it's a living death on them stinking ships. It's more likely the sickness gets 'em than the fighting. They'd not stand for ought like this in France.'

The woman laughed. 'In France it's not the king they serve, it's folk like thee and me. Maybe they treat their sailor lads better now that their king may whistle for his head.'

'Oh I don't know as this Napoleon fellow's much

47

different to a king,' said Maggie more gently. 'At least our king's not wild wi' his money. They say he wain't eat sugar, and forbids it at court; all to help the poor slaves and stop the slavers getting rich on sugar cane.'

'Nay, don't believe it! He just wain't spend the money and he's going mad again! They've called those Willis doctors in I hear!'

But Maggie wouldn't have it. 'I'd rather have Farmer George for king than his son, I can tell y' that.'

'Eeh I'd gladly do away wi' both,' the woman replied. 'If I'd been there when they pulled that Bastille down, I'd have been first inside.'

The woman's face was very grim. A shiver ran down my back for I suddenly knew that she really meant what she said.

'Aye,' said Maggie suddenly thoughtful. 'True we've no Bastille, but we've got that place,' she nodded her head towards the press-gang's rendezvous.

All at once their conversation was interrupted by the sound of raised voices and shouting. Mam and Lyddy appeared. They were escorted roughly down the steps of the rendezvous and thrust towards the muddy gutter that ran down the middle of the street.

'Bide here by me!' Maggie hissed and caught my hand in hers. Then she turned to the kipper woman who she'd been talking to. 'If you clap eyes on Hester Welford, tell her that her cousin's wife's in a bit o' bother.'

'I'll go directly to fetch her,' the woman spoke low and at once set off down the street.

'My Mam!' Polly cried aloud in outrage, seeing our mother treated so disrespectfully.

Mam and Lyddy turned on their escort with clenched fists and loud complaints, but the press-gang's lieutenant strolled over towards them, leering. Suddenly pistols were drawn all about the two women and the lieutenant was growling at them in a low voice. We could not hear clearly, but there was mention of the constable and the stocks. I saw Lyddy take Mam by the arm and back away. The lieutenant roared with laughter, as did some of the other men, but many of the Whitby folk stopped their work and chatter, standing in grim silence watching. Even the traders paused in their selling, showing little mirth at the sight of two desperate mothers so roughly treated and insulted.

''Tis their sons the gang have taken,' Maggie whispered. 'Two lads barely fourteen.'

'Two lads!' low voices repeated it up and down the street.

Chapter Eight

SOMETHING'S GOING TO HAPPEN

At last Mam and Lyddy came over towards us dusting themselves down, red faced and angry. 'Oh Mam!' Polly cried, grabbing her arm. 'Have they hurt you? We've been so scared.'

'We've failed our bairns,' Mam's voice turned shaky, her hands trembling. 'That's what natters me most. They say it's up to us to prove our lads are under age, they'll not take our word for it.'

Lyddy was shaking too. 'They're threatening us all ways. If we make more fuss they'll fetch the constable and have us put in the stocks,' she said. 'They claim they've orders from t' Admiralty, all protections cancelled. How can we prove their ages if they'll not take their own mothers' word for it?'

'I believe they'll take sworn statement from a parish priest,' Maggie tried to help.

'Aye,' Mam agreed. 'But they'll have sent the lads off to the Thames before we can get that done.'

'Eech Lyddy, whatever are you up to?' A small woman in a fishing bonnet came shoving her way through the crowds towards us.

'Hester?' Lyddy flung her arms about her husband's cousin and, all talking at once, we tried to explain what had happened.

Hester looked worried. 'We mun get you out of here,' she told us. 'Comeback home wi' me. This here press-gang are more vicious and feared than any other that's come our way. All protections ignored they say, and they're even taking the lads off the whaling ships. Isn't that true, Maggie?'

'Aye, right enough,' Maggie agreed.

Mam's eyes flashed and her voice was firm and angry. 'It cannot be right that they take such young lads.'

'No, honey,' Maggie agreed. 'Whatever t' Admiralty says, I say it's wrong, and there's plenty round here would agree wi' me. But your Hester speaks true; there's nowt else thi can do now. Go and rest at her cottage, tha's both done in.'

Lyddy nodded her head, distressed, but seeing the sense in it.

Maggie bent forwards and touched her shoulder. 'This ain't the end Lyddy. There's many a whisper flying about these yards. Many a strong man cramped away in hidey-holes, desperate to burst out. Like a tinder box Whitby is, just wanting a match.'

Mam and Lyddy listened thoughtfully, a touch of hope seeming to creep back into their eyes.

'I speak truth,' Maggie nodded. 'Whitby's like to flare up and burst into flames. All due to them!' She spat furiously and dipped her head towards the men of the press-gang, who'd gathered together and were climbing into a cart.

We all went quiet then, staring at Maggie, wondering just what her words might mean.

Hester broke in. 'Come thy ways,' she told us firmly, so we nodded and followed her obediently up Kirkgate and into Welfords' yard.

'Y' mun stay the night, there's room in our attic,' Hester insisted.

Mam shook her head, wondering what to do. 'I can't go back without Joseph, but Thomas will be worried sick. I'm feared he'll come looking for us and get himself impressed too.'

'The carrier'll take a message,' Hester told her. 'Though he'll be setting off at noon and that can't be far away.'

'We can find him,' I offered. 'Me an' Polly.'

'Good lasses,' Hester nodded. 'It's a strange day I say, when lasses are safer on the streets than lads.'

Mam looked a little uncertain, but Lyddy put an arm round each of us. 'They'll be fine. Yer should've seen them yesterday,' she said. 'Ready to take on the press-gang single-handed they were.'

Lyddy's praise made me feel stronger, so when Mam nodded, I grabbed Polly and we rushed outside before she changed her mind.

We went fast up Kirkgate towards the White Horse and Griffin, for we knew that the carrier would be stabling his horse there. It was one of the main setting-off spots for coaches and carriers' carts, travelling in and out of Whitby.

'We've not got long,' I said, grabbing Polly and breaking into a run. The sun was high in the sky above us and we were just in time for the bell was ringing, warning passengers that the carrier was about to set off.

'Please tell Father that we're safe and staying here the night,' I cried as the cart rumbled out of the yard.

'I will, my lass, if I can get out of Whitby through this lot,' the carter shouted back to us.

It was only then that we really saw what he meant. We'd been so frantic to find our man that although we'd been pushing past people we'd not really noticed how many there were out on the streets now. The crowds usually built up a bit in the afternoon, but this gathering was different. The market traders were quiet for once, with few customers looking at their wares. Instead many women, both young and old, seemed to be milling around the rendezvous and the opening of Grape Lane. We could see the carter ahead of us, battling his way across the bridge. When people noticed him they moved aside, willing enough to let him through.

The uncomfortable feeling that I'd had as I'd listened to Maggie talking to her friends earlier came creeping back to me. 'Summat's going to happen,' I whispered.

'Aye,' Polly agreed, slipping her arm through mine and moving closer. 'Is it summat bad?'

'Don't know.'

I couldn't think why we both felt so scared, but then I realised that what was so strange was the quietness of the crowd. People were talking, but their voices were low, almost with church-like softness. A great deal of whispering and signing went on from window to doorway, from trader to shopkeeper and back again.

Then there was a stir in the crowd at the bridge-end and an old man climbed on to a stool, close to Maggie's stall. He was shaky in the legs and had to be helped up by Maggie but as he began to speak all heads turned towards him.

'It's William. Old William!' The whisper flew around. 'What's he up to?'

We pushed slowly forwards, trying to catch what the old man said. Polly kept tight hold of my hand.

We couldn't hear him clearly but even the whispering stopped while people struggled to hear. The man waved his fist and pointed down Grape Lane to the rendezvous. We pushed closer so that we too could see down the lane, as all heads turned to glare at two armed guards, standing on the steps of the timbered building. They glanced at each other in sudden alarm, then fled inside, closing the doors tight shut behind them.

Polly and I wriggled forwards again, straining our ears to hear.

'Look about thi,' William cried. 'What do y' see? Where are yer men? They live in hiding.'

There was much agreement, and cries of 'Aye! Aye, they do!'

'Skilled whaling men's been taken, harpooners and even youngsters! This gang has turned Whitby into a place of fear. We'll treat this rendezvous as the French did their Bastille!'

'Aye! Aye! We will!' Angry muttering rose.

'Now's the moment!' We heard Maggie's voice raised. 'Now, before they get back wi' their weapons and their victims. No more stolen Whitby lads I say!'

'No!' The quiet broke and roars of angry agreement came from all around. There was a sudden surge of movement down the lane as the furious crowd of old men and women rushed towards The Grapes Hotel, hurtling themselves at its door.

Chapter Nine

OUR OWN BASTILLE

As angry women streamed past us I was terrified and delighted both at once.

'Hooray!' Polly yelled, her face flushed, eager to join in now.

I hauled her back, fearful that she'd dash into the middle of the throng. 'No,' I told her. 'We ought t' go and fetch Mam!'

'It'll all be over and we'll miss it,' she cried. She was carried away by the wild determination about her now, and didn't seem to see the danger.

Great crashes and thuds reached us as the doors of the rendezvous were battered and thumped. The men left behind to guard the place broke the small glass panes and fired shots from the windows, so that the attackers were forced to turn and fight their way back up the lane. It went quieter then, and the women seemed to be struggling in all directions.

'Is it over?' I whispered.

Then shouts rang out behind us and all at once a second, more powerful wave of rebellion began. Suddenly the men were there, pouring out of the yards and alleyways. News of what was happening had flown through the town so that cooped-up seafarers joined their women folk, with anger in their hearts and home-made pikes in their hands. Strong men from whaling ships broke free from the misery of their cramped hidey-holes, pushing past us, joining the attack with gusto. I knew there'd be no stopping them. The doors were quickly broken open and the guards disarmed.

'T' prisoners – fetch 'em out!' the cry went up.

I didn't know whether to run for Mam or stay to see what happened.

'What about Joseph?' Polly wailed.

'Aye, we must find him,' I agreed, still unsure what to do for the best. But then we saw that people nearby were pointing upwards to the rooftops, and as we watched we saw young men and lads pop out of one of the chimneys, high above The Grapes Hotel. A trail of sooty fugitives went clambering and skidding across the rooftops, leaping fast from neighbouring house to house, down towards the farthest end of the lane that would lead them back to Kirkgate.

'Joseph, that's him!' Polly cried.

'Aye, and there goes Tommy,' I shouted, then all at once my eyes filled up with tears and I could not see clearly any more. I don't know whether they were tears of relief that they were out or fear for what might happen next.

'What shall we do?' Polly asked me.

I dashed the tears away and tried hard to think. 'If we run back up Crossgate we'll maybe meet them back on Kirkgate.'

We turned around and hurried back up the street, struggling against the flow of angry men that still poured from the houses, heading for the fight.

As we turned the corner we saw Joseph and Tommy still up on the rooftops, hesitating as to which way to turn, where Tin Ghaut Alley leads down to the river.

'No,' we bellowed. 'Not down there!'

The streets near the alley were quieter, as everyone still milled around the rendezvous.

'Come here!' we cried.

They heard and saw us, relief in their faces.

'Get down! We've somewhere safe to take thee!'

They scrambled down, finding footholds on the rain-water pipes and at last they were there on the street with us. There was no time for hugging or joy. 'We've to get t' your Aunt Hester's,' I told Tommy.

We could hear cries and the dull thuds of flying bricks and stones coming from Grape Lane, and as we tore up Kirkgate nobody stopped us or even seemed to notice us.

'Fire it! Fire it!' we heard them shouting.

We burst into Hester's kitchen, making Mam leap up from the settle, spilling warm ale all down her gown.

'Bless thee, Lady Hilda,' she whispered, pulling our Joseph into her arms, careless that his breeches were more ragged than ever and he was covered with soot.

'Mam, Mam,' Tommy cried, clinging to his mother. Big lad though he was, tears poured down his face, making clean pink trails on his dirty cheeks as Lyddy hugged him.

I had an urge to hug him too but I was too shy and besides I knew that there was much more that needed to be done.

Polly felt the same. 'We've no time for fussing,' she cried.

'No,' I tried to speak calmly. 'There's a great gang o' Whitby folk broken into the rendezvous!'

'We heard the row,' Joseph gasped. 'When t' guards went out to see what were up, we took our chance and shot up the chimney and got out on t' roof.'

'I can see that,' Mam dusted him down, still delighted just to see him.

'Listen!' Polly cried. 'There's guns being fired!'

'People going mad,' I added. 'Tearing The Grapes Hotel apart. They're calling it their Bastille and saying they'll fire it!'

'I knew it . . . bound to happen,' Hester shook her head. 'But there'll be hell t' pay!'

At last they were listening to us.

'They've done it while most of the press-gang are out and about their business,' I told them, 'But what'll happen when they get back tonight?'

Then Hester spoke slowly. 'Why lass, if what yer say is true . . . I dread t' think!'

Mam looked at Lyddy. 'We ought t' get these lads out o' Whitby fast,' she said.

'Aye,' Lyddy agreed. 'They'd maybe call 'em deserters now! Yer know what that means?'

'They'd shoot us,' Joseph went white beneath the dirt on his cheeks.

'Don't y' fret lad,' said Hester snatching up her shawl as she spoke. 'We have our secret ways o' moving goods and people safely out o' Whitby.'

'Should we not wait for darkness?' Lyddy asked.

'Nay,' Hester insisted. 'That's when the damned press-gang will return, and who knows what'll happen then. We'll go at once.'

'Won't we be seen?' I asked.

'Nay! Not the way I'll take thi, honey, and by the sound o' it, the constables will have their hands full enough and not be hunting these fellows just yet.'

So without wasting any more time we all set out. Hester looked down Kirkgate and waved us to follow. We walked quickly along to the bottom of the Church Stairs, then turned up the steep donkey path, that curved round and up to the cliffs above. I was surprised at the direction she'd taken, but kept my mouth shut and followed the others. We'd not gone far when she went off to the right, along a small pathway beside a terrace of tiny cottages and down a steep flight of steps. Now I began to understand what Hester meant by secret ways; the path we took wound in and out of yards and gardens, up and down steps and alleyways, but always following a narrow hidden route, with high walls on either side of us.

'It's the free-traders route,' I whispered.

Polly nodded and smiled. We seemed to be discovering quite a bit about smugglers' ways, since our lives had become so frightening. At one point we knocked on a door and marched straight into somebody's kitchen. The woman of the house was just setting out fresh bread to cool on her windowsill.

'Don't mind us, Lizzie,' said Hester. 'It's the press-gang!'

'Bless thi,' Lizzie told us. 'Has tha far t' go?'

'Sandwick and Burning Mountain,' Lyddy spoke.

'Here take a loaf, honey,' she thrust a cooling bread loaf into my arms. 'Tha'd best not stop to seek out food.'

There was no time for thanks for quickly and quietly we were out of her side door and again up a long passage, then down another steep flight of narrow steps. On we went, through a fisherman's shed, where the old man stood up without a word from mending his nets and pushed aside the wooden chest that he'd been sitting on. He lifted a trapdoor hidden beneath and we hurried down a strong wooden ladder, arriving in a very long building that smelled of sacking and glue. The building was full of workers who walked steadily back and forth, but nobody stopped their work to question us.

Chapter Ten

A POPE'S CURSE

I stared about me. This strange shed-like place that we found ourselves in seemed to stretch away into the distance forever.

'The ropery,' Tommy whispered and I realised that he was right.

We marched on past the oblivious rope-makers for what seemed ages and at the far end of the building we headed down some cellar steps and into a dark tunnel where we had to feel the walls to stop us stumbling.

'Under the street,' Hester whispered.

When we came out again into daylight she was grinning at our amazement. Then came another stretch of narrow pathway with high walls on either side, then up a ladder to a sail-loft built into the hillside. We stepped out from the back of the sail-loft into fresh green wood-land, high above the banks of the River Esk. We had somehow managed to pass right through Whitby Town without ever going through any open street.

We gasped with relief as we looked back and saw Whitby in the distance behind us. 'Now then, keep head-ing up river till yer reach Ruswarp Mill,' said Hester.

'But that's inland, far away from Burning Mountain!' Mam was puzzled.

'It's not the quickest way.' Hester agreed, 'I grant yer that, but believe me, Mary, it's the safest. Cross the Esk by the bridge at Ruswarp, then over the Carrs and north up Featherbed Lane, on towards Newholm and Dunsley. Tha'll be heading back towards the sea b' then an' making for tha home by way of woods and moors and hidden paths. Tha'll never need to travel by road until ye'r back at Sandwick Bay.'

We kissed Hester and thanked her greatly for her help, but she was in a hurry to get back, uncertain of what might be happening in Whitby. We headed off up river, keeping well into the sheltering woods as she'd told us to. Then crossed the Esk at Ruswarp and marched over the low hills that she called the Carrs. We struggled up narrow Featherbed Lane to Aislaby in single file, safe and hidden, though it was steep and made us breathless. I knew then what Hester had meant by secret ways.

It was growing dark by the time we reached the out-skirts of Dunsley village.

'I can't take another step,' Polly complained. 'And my stomach is crying out for food.'

I was glad that she'd said it, for I felt the same, though I didn't like to moan.

'Fair enough,' Lyddy agreed, throwing herself down upon the drying bracken that surrounded us. 'We'll share the bread and get up our spirits for Lythe Bank, though we'd best keep away from the road and stay in the shelter o' Mulgrave Woods.'

'You lads are quiet,' said Mam. 'Did they feed yer in that place?'

The two lads looked at each other in silence. Joseph shuddered. 'A bit o' mouldy bread and disgusting broth,' he told us. 'Some of 'em wolfed it down, but I couldn't touch a drop. There were fellows as had been there a week in that filthy den.'

'How many?' Mam asked, her voice soft with concern.

Tommy shrugged his shoulders. 'Mebbe fifty,' he said. 'The gang were bent on getting a hundred, so we'd heard.'

Lyddy nodded. 'Hester told me they'd taken her neighbour Robbie – boarded his whaling ship as it returned and grabbed the whole crew.'

'Aye, we were with Robbie,' Tommy told us. 'He were desperate and wept all night. He'd never got a chance to see his new-born bairn.'

There was silence for a moment as we all grieved for Robbie's desperation, then a touch of wicked joy crept into Joseph's voice. 'He's out o' there now, though,' he said and we all laughed. 'He were first up on the rooftops!'

'And I pray he stays out,' Lyddy whispered.

Tommy sighed and shuddered. 'Can't believe we're free. Thought we'd had it. I've never liked being out beneath the sky as I do tonight.'

'But it's getting very dark,' I whispered, shivering.

'Don't be feared o' that, we'll have a bright moon by the looks of it,' Lyddy told me, nudging my elbow. 'We're getting close to home now and I know every tiny pathway, for I've done quite a bit o' walking in the moonlight,' she patted my face, chuckling. 'Now can we have a bite o' that bread, my lass?'

'Eh Lyddy,' Mam shook her head, laughing. 'I never thought tha midnight dashes could come in so useful. Of course, I know nowt of such things!'

Their cheerful fooling made me feel better.

'I could hold yer hand,' Tommy offered.

Polly giggled at that.

'Oh could you?' I replied huffily, but secretly I was pleased.

It was early in the morning when we stumbled back to Burning Mountain, giving Father a terrible fright. Lyddy and Tommy came with us and bedded down beside our hearth, for Mam insisted that the lads could not safely stay in their homes for long and that we must plan carefully what to do in the morning.

I was worn out but couldn't stop thinking about what

had happened. It had been a dreadful day, but for the moment we seemed to be safe. It hadn't all been bad; I had let Tommy hold my hand as we stumbled uphill through the woods, and his strong warm grip had felt very pleasant to me. I'd been glad that the darkness covered up the big smile that I'd got on my face.

We tried to sleep but it seemed impossible despite our exhaustion, so we all got up and sat around our fire while Mam made oatcakes instead.

'I cannot believe they'd shoot these two lads as deserters,' Father shook his head.

'If you'd seen that fierce lot that have set up their rendezvous in Whitby, you'd not put anything past them,' Mam could not settle her misgivings. 'Do you think that I wish to send my lad away from his home? I do not, but I want him alive.'

Lyddy was deep in thought, listening to the argument that swung between Mam and Dad.

'It's the damned curse,' Mam insisted. 'Waint go away. A pope's curse is a terrible powerful thing. Mother always warned me not to marry an alum worker. I should ha' married a weaver, that's what she said, then we could spend our days peacefully spinning and weaving together.'

Polly and I sighed and exchanged glances. We'd heard this many times before.

'Don't talk so about the curse! It's foolishness!' Dad insisted. 'Nowt but a fairy tale.'

Dad had never taken much notice of the alum

workers' curse, but the thought of it made me shudder. Many of the workers believed doggedly in the thing.

The story went that Sir Thomas Challoner, way back in the time of Queen Elizabeth, had gone off travelling through the countries of Europe and that he'd seen the pope's alum works placed amongst similar rocks and cliffs to the ones that we have here in Yorkshire. The secret of making alum belonged to the Vatican, but Sir Thomas persuaded one of the pope's workers to come away with him and set up alum works here in Yorkshire. When the pope discovered what had happened, he was said to have laid a terrible curse on all those who meddled with alum.

'Rubbish!' Father insisted. 'The pope must ha' been angry,' he agreed. 'And maybe he excommunicated Sir Thomas, for until our alum workings were set up in Yorkshire he'd been able to charge whatever he liked for his crystals. But the curse is just superstition. I'll never believe in such things; plain ignorance it is!'

Lyddy suddenly looked up from the fireside and spoke to Mam. 'My lad's in danger too, Mary, and we fisher-folk have no curse on us – yer can't believe that rubbish?'

'Now who's talking?' said Mam. 'Whose husband turns about and goes back home if a woman looks at him when he's walking down to his boat? And if a pig runs across his path . . . well?'

Lyddy had to chuckle then for the fisherman's superstitions were well known. 'Aye, tha's got me there, but curse or no curse, pig or no pig, what are we going to do about these lads?'

Suddenly Father got up from the settle and knocked the ash out of his pipe. 'I think I might just have an idea,' he said. He rushed out of the cottage and was back within moments. 'Aye, she's still here! They're loading up *The Primrose*, Captain Camplin's boat. He's bound for the Thames. These lads could be off to London on *The Primrose*, delivering our alum crystals, then come safely back with the urine pipes, when things have cooled down a bit. If there's any trouble, I daresay Captain Camplin would find space for them in the gin-smuggling holes!'

Chapter Eleven
THE PRIMROSE

There was silence for a moment, then Joseph pulled a disgusted face. 'What, go off in a piss-pot?' he cried.

Piss-pots, was the ruder name for the sturdy Whitby-built boats that came and went from Burning Mountain. *The Primrose*, despite her sweet name, did a very heavy job of work, bringing coal from Newcastle, then taking alum crystals down to the Thames and returning with a cargo of Londoners' urine, stored in long barrels that we called pipes. The stench of *The Primrose* cut through the other foul smells of Burning Mountain, and we all knew when the boat had arrived.

Lyddy grinned. 'That's fine coming from one who collects the stuff every morning. I'm surprised tha's so delicate.'

We said nothing, for we knew how deeply Joseph hated his work.

'That boat might stink, but it could save yer life,' Lyddy clearly thought it a good idea.

'Never mind whether it stinks or not,' said Mam. 'I don't want him going down to the Thames, that's where they take the impressed men. They'd be sailing straight towards danger.'

'I'd maybe agree,' said Father, 'if it were any other than Captain Camplin, but the man's as skilled at his job and as crafty as they come. He'll not let us down. Besides, none of the naval ships down there will recognise our lads. It's this lot up here that we've got to keep them away from.'

'Well,' said Tommy. 'I daresay *The Primrose* would be better than one of his majesty's ships. And it'd definitely be better than being caught and shot.'

'Aye,' Joseph agreed glumly.

'Are you going, lads?' Father was agitated. 'There's no time left, and I'll have Douthwaite round here in a minute, angry that I'm not there in the boiler house!'

They looked at each other. 'Aye,' they agreed.

'Then there's not a moment to lose.' As they rose to their feet, Father snatched up a strong hempen bag that Mam had made from her own spun threads and pulled down a pair of breeches that were hanging over the fire to dry, thrusting them into the bag.

Mam was on her feet and racing around our house-place, snatching up a knife, a loaf of bread and two earthenware water bottles. 'Aye! Aye! It's the best that we can do,' she cried. 'Captain Camplin will be off as soon as he's loaded; he'll not want to hang about.'

Lyddy hovered uncomfortably by the hearth, wanting to help but uncertain how. 'I should fetch things from Sandwick,' she fretted.

'Don't worry, Lyddy,' Mam saw her fears. 'There's no time. All that can be taken will be shared with Tommy.'

'It will,' Joseph agreed.

He was trembling as he took the bag from Mam. He's scared, I thought, and for once I was glad that I wasn't a lad. Then as he turned to kiss me, I saw that he was excited too. 'Goodbye to the collecting barrels,' he whispered.

Lyddy stayed to watch her son sail away on *The Primrose*, then marched back over the cliff tops to Sandwick Bay. Father went back to his work in the boiler house. At last it seemed that we might have time to draw breath.

'They're safe as they can be now,' said Mam. 'Safe for a time at least, and now my two fine lasses, yer must take your brother's place and do his work.'

Polly and I looked at each other in horror. We hadn't thought of this.

'Oh yes,' Mam insisted. 'Joseph's job must be done in the morning and gather a bit o' seaweed in the afternoon. Urine pays better than seaweed and until your father finds the best way o' using kelp, urine has to be collected same as ever. Now then, fetch the mule and set off at once. The other collectors are at their work already.'

Just for a moment I'd have risked anything to have our Joseph back.

Polly wrinkled her nose. 'I wish I were a lad. It should've been me that went sailing away over the sea.'

'Not where they're going,' Mam told her firmly. 'Captain Camplin'll make them work their way, I've no doubt o' that. Now come on, off yer go!'

'Why can't Father use kelp?' I muttered. 'Other works do!'

'Aye, and they keep their secrets to thissens!' Mam growled.

So we walked round to the stables to find Patience the mule, the most bad-tempered, awkward beast on earth.

'You can strap the barrels on,' I told Polly.

'I'm not. You're the oldest. You do it!'

I sighed. 'We'll do it together,' I said.

The days that followed were packed with distasteful work. Collecting urine from cottage doorsteps was not a job that we relished any more than Joseph did; we'd rather face the back-breaking seaweed-gathering all day, though it seemed that now we must do both.

'Can't we do wi'out collecting for a while?' we begged that night as we sat in front of the fire, exhausted.

Father shook his head, wrinkling his brow with worry. 'We shall have urine shortages soon. One thing leads to another, I've seen it all happen before. The press-gang take seamen off the boats, then all sea traffic slows down, and our stocks of raw materials run low. Thank goodness that we've plenty o' coal for the time being. If the press-gang move north, troubling folk in Newcastle, the next thing will be coal shortages.'

I sighed.

'Nay, we need every drop of local urine we can get. Saltwick and Peak Works are taking what they can in Whitby, I hear they've set collecting barrels in the streets.'

'Aye,' we nodded. We knew only too well how true that was.

Father drew a hand across his brow and sighed. 'Sir Rupert owes us three months' wages and isn't like to put things right very fast at this rate. He complains about the war and shortages and says that we must somehow keep production up. All he sent down as payment last week was two fleeces. You knows what that means.'

'We know, Father,' we both replied.

My shoulders drooped at the thought of it. It meant that Mam must spend her daylight hours washing and combing and spinning wool before we could take it to sell on to the dyers up the River Esk.

Still, I hated to see Father so fretful and anxious. 'Don't fear,' I told him, kissing the deep folds in his brow. 'We'll get the stinking stuff for yer.'

We knew that there was good reason to worry; the market for alum could be very uncertain. Father had often told us about the terrible time when he and his brother Robert were lads. The price of alum had dropped very low and the Alum Master paid his workers with produce instead of money.

'I wouldn't have minded so much,' he'd say, 'but most of the stuff was old and beginning to rot, so me and Robert were sent off to market with a cart full o' rotting turnips and sprouting grain. We ended up almost giving it away and earning nowt. Rotting turnips don't sell easy,' he'd shake his head, remembering. 'We worked and worked and we damn near starved.'

It seemed to us those desperate times might be returning. In recent years the workers had begun to set up their little gardens and cultivated vegetable plots. Father insisted that there'd been many a time that the rows of kale and cabbages had saved our lives.

As summer passed and the weather chilled a little Father became very busy each evening, carefully gathering seeds from the few vegetable plants that he'd allowed to flower and go to seed. He dug over new patches of earth to extend our garden and planted extra rows of cabbages and kale, for as he said, 'It's better to prepare for the worst in uncertain times like these.'

Chapter Twelve

THE COLLECTING LADIES

So as the weeks passed, Polly and I gritted our teeth and fought over which of us was to lead the mule and who should collect the jugs. We both thought collecting the worse job, for it meant carrying the jugs and pouring out the contents, which slopped on to our clothes if we didn't pour carefully enough, or if Patience moved, as she usually did. There wasn't much to choose between the jobs though, for the mule driver would often get bruised shins from Patience's kicking, as well as a soaked apron.

'I really know now how Joseph felt,' I said.

'Aye,' Polly sighed. Though we still squabbled, for the most part we were better friends, struggling over the cliff-tops together with our smelly load.

Father praised us for our efforts and called us the Collecting Ladies.

'Lady Poll and Lady Nan,' we giggled.

It was while we were collecting from Sandwick Top Green that we heard from Parson Eardy that the rendezvous in Whitby had been destroyed.

'Almost gutted,' he told us. 'The militia's been brought in to keep the peace and an enquiry set up. Oh yes, Whitby's full of soldiers and it seems they'll stay a while. The press-gang's moved on to Newcastle to try their luck there, but I heard that an elderly farmer's been arrested, charged with aiding and abetting rebellion.'

'Old William?' I whispered.

Polly dug me sharply in the ribs lest I gave more away than I should, but the parson took no notice and shook his head sadly. 'I cannot see how one old man can be responsible for that,' he murmured. 'It's more that some-body must get the blame and be used as an example.'

Feeling his guarded sympathy, I dared to ask the parson more. 'Did all the impressed fellows get away, sir?'

'I believe that they did, my dear,' he nodded.

I sighed with relief for poor Robbie and his wife.

'And I hear,' the parson carried on, smiling meaning-fully, 'I hear that some of them have chosen to voyage in a different direction,' he winked. 'I keep such fellows in my prayers,' he nodded piously.

'Even the parson hates the press-gang,' I whispered as Polly and I stumbled away down the track.

*

As late summer turned to autumn, Polly and I struggled hard to do Joseph's job, but Mam was always ready with a good warming stew of vegetables after we returned at noon with full barrels. More often than not it had a taste of fish to it if Lyddy had sent over one of the younger Welfords with a parcel of fish tails.

Mam let us sit by the fire with our feet up while she spun one spindle of washed sheep's wool.

'Keeping spinning! Keep spinning, Mam!' we'd beg, but as soon as that spindle was empty, the wheel would stop and she'd turn aside from her work to lift our kelp baskets from the wall nails.

'Off you go again!' she'd cry, shooing us off down the steep cliff path with our baskets on our backs.

All afternoon we gathered the seaweed that we call tangles and carried it to Annie, who spread it out to dry in the kelp hut. She'd burn it carefully once it was dry enough and collect the ashes to make the kelp for Father to try his experiments with.

We grubbed about, slipping and sliding on the rocks, our baskets growing heavier at each handful of tangles that we added. As we gathered we often glanced out to sea, hoping to see the familiar shape of *The Primrose* on the horizon returning with her cargo, but we looked in vain. We worked until the light began to fade, then stumbled back up the cliff path, desperate for warm porridge and the mattress that we shared.

On Sundays we went to the chapel near Sandwick Bay Top Green, then after our dinner we helped Father with the vegetable plot. That was the best time of the week, digging and planting and Father in a good humour, with fine full bellies for once.

We heard nothing from Joseph and Tommy, but Father said that was a good sign, for Captain Camplin would certainly let us know if they'd fallen foul of the Admiralty.

Sad news came from Whitby; old William was convicted of aiding and abetting rebellion. He'd been taken off to York, a condemned man, due to be hanged at Micklegate Tyburn. There was a great deal of distress and crying 'Shame' about it, for William was seventy years of age and much respected, though it was also whispered that he'd been a wild rebellious fellow in his youth.

Lyddy came up the cliff path to Burning Mountain to tell us of his death. 'It's strange,' she said, 'but somehow there's relief in it. They say he died in the prison cart and when they opened it up at York to get him out, all they found was a peaceful corpse.'

'Aye,' Mam agreed, wiping sudden tears away with the back of her hand. 'It is better that he died before they could hang him.'

Lyddy chuckled, her arms folded tight across her chest. 'Trust William – he got the better of them in the end.'

Weeks of steady rain made us more miserable than ever, for work must go on at the alum works, rain or not.

Everything was harder and more uncomfortable. The jugs of urine must be kept covered, for the stinking stuff must not be diluted at any cost.

'As I often reminded our Joseph,' Father told us as he sat beside the fire in the evening, smoking his pipe. 'You must be sharp when collecting. The poorer folk will use every trick in the book to make their piss seem more. They'll try diluting it with sea water, just to get their penny at the end o' the month.'

'But how can we know?' we asked him.

He shrugged his shoulders. 'You must get a sense of it,' he insisted. 'And watch your suppliers closely; the twitch of the mouth, the blushing cheek. You cannot tell by looking or smelling but we can tell soon enough when the stuff is poured into the alum liquor.'

'Why?' Polly asked. 'What happens?'

'Not a damned thing!' he told us thumping his fist down upon the wooden arm of the settle, while Mam clicked her tongue and shook her head as she turned the spinning wheel. 'If they've been diluting their urine and deceiving us – not a thing happens when it's poured into the alum liquor. If it's good strong stuff it makes the liquor fizz like yeast put to sugar.'

Mam shook her head. 'You'd think he loved the stuff,' she chuckled and sighed.

Father spoke with pride. 'We possess the secrets of alum making, handing it down through our families, and besides it makes us money.'

'Sometimes,' Mam quickly butted in.

We'd smile when Father started talking like this, but I did understand a little of how he felt. Though we hated the smelly process of making alum, we loved to go into the sheds to watch when the men were breaking open the wooden barrels of finished crystals. As they lifted off the truss hoops and stripped away the wooden staves, crystals came tumbling out sparkling and true, white as snow. That moment was always magical; you couldn't believe that anything so pure and bright could come from greasy shale and piss.

Chapter Thirteen

SUCH A NIGHT

The riverbanks flooded as the rain continued, but then one morning early in October we woke to sharp, bright sunshine, the rain had ceased. Suddenly the world seemed to be a wonderful place once again, for Father returned home at noon with a huge beaming smile on his face.

'The London stage has brought news o' *The Primrose*,' he cried. 'She's gained the best prices in the market – the only alum boat that's got through with a full cargo o' crystals to sell. Douthwaite tells us that Sir Rupert has promised to pay all he owes.'

Mam couldn't believe it. 'It's an ill wind,' she said. 'The press-gang seems to have done us some good. They've stopped other alum boats getting through and we are the winners in that war.'

'Aye, it's all mad,' said Father. 'The world is going mad but we'd best be grateful for small mercies.'

'I'd rather have my lad back home,' Mam whispered.

It seemed that the press-gang's activities had brought many of the other alum works to a standstill and so the London prices paid for our goods had really shot up.

'Things are looking bright,' Father insisted. 'There's to be a fine meal to celebrate our good fortune, with meat and ale provided by Sir Rupert. Look at me, Mary,' he said, grabbing Mam round the waist and making us giggle. 'Who says now that we're cursed?'

'When is this meal to be?' Polly bellowed.

'At once! Today! For a change, Sir Rupert's full of praise for his manager and his workers. We've kept up production whilst others slumped. So work is stopping and we're to be rewarded.'

'Oh,' Mam sighed, her cheeks pink with pleasure. 'If only our Joseph were here, then all would be well.'

'Never mind what can't be helped,' Father told her, kissing her forehead. 'Get making some of your famous oat-cakes – and lasses, will yer clean carrots and potatoes for the pot? Sir Rupert is supplying us with roast beef, mutton and barley ale. I've got to get back to the boiler house now, for there's much to be done if we're to leave the pans later.'

None of us needed telling twice, such good news travelled fast. The pickmen and barrowmen came home early. The clang of Bart Little's hammer ceased and he came out from his smithy wiping grime from his face and hands. The coopers set half-made barrels aside. Father and the other housemen were the last to leave their work, for the coal fires beneath the boiling pans were to be dampened down for once and couldn't be left for long. I couldn't remember another time when work had ceased in daylight hours. Even the seaweed gatherers were called up from the beach.

Workers and their families rushed excitedly from cottage to cottage, delighted with their good fortune. Trestles and tables were dragged outside into the bright October sunshine and wooden settles, stools and benches fixed up all about. The littlest children were sent up the cliff-side to stand by the spoil heaps, ready to give warning when they saw the food arriving.

A good smell of fresh-made oat-cakes, roasting potatoes and vegetables came from every open door. At last the sound of distant clapping and cheers from the lookouts told us that they'd spied a great train of servants coming down from Whingate Hall. Sir Rupert and his lady carried in sedan chairs headed the procession. The butler and four cellar-men walked beside them, stumbling downhill, bearing huge flagons of ale. The procession moved slowly but surely, wending its way down past the steadily burning clamps and the steeping-pits, towards Alum Row on the lower cliff ledge.

The workers came from their doorways with hot bowls of cooked vegetables in their arms and the few scraps of cutlery that they possessed. We all took our places at the tables, cheering wildly as great platters of meat were placed before us.

Sir Rupert and his lady stayed just long enough to receive our grateful thanks and to see mugs raised to them. They invited Mr Douthwaite to go back to the hall to dine with them. He accepted readily, his face flushed with the honour. The Master of Whingate and his wife stepped back into their sedan chairs and returned to their home on the cliff top, waving graciously from the windows, carried by four strong stable lads, rather red in the face. Mr Douthwaite walked behind them, used to making the trail up the steep cliff-side. The servants soon followed while we hungry workers gave all our attention to the delicious food, politeness forgotten.

The meat was tender and well cooked, with jugs of rich gravy to accompany it. We ate and drank with relish, for we'd all suffered empty bellies in recent weeks, whilst we'd worked harder than we'd ever done before.

'God bless Sir Rupert!' Annie cried, waving her mug in the air.

'God bless Old Rupe!' we cheered, clattering our wooden mugs together, full of sudden charity to the master who'd left us hungry and unpaid for months. It was just at that moment that we heard a gentle rumbling above us coming from the cliff tops and suddenly the table shook, knocking over mugs and spilling ale. Three of the cottage doors on Alum Row slammed shut, one after the other, then all went quiet for a moment.

'What was that?' Polly asked.

I looked up towards the spoil heaps and burning clamps that loomed above us.

'Just a bit o' shale,' Father told us. 'Just a bit o' spent shale slipping down from the heaps, as it often does.'

'More than likely,' Mam nodded.

'Don't fret, Mary,' Annie told her. 'Hold up yer mug for me to fill again. We must make the most o' this night. Who knows when such a feast may come again.'

So the feast went on until the sun began to sink down behind Burning Mountain, and we could no longer see clearly the big dark shapes of the clamps set in the open quarry above us. We sat there with our bellies full to bursting, I couldn't remember ever feeling so full before.

'Come on our Henry, bring out that fiddle,' Annie cried, and when we all begged him, Henry did fetch his fiddle and started to play for us.

A cool breeze sprang up as Annie started to sing, and everyone clapped to keep warm while Polly and me got up to dance. Though my stomach was still full, the more I danced the more I seemed to shake the food down and feel comfortable again. The faster Henry played the faster we danced, swinging our patched skirts about and stamping our clogged feet on the trampled shale that formed the ledge on which our little hovels perched.

Polly shrieked with excitement as we tottered back and forth, then all of a sudden we fell over, rolling together wild with laughter on the floor.

'This ground's moving,' Polly gulped and giggled.

'Far too much ale for a little lass,' Father told her.

I pulled her to her feet, though I seemed to feel giddy enough myself. We stumbled back to our places as everyone clapped and cheered us.

'Now Mary,' Annie cried. 'Give us a song. We want to hear that fine voice o' yours! Come on!'

So Mam got up to sing a song that we'd loved when we were small. A song deeply linked with the place that we called home.

> *Whin bush, whin bush,*
> *Bloom on Easter Day,*
> *Paint our eggs all golden,*
> *To roll along the way.*
>
> *Whin bush, whin bush,*
> *Sweetly bloom through May,*
> *Fill our hives with honey,*
> *To eat in summer hay.*
>
> *Whin bush, whin bush,*
> *Burn for us today,*
> *Black sticks, black sticks,*
> *Burn our shale away.*
>
> *Whin bush, whin bush,*
> *All winter, green you stay,*
> *Feed our goats and feed our cows,*
> *Right through to Easter Day.*

There was happiness all about us, but I glanced up and caught my father straining his neck, distracted from Mam's deep pleasant voice. He was looking anxiously towards the clamps and spoil heaps above us, then when another, louder rumbling sound came he was up and out of his seat in an instant.

Mam stopped her song. 'What is it?' she cried, as the feasters fell silent.

'Second clamp at Ridge Top,' Father told her. 'It moved! I swear it moved!'

There were gasps, but nobody spoke or cried out – faces were full of disbelief that Father should cause panic at such a wonderful feast. We were used to small land-slides, living up there on the cliff ledges, with the sea battering at our feet we couldn't expect anything else.

Bart Little rose from the table and went quickly to stand beside Father. He was a tough, strong fellow, but we all knew that he'd got a horror of landslides ever since he'd lost his family in one as a small lad. He rubbed his hands together fretfully, staring up into the gloom above.

Henry tucked his fiddle under his arm and went to join them. 'I'd say y're right, Thomas,' he agreed, his voice hushed and a little shaky. 'See where yon clamp is glowing red, I'd swear it's breaking up. We'd best take a gang o' fellows and go up t' see if we can steady it? Where's Douthwaite when you need him?'

'Aye,' Father agreed. 'We don't want that lot tumbling down on us!' He looked quickly about and seemed to take charge, nodding his head at certain men who rose at once from their seats and went to him. 'Don't fear,' Father told us, his voice calm enough now to reassure us a little. 'Best clear away our feast – light's gone anyway now. Fetch lanterns can you, Henry?'

'Aye.' There were murmurs of agreement and as the men set off to climb the steep slope, we busied ourselves collecting up our precious knives, forks and wooden trenchers. We dragged stools and benches back to our homes.

Chapter Fourteen

ARE WE CURSED?

As I hauled two stools back into our house-place I heard another rumble, heavier still, and swore that the very ground beneath my feet gave a shiver. Sharp wrenching, cracking sounds made me drop both the stools in fright and stare about me until I saw a jagged break that had appeared in the timbers of our cottage door posts. I ducked my head and ran straight outside, hearing it creak as I passed. Everyone was staring up through the fading light towards the top of Burning Mountain once more.

'God help us,' Annie cried. 'That top clamp is going and the next!'

Now there were cries of deep distress and alarm as we saw that she was right. The whole clamp toppled sideways as we watched, its burning centre glowing red as it broke apart, thick white smoke belching from its belly and rolling down the hillside towards us.

'Cursed! Cursed!' Annie cried.

'Aye this is it! This is our curse dear God!'

'What shall happen to us?'

Desperate shrieks went up and my heart started thundering loudly as I felt the ground move again beneath our feet. Lanterns bobbed wildly about in the distance telling us that the men were running back, slithering and sliding down the path as the clamps began one by one to topple and fall. Another great thundering tremor brought the dark mass of spoil heaps shifting down the hillside in our direction.

There was panic, people ran into their houses to snatch up their most treasured possessions; then, as cracks appeared in their walls they ran out again, screaming and grabbing at their children. Where could we go? We could not go upwards, we could not run towards Sandwick for the whole cliff-side was falling, and beneath us there was nothing but the freezing North Sea.

Father came pelting back to us, the other men following, frantically seeking their wives and children. I'd never seen Father look so frightened and bewildered.

'Where can we go?'

'What can we do?'

Polly grabbed my arm, pinching me so tight that it hurt. 'We're going to die,' she gulped.

'Hush!' I cried, hugging her tightly. Then with a

terrible cracking, wrenching sound, the wall of the boiler house caved in, sinking straight down into a pit that appeared in the crumbling ground. There was a great thundering bang as the leaden boiling pans tipped and alum liquor, still hot, came flooding out through gaping holes in the side of the building. Braying and thumping came from the stables, and one mule broke loose and crashed past us up towards the tumbling spoil heaps.

'Get out o' the way! Shift thissens!'

The boiler house roof came crashing down.

'All's going,' Mam cried. 'Everything! We're cursed – we'll die!'

We moved instinctively towards the edge of the lower cliff away from all the terror above us. But it seemed that there was no escape for the ground by the cliff-edge began to give. Father grabbed hold of both Polly and me, hugging us tightly to him, trying somehow to comfort us. I shut my eyes, waiting to die. But suddenly I felt Father breathe more freely, 'Thank God! Thank God!' he whispered.

'What is it?' I asked.

Father laughed. I thought he'd gone mad with fear.

He laughed again and drew us stumbling and sliding further on towards the sinking edge of our cliff ledge. I still kept my eyes tight shut, for I did not want to see what lay below us.

'No, Father! No!' we cried, thinking that maybe he was going to throw us over into the sea, thinking that might be a more merciful death.

But Father kissed us both, his arms clasped tight about our waists. 'We are not cursed!' he shouted cheerfully. 'We're not going to die! Open your eyes, my lasses, and see your salvation.'

And when I did at last dare to open my eyes, tears of joy flooded them, spilling down my cheeks. There beneath us, with oil lamps lit, gleaming golden in the dusk was *The Primrose* nosing her way towards us through the narrow rocky cut in the scar that acted as a dock.

Never was the sight of a boat more welcome.

'This way,' Father shouted back to the others. '*The Primrose!* Follow us down to the sea.'

'*The Primrose!* We're saved!' The cry went up from all those behind us.

Suddenly we were all tottering towards the crumbling cliff edge, feet clogged with mud, grasping at bushes and handfuls of grass and earth. But we were not so fearful now, for although the path and steps were gone at least as the damp earth slid beneath our feet it carried us down towards the safety of *The Primrose*.

Captain Camplin dropped anchor out where the water was still deep. He stood on deck, shouting out sharp orders while his crew ran fore and aft, hauling on ropes, bringing down the sails.

'No nearer!' he shouted. 'No nearer!'

The small boats that we kept at the dockside had vanished beneath growing piles of rock and shale. There was nothing for it but to go wading out into the freezing foam while ropes and ladders were thrown down from the deck. The two small rowing boats were lowered, but they could only take a few of us. I lost Polly then, though I could hear her shouting my name. I rushed into the sea along with the others, and fell stumbling on the slippery scar. I'd lost both my clogs. Soaked and gasping, with a mouthful of seawater, for a few moments I thought this means of rescue worse than death, but Father's arms went round me and hauled me up again.

'Polly!' I cried. 'Where's Polly?'

'She's here,' Father bellowed. 'Just behind. Mam's got her.'

And then I was reassured by Polly's clutching hands.

'You must climb!' Father told us, putting one of the ship's ropes into my hands.

'I can't,' I cried. My hands were numb and I could do nothing but shiver and shake.

'Climb or die!' Father's voice was urgent. Then he spoke low and calm. 'You can do it, lass, Polly follows close behind, hold tight and climb! Don't slip back, you'll crush your sister.'

Then I knew that I must somehow find the strength and slowly, step by step, shuddering and clinging tightly, I began to shin up the rope, pressing my bare wet feet into the thick rough coil, then against the side of *The Primrose*.

At last a strong hand above caught my apron straps and hauled me bodily upwards and I went scrambling over the side of the gunwales. I thought that a quick and smacking kiss landed on my cheek as I staggered about the decking, stunned. I couldn't see properly and thought that I must be dreaming, for whoever had hauled me up and kissed me so fast had vanished.

'Nan!' I heard Polly's desperate cry and went back at once to the gunwales. Polly's drenched, white face appeared, and I saw that it was Joseph that was heaving her up and over the edge. I grabbed her arm to help and Joseph turned to me with another quick kiss.

'All right,' I said. 'Tha's kissed me once.'

'Nay,' he frowned. 'Take Polly and try to warm each other!' he told us, his voice full of authority.

I saw Henry Knaggs hauled aboard, his precious fiddle tucked under his arm and the bow clenched tight between his teeth. I shuddered as he fell on to the deck, dragging his left leg, groaning with pain but still gripping on to his fiddle. His mother followed but as soon as she staggered on to the deck she pulled off her shawl, wrapping it about Henry's shoulders.

'Come away,' I told Polly. 'We'd best do as Joseph says, and try to get warm.'

Mam followed us and we were all soon huddled together beneath a woollen rug that Captain Camplin had taken from his own bunk. When at last every one of the alum workers was hauled aboard, all cries subsided and a grateful quietness seemed to spread amongst us. We were battered and bruised, with nasty cuts and wrenched muscles, freezing cold and wet, but we were alive.

Captain Camplin ordered the anchor to be raised and *The Primrose* was poled away from the rocks. 'We must be off into deeper sea roads,' he told us. 'If we wait a moment more we'll be stuck fast in shallow water; trapped beneath the muck that's coming down.'

He suggested that we go below deck to find better warmth, offering the use of his own cabin, but though we were freezing cold, we could not take our eyes from the dark moving land that was all that was left of our homes. High on the cliff top we could see the lights of Whingate Hall. The stone wall that edged Sir Rupert's gardens seemed to be ablaze with moving lanterns. Sir Rupert and his family and servants must be up there gazing down on the destruction of Burning Mountain.

'Aye, Douthwaite has done well to be up there!' Annie snarled.

'I don't know,' Mam shook her head. 'Is Whingate Hall coming down as well?'

We stared into the darkness, but couldn't see anything clearly. We knew that the coal yard had vanished, along with the boiler house and the tun house and warehouse; our cottages had tumbled down too. The alum channels and the steeping-pits must surely all be broken and destroyed. How could we ever work there again?

Again the whispering began. 'Cursed – we're cursed, and always shall be.'

But Father wouldn't have it. 'Stop that!' he cried. 'We'd be a damned sight more cursed without *The Primrose*,' he insisted. 'Go below deck now.

Get warm. Thank Captain Camplin for your lives!'

Father seemed to have taken on Mr Douthwaite's role in his absence, and everyone quietly obeyed his orders.

Chapter Fifteen

CAPTAIN OF A PISS-POT!

Captain Camplin took *The Primrose* out to sea, the sails carrying us along fast with a westerly wind behind us — that had added to the havoc on land but now helped us along nicely. We huddled together dazed and shivering. The crew of the sturdy alum boat cheered us with their rough kindness. A steaming mug of broth was thrust beneath my nose.

I shook my head. 'Not hungry,' I muttered.

'No, but cold,' a familiar voice answered. 'It'll warm thee up – get supping!'

I looked up to find Tommy Welford hovering over me dragging a great iron stew pot in one hand, ladle and mug in the other. He looked older and somehow more of a man.

I was so glad to see him there, looking so strong and at home aboard the alum boat.

The ladle clanged down on to the floor as he bent to kiss my cheek. 'There's another kiss,' he whispered. 'Don't fret. Y're safe now.'

'Another kiss?' I asked. Then I realised that it must have been Tommy who'd hauled me over the gunwales and on to *The Primrose*. 'Was it you pulled me aboard?'

'Aye,' he nodded. 'I had to see thee safe, didn't I?'

I smiled up at him, forgetting that my hair and face were filthy.

'Give us a sup o' that broth,' Mam butted in. 'Bart here can't stop shaking, and Henry needs warming too.' Tommy turned away from me to serve the other frozen folk.

We spent a cold choppy night out at sea, with the sails down and *The Primrose* hovering in the Whitby sea roads. Nobody could sleep.

'Well I never thought I'd be so glad to see the Captain of a piss-pot!' Annie insisted, making us all laugh at last.

'I never thought I'd be so glad to get aboard a piss-pot!' Mam agreed.

It was only then that I realised that though the boat must stink to high heaven, I'd not given it a thought.

'Why it doesn't seem to smell so bad,' I murmured.

'Y're right lassie,' Annie cried, breathing in deeply. 'I must say, I'd have married the captain myself if I'd known his boat'd smell so nice!'

Annie made fun of Captain Camplin all through the

night, and would not allow us to weep; she even made Henry laugh and curse her by telling him to play us a jig. Then early in the morning, as the tide filled up the harbour, we sailed into Whitby Town.

There was quite a crowd there to meet us for the news of our disaster had travelled fast. Mr Douthwaite was there, along with Sir Rupert who looked white-faced and worried. They talked low-voiced with Father and Captain Camplin, all four men shaking their heads. I almost felt sorry for Sir Rupert just for a moment, but then I remembered how hungry we'd been in the last few months and the great jellies and pastries that I'd glimpsed in his kitchen.

Mam clearly felt the same. 'And what help is he offering?' she growled to Annie.

Father came back to us, his face drawn. 'Whingate Hall gardens have collapsed,' he told us. 'He and his servants fled over the cliff tops. They don't know whether the house is stable and they're fearful to return. He's sent his wife and daughters off in a carriage to Pickering where his sister lives.'

'He's not suffering like us!' Mam insisted, her chin trembling. 'He's got the means to see his family safe and comfortable.'

'Now then, Mary!' Lyddy Welford came pushing through the crowd to reach us and flung a warm shawl round Mam's shoulders and gave her a good hug.

'Lyddy,' Mam was suddenly tearful. 'How are you here?'

'I walked all night,' she said. 'We spied *The Primrose* from Sandwick Bay, and we just stood there helpless, watching Burning Mountain fall,' she choked on her words and shook her head.

'Bless thee for coming,' Mam whispered.

Lyddy turned to hug us girls. 'Have you seen our Tommy?' she asked.

'Aye,' I told her. 'He's fine and well and looks like – a man!'

Lyddy smiled and kissed my dirty cheek.

We must have made a sad sight as we were stood there in a forlorn group on St Anne's Staithe. Our patched clothes were now in shreds, barely decent and caked in thick mud. My feet were bare, so cold and numb at least they didn't hurt much. Our hair was matted with mud that began to set hard as it dried. Most of us could only hobble slowly about, so many bad bruises and wrenched ankles were there. I could see that we were lucky compared to poor Henry who bit his lip, refusing to make a sound, though his cheeks were deathly white and he grimaced at every movement.

Polly clutched my arm. 'I want to be clean,' she whimpered. 'I want to be clean.'

Lyddy found Tommy at last and admired his strong seaman's breeches and woollen hat, but it was then that the full meaning of our loss began to sink in. We had lost everything, our home, our beds, our cooking pots and our Sunday clothes. We'd lost our hens and goats and even the pack mules. These filthy rags that barely covered us were all that we'd got. There was nothing to change into. Would we have to spend the rest of our lives in these foul clothes?

Then suddenly Lyddy saw our distress and understood. 'Come back wi' me to Sandwick,' she said.

'Y've not got room,' Mam shook her head.

'I've been trying hard to think all night,' Father said. 'My brother Robert would help us, I'm sure he would. But it'll take time to get a message to Peak. If we went there I could help him with his work and maybe find a way to pay him back. I thank you most kindly, Lyddy, but we know nowt o' fishing life. We're better to go to another alum works if we can.'

Lyddy nodded her understanding.

'Aye,' Mam agreed. 'But where do we go today?'

'Today tha comes to me.' It was Hester Welford speaking. She stood there behind us on the quayside, fish basket on her head and the other hand on her hip. She looked so determined that just the sight of her made me feel better.

'Oh Hester,' Mam hesitated. 'Y've helped us enough already.'

But Hester would not have any argument about it. 'Sin' that day when the press-gang took thy lads, Whitby is a different place. Thy lads' misfortune brought all t' trouble to a head. Oh aye, we've soldiers marching about keeping us in order now, but the press-gang has been moved on and our yards are full of work and whaling men again. You come wi' me, now. We'll make on it's wash day and we'll get thee feeling fit and fine again.'

Joseph and Tommy insisted that they stay with Captain Camplin, for there were errands to run and much to do. With the collapse of Burning Mountain the Captain had lost his buyer for the cargo of urine, so he must look about fast to see if he could find another market for the stuff.

Father went to find the Scarborough Carter and beg him to take a message to his brother at Peak alum works.

We lasses and Mam set off stiff-legged to follow Lyddy and Hester over the bridge. As we crossed and looked up the river, we could see that what she'd said was true. Whitby was a different place from last time. The yards were full of workers from the Greenland Fishery, cutting up blubber, scraping whalebones and pressing oil. Cheerfully and openly going about their work, though the stink that came from their yards was almost as bad as our alum works.

We followed Hester back to Welfords' Yard. Her three daughters were just setting off to the scar, with their wooden pails and baskets, for the daily round of bait-gathering.

'Eeh bless 'em!' they murmured, greatly concerned when they saw the state of us. 'How'll they ever get thissens clean?'

'It'll be done!' Hester told them firmly. 'I'll not come flither-picking today, nor Alice. She can stay and help.'

'Oh thank you, Mam!' Hester's youngest daughter cried, flinging her basket down in a corner of the yard.

'Tha'd best not be thanking me so soon,' Hester smiled. 'It's like to be harder work than any bait gathering, I'd think.'

Hester served us out there in the yard with warming porridge, which we ate with relish. While we ate she pulled out a wooden tub and little Alice ran back and forth to the pump, fetching buckets of water until it was half-filled. Rachel, a skinny old woman who lived across the yard, brought out a second tub for us to use.

'Now then, drop tha poor clothes into t' tub,' she told us, pointing a gnarled finger at our rags. She also brought out her ash pot and sprinkled handfuls of white wood ash into the clothes tub. 'That'll mebbe help loosen t' muck.'

I began to wonder how our rags could be washed without us being left stark naked, when Hester pulled a wooden screen out into the yard from her house-place.

'Have we to stand naked behind that?' Polly whispered.

'Just while tha gets washed,' Hester told us. 'Once tha's clean I'll fetch out our lass's Sunday petticoats and shawls for thee.'

Letting us wear their best clothes was a big sacrifice; Sunday clothes were treasured beyond all.

Hester topped up the wash tub with a bit of hot water from the kettle that bubbled constantly on the reckon above her fire.

'Now then,' she asked. 'Wha's first?'

We hesitated for it was terrible standing out there in the yard with thick mud slowly drying and chafing all over us. I was desperate to be rid of it, though I didn't relish stripping off either.

'Lasses first,' said Mam.

'No, you Mam!'

'Water's getting chilled!' Hester complained.

Mam didn't wait around then. She stripped her top half off boldly and set to washing down her hands and face in the tub. 'Warm,' she smiled, then she ducked her head in, hair and all, while Hannah and Lyddy stood by with a soft drying cloth and warm rugs to wrap us in.

'Come on, lasses,' Lyddy encouraged. 'Once tha's clean, Hester'll let thee go inside.'

Chapter Sixteen

IN SAD NEED OF REPAIR

At last we were all washed and dressed, our hair steaming gently as we sat around Hester's fire. We felt better but still whispered fearfully, wondering what was to become of us. We dozed a little for the fire made us sleepy, remembering that we'd had no rest at all the night before.

Hester, Lyddy and Alice had gone down to Tate Hill Sands with our dirty clothes in their wash tubs, wooden beetles tucked under their arms. The two women returned at noon.

'Thank goodness the rain's holding off,' Lyddy cried. 'Eeh, yer ought t' see thy gowns and petticoats, they're scrubbed and beaten clean and all stretched out on Tate Hill t' dry. We've left Alice there to mind 'em.'

'Is there ought left of 'em?' Mam asked doubtfully. 'They've been darned to death already.'

'Now then, don't you worry,' Rachel told her. 'Though they're in sad need o' repair I've used m' needle and thread to fix up worse clothing than what's out there on t' sands and I've a fine sack o' patches under my bed.'

'But we can't pay thee – though we do have money owing to us.'

'Nay – I don't want pay,' Rachel told her firmly, then added wickedly, 'Mind a parcel o' alum crystals to fix my dyes 'ud be a grand reward.'

Mam's face crumpled up and I could tell that she was swallowing back tears. 'So kind,' she muttered. 'Everyone's so kind. You'll get yer alum crystals, make no mistake; my brother-in-law will fetch some from Peak, even if we never do get them from Burning Mountain again.'

We were lucky that the sun came out quite bright that morning, and Alice returned soon after noon with her arms piled high with torn but dry clothes. After a good dinner of oat-cakes and bloaters, all the women settled around the fire with needles and threads, and a basket of cloth patches, ready to tackle the tricky job of stitching our rags together again.

Suddenly the yard became full of voices and bustle and the smell of fish as the two older girls returned from their bait-gathering.

'This is summat!' Dolly bellowed. 'A little alum lass in my best petticoat and clogs!'

But when I started to unfasten it, she hugged me and swore that she was teasing. They ate their dinner, then set about fetching knives and buckets of water to shell the bait and fix up their dad's fishing lines. They shouted and laughed and shoved us about as we got in their way.

'I tell yer what,' said Hester. 'Alice, leave the line-baiting be. I need a few errands fetching. Take these poor lasses and let them have a little wander round t' town.'

Alice grinned at us. 'Tha' best come every day,' she told us, then added hurriedly, 'though I wouldn't wish yer such ill fortune again.'

We were glad to get ourselves moving, though I was shocked to find that my shoulder and back ached so badly. I could only hobble on my bashed ankle.

'Aye,' said Mam, stitching fast as she always did. 'Keeping moving's best thing.'

So we limped down Kirkgate to the market place, each with a basket on our arm. Whitby was a lively place, much more so than the last fearful visit that we'd made. The stink of smoked fish and boiled whale blubber was everywhere and the shipyards were full of carpenters sawing and hammering like mad. The market was crammed with farmers and their wives, who'd brought fresh produce into Whitby to sell. A few soldiers paraded through the streets, rifles at the ready. They smiled at the pink-cheeked fisher lasses, seeming rather pleased to be there in Whitby keeping the peace and not down in the southern part of the country, preparing to fight the French.

We headed for Maggie's fish stall to tell her what had happened to us.

'Bless yer honey,' she said putting crab claws into our hands. 'Haven't yer had troubles enough. I always say t' never rains but it pours!'

We returned with our baskets full and found that Father was back, sitting by Hester's fire. He was washed and pink-cheeked and wearing a worn blue fisherman's smock and breeches.

'What's happening, Father?' I asked.

For all his improved appearance he still looked very drawn and worried.

He smiled then. 'We'll manage sweetheart. Somehow we shall manage.'

'Will Uncle Robert help us?'

'I'm sure he will, but it looks as though we'd best take a chance and travel on to Peak works, whether he will or not.'

Mam was rushing about with hot irons and we could see at once that the women had done a grand job with our clothes. My petticoat was patched with faded pink cotton, my pinafore with blue. They'd managed to scrape together enough patches that matched, so that they almost looked good as new.

'Quickly now,' Mam cried. 'Change back into your clothes. We must catch *The Primrose* again, before the tide changes.'

'What?' we cried. 'Are we off again?'

'Aye, Captain Camplin's taking his pipes round to Peak,' Father told us. 'We may sail with him and trust that our Robert will give us shelter. He should have heard our news from the carter by now.'

'It were thee that wanted to go sailing over t' sea,' I told Polly.

'Aye,' she answered. 'Not like this though.'

'There's a bit o' worrying news,' Father stroked my hair gently. 'Sir Rupert cannot be found. It's said that he headed off to York, for he's another smaller house there. Douthwaite is furious and insists that he can't do anything for us. I fear we've little hope of quickly getting the money we're owed. We must all fend for ourselves as best we can. This curse, it does seem to . . .'

Mam couldn't believe it. 'Now don't you start that,' she told him wagging her finger in his face. 'How many times have you sworn to me that it's nowt but a fairy tale? Captain Camplin and *The Primrose* are our good luck – are they not? You said so yourself!'

'Aye,' Father had to smile at the sudden reversal of Mam's belief. He got up from the fire and hugged her tightly. 'You are my good luck,' he told her. 'You and these fine bairns of ours.'

I was happy again to be back on *The Primrose* with Joseph and Tommy, and happy to know that my new washed hair shone and even though my gown was patched, it was patched in bonny colours so that I couldn't remember when I'd felt so clean. Dolly had given me her working clogs and sworn that she was pleased to have a reason to wear her best ones every day.

Lyddy set off to walk back to Sandwick, leaving her son to fulfil his duty by Captain Camplin. The ship's master told both him and Joseph that their willingness and seamanship had been good enough for him to count them as crew, and that meant pay at the end of the voyage.

Hester waved us off from St Anne's Staithe and Mam thanked her over and over again. I went very watery eyed myself. The loss of my home had left me dry-eyed and empty, while the kindness of the fishing folk, who'd little to spare, touched me deeply, making me want to weep.

I stood on the deck of *The Primrose* with Polly beside me, watching the steep cliff sides of Whitby shrink into the distance in the fading light. Although it wasn't far to Peak, Captain Camplin had to go out into the deeper water to avoid the dangerous rocky shore.

I'd have given anything to be turning north and sailing back to Burning Mountain, but I knew that such a thought was stupid. What would we find there if we did?

Aunt Margaret had always been kind, but she did fuss so and she liked her house-place to be kept very spick and span. Last time we'd visited them I was quite small. We'd stayed for two nights, then returned home with Mam declaring that she'd had enough o' fuss, fuss, fuss. What would it be like to stay for weeks, maybe months and would they want us there for such a time, crowding out their home?

At last I turned away with a sigh and saw that Polly

was staring up at the tallest mast in the middle of the ship while the crew hauled on ropes and Captain Camplin roared at them from the bridge. She nudged me and pointed 'He's swinging about up there like a squirrel.'

'Who?' I asked, trying to see what she meant.

'Your Tommy!'

'Hush! Not my Tommy.' I blushed.

'I swear he'd like t' be,' she insisted.

I couldn't resist watching him skilfully unfurling the main sail and letting it down, while Captain Camplin yelled instructions to Joseph who rushed about the deck below, pulling the great sail round and making it fast so that it filled with wind and sent *The Primrose* moving steadily south.

Chapter Seventeen

AT PEAK

It was dusk when *The Primrose* sailed into the dock at Peak alum works, carried by the evening tide. We stared up at the great dark bulk of Peak House on the south cliff. It was a fine big mansion belonging to Captain Childs, the Alum Master, surrounded by gardens and built on the high rocky headland that stretched out into the North Sea.

'Like a castle,' Polly breathed.

'Aye. You were a bairn, Polly, when we last came to visit,' Mam reminded us.

'I can remember it,' Polly insisted. 'Like a castle in a fairytale.'

We soon turned our attention away from Peak House, for many of the alum workers came down the steep cliff path to meet us. They'd seen *The Primrose* from afar and curiosity brought them hurrying down. *The Primrose* was soon surrounded by small rowing boats.

Uncle Robert clambered aboard, not at all surprised to see us. 'I told our Margaret that you might be here. It'd make sense, I told 'er. We got yer message at noon and I damn near set straight off to Whitby t' see if I could find yer.'

'And can yer do with us turning up s' desperate at your door?' Mam's voice had gone very shaky again.

Robert wrapped his arms around her. 'O'course we can. Our Margaret's been nagging and nagging me, wishing to see these lasses,' he winked at us, and Mam was off sobbing again and wetting his shoulder.

It was a very steep climb up to the workers' cottages and I kept glancing back to see *The Primrose* anchored out in the sea roads with Joseph and Tommy still aboard.

Though Captain Childs was disappointed that our cargo wasn't coal, still he agreed to buy the London urine. Though his works were mainly using kelp, his supplies of seaweed were low and urine would be better than nothing. By the time we reached the rocky ledge with its row of houses and smoking clamps above it, it was growing dark and we were exhausted.

'Is this cliff safe?' I caught Father by the sleeve, suddenly seeing again our crumbling cottages and toppling clamps.

'Aye honey,' he whispered. 'Well, it's as safe as any alum worker's haunt.'

Then I forgot my fears and felt relieved as Aunt Margaret fussed and fretted over us, kissing us and crying out her thanks for our survival. It was clear that we were very welcome, at least for a while.

'I was stuffing more mattresses,' she told us, waving her arms at the sea of straw that filled her house-place. 'I thought you would be here tomorrow and I wanted all to be neat and ready for you.'

Mam kissed her again. 'Just to be safe and warm here with you is like heaven,' she murmured. 'I can't tell you what heaven it is.'

That night we did manage to get to sleep, even though I was squashed together with Polly on one of Aunt Margaret's narrow, hastily stuffed mattresses. When I woke up in the morning, I thought for a moment that I was safe back at home on Burning Mountain. I poked my elbow into Polly's ribs. 'Go, fetch the mule!' I murmured.

Then I sat up and looked around me, puzzled. It was clean and cosy in Aunt Margaret's house-place, and she was up and had built up her fire, the kettle swinging over it, hooked on to the reckon. But even though it all looked so warm and bright, my heart sank as the frightening memories of the last two days flooded back into my mind.

'Not Burning Mountain,' I whispered. 'No Burning Mountain left . . . all gone.'

'You fetch t' mule,' Polly murmured.

'No,' I spoke sharply then. 'There *is* no mule, it's dead I'd think. Dead and gone and everything else with it.'

Polly suddenly sat up remembering it all. 'Patience,' she said. 'Will she be dead?'

I could do nothing but shrug my shoulders, hearing again the terrible cries that had come from the stable block and seeing once more the glowing clamps toppling down. 'You never liked her,' I said.

'No,' Polly admitted. 'I didn't, but I wouldn't wish her dead.'

Mam came into the house-place with a pail of water. 'Right now, lasses,' she said. 'Get up and we'll find some work t' do. It's best thing I swear, it'll take our minds off our troubles and leastways we'll do our best t' pay our way.'

'Now tha's no burden,' Aunt Margaret insisted. 'Let the lasses sleep after what they've been through.'

'No,' Mam insisted. 'Come on, get up, lasses. Yer don't want those legs stiffening up!'

We got up willingly enough and ate some of Aunt Margaret's fresh oat-cakes. 'Now then,' Mam asked. 'What can they do to be useful? They're fine seaweed pickers and they can do the burning.'

'Well,' Aunt Margaret looked hesitant. 'If they're really willing, there is summat that's needed badly, though I daresay they won't relish it. There's just one lad left that collects the urine from the villages with a cart but he's broken his leg and cannot get about.'

I looked at Polly and Polly looked at me, then suddenly we burst out laughing.

'Whatever's got into them?' Aunt Margaret was

puzzled at the way we howled. 'We've been taking turns to do it,' she said. 'And it's quite a struggle, for we've to leave the other jobs undone, but I wouldn't blame you lasses if you don't fancy . . .'

We both jumped up from the table and kissed Aunt Margaret. 'We'll take the cart round and it'll be a pleasure,' I told her.'

She smiled at Mam, surprised.

'We're the famous Collecting Ladies, didn't you know?' Polly giggled.

And strangely enough, though the route and cottages were unfamiliar, just at that moment to be out in the fresh air, trundling along the cliff paths with a cart full of piss seemed to be the best job in the world.

That evening Joseph and Tommy came up the cliff path to see us. Joseph proudly handed over to Father the payment that Captain Camplin had made to him.

Father hesitated, but we all knew that the few shillings were badly needed. Father's hand at last closed over the coins. 'Tha's acting like a man, our Joseph,' he said.

Captain Camplin had offered Joseph and Tommy a place amongst his crew for the next voyage. He was determined to sail *The Primrose* up to the River Tyne and come back with a cargo of coal, as all the alum works were now desperately in need of the fuel. There should be good money in it.

'But up to Newcastle,' Mam was fretful. 'That's where

the press-gang's gone,' she cried. 'Y're determined to get in their way!'

But Joseph was keen to go. 'Captain Camplin is clever and cunning, Mam,' he told her. 'We've heard the press-gang've gone up the River Tyne, seeking for the keelboatmen, who bring coal down river from the mines. They've not had much success in ports, so now they try inland.'

'But that means even less coal coming out o' Newcastle,' Father was puzzled.

'Aye,' Tommy grinned wickedly. 'So Captain Camplin knows that if he can manage to get a load, it'll fetch the highest possible price.'

'Aye well,' Father sighed. 'We've nowt to offer here. Captain Camplin seems to be turning pirate more than merchantman, but mebbe y're as safe with him as anywhere.'

Both lads laughed. 'He *is* more of a pirate,' said Joseph, 'but at least he treats his men decent and pays us fair. We've faith in his seamanship – we'll not be caught.'

'You see that yer not,' Mam growled.

We went down to the dock the following morning to wave them off. I knew that I'd miss Tommy as much as I'd miss Joseph and I'd worry about them both.

Chapter Eighteen

THE OLD MAN

All through the winter months we stayed with our aunt and uncle doing our best to help them and work hard, but it was cramped in their little house-place and freezing cold outside. Father was very quiet and we could feel his unhappiness, the only thing that really seemed to rouse him was when Uncle Robert took him into the boiler house and shared his secrets, showing how he was managing to use kelp instead of urine in some of the boiling pans.

Every few weeks Father went off to Whitby to see if there was news of Sir Rupert. Each time he came back unsatisfied, looking greyer and sadder than ever. He brought us news of Annie and her sons who were living with her sister in Whitby, but they were very cramped and short of food. Henry's leg had mended, but crooked. Father sighed. 'He'll never run wi' a barrow again,' he said.

I felt a great sadness to think of the strong young man so stricken.

'Can he still play his fiddle?' I asked.

'Oh aye,' said Father. 'He's making a few pennies playing in Whitby Market.'

It was horrible to think of him playing while others danced and he could not, but I guessed that being able to make his music was more important to Henry than anything else.

All the old workers from Burning Mountain were suffering hardship and desperate for the money they were owed. 'Douthwaite's been offered the manager's job up at Boulby Works,' Father told us. 'So the man's doing all right for himself and I can't see him bothering wi' us.'

It was early in April that a fast sailing brig arrived at Peak on the evening tide, dropping anchor close to the dock. Father stood on the ledge of the cliff looking down through the fading light.

I went to stand beside him. 'Has coal arrived?' I asked him, knowing how eagerly the manager at Peak was looking each day for such a cargo.

He scratched his head, puzzled. 'That's no coal brig,' he said. 'That's no merchantman of any kind that I know of.'

I could see a rowing boat heading for the dock, with three men as passengers. We watched as they clambered out and started slowly ascending the cliff path. There was something secretive about the hurry and silence of it all that made me think that we should not be watching.

I grabbed Father's sleeve. 'We shouldn't look,' I whispered. 'Are they bringing in the gin?'

'Nay!' Father shook his head. 'They'd hover out in the sea roads till darkness falls for that.'

The smaller boat returned to the brig, then came back twice more to shore with three other passengers and a large quantity of baggage. Father and I watched as a coach and four came slowly down the cart track from Peak House, stopping by the steep cliff stairs. The three cloaked men who'd arrived first appeared at the top of the stairs. One of them looked old or ill, leaning heavily on the other two, all muffled in hat and cloak. They got into the carriage and were taken swiftly back to Peak House.

Father shook his head. 'Must be the owner's father-in-law,' he said. 'Margaret told me that he lived in Lincolnshire. Mebbe they've sailed round from Grimsby.'

He took my hand and we wandered back to the cottage, a good smell of stewed vegetables drawing us in. 'Look's like the father-in-law's arrived by sea,' he told Margaret and Mam.

'By sea?' Margaret looked surprised, then suddenly curious. '*The Swallow*? Is it *The Swallow* come back?'

Father shrugged his shoulders, but Uncle Robert got up from the settle, knocking the tobacco out of his pipe in an agitated way. 'I'll go and have a look,' he told his wife.

He was back in a moment, eyes wide with excitement. 'Aye, it's *The Swallow*. I'm sure of it.'

'Has the old man come back then?' Margaret asked.

'We did see an old man,' I told them. 'He was wrapped up in a great cloak, and his back was bent. It was hard for him getting up the steps.'

Margaret and her husband both looked at each other, raising their brows and sighing. Mam put down the old bed-gown that she stitched. 'What does it mean?' she asked.

'All sit down and eat,' Margaret told us. 'I think we'd best tell them, Robert. We don't want them saying the wrong thing to anyone.'

We gathered round the table then, full of curiosity.

'You know who the Alum Master's daughter married?' Margaret asked.

Father nodded vaguely. 'Some gentleman clergyman, isn't it?'

'I thought someone told me it was a doctor?' Mam frowned.

'He's both clergyman and doctor,' Margaret told us. 'And his name is the Reverend John Willis. His father Francis is clergyman and doctor too, though the Reverend Francis is very old now.'

'So he's the old man!' I cried, thinking that I'd understood.

'Well, I don't know,' Mam sighed. 'Why do they bring the old fellow by boat at night and make him walk all the way up that steep path?'

'Ask why indeed?' asked Margaret, looking very mysterious.

There was silence for a moment, then Uncle Robert spoke again. 'We always speak o' this visitor as the old man and that's on Captain Childs' strict orders. Y' must be careful to do the same, but Captain Childs can't stop the whispers!'

We were all wide-eyed and listening now. 'It's the free-traders!' Polly suggested. 'They hide their stuff in Peak House!'

Aunt Margaret snorted with laughter, 'Y're partly right, lass,' she agreed. 'The kitchens and pantries up there are full o' fine goods that oughtn't t' be there, but that's kept below stairs. It's what's going on above stairs that's the biggest secret. Doctor John is a mad doctor and he brings his most important patient here for rest and quiet and a bit o' sea air.'

'Some say the scent of stale urine does no harm either!' Uncle Robert chuckled.

'Who is it? This patient?' Mam thumped the table, unable to bear the suspense anymore.

'The most important patient that any mad doctor could possibly have,' Aunt Margaret suddenly whispered. 'Most important in all the realm.'

Suddenly Father thought that he understood and his mouth dropped open wide. 'No,' he breathed. 'No surely not!'

'We have not said it,' Uncle Robert warned wagging a finger at him.

Mam got up and grabbed hold of Father by his neckerchief. 'Who?' she growled.

'Hush Mary . . . it's the king,' he whispered. 'They've got poor old Farmer George holed up in there. Fancy dragging him up all those steep steps!'

We all gasped and Mam went quite white and sat down with a thump. 'Nay,' she whispered. 'Nay! They'd not do that to him.'

'Treatment o' the mad were never gentle,' Aunt Margaret shook her head. 'And I believe the queen has given permission for these Willis family doctors to do whatever they think is best. The government believe him locked up at Kew with his doctors, that's what the news sheets say, but we mebbe know different.'

Polly and I looked at each other, lost for words.

'Now you've not heard it from us,' Uncle Robert warned, his voice solemn with the seriousness of it all. 'If you ever refer to him, you call him the old man and he's best not referred to at all.'

It was hard to sleep that night, thinking that bent and frail figure that we saw rushed up the steps might be His Majesty King George. Polly and I tossed and turned and whispered together, even though we were so tired and must get up to start work at dawn.

At last Polly heaved herself up in bed.

'What is it now?' I asked.

'I'm going to get a look at him,' she insisted.

'You can't,' I told her.

'Yes I can. When we bring the cart back tomorrow we

could offer to go seaweed picking, then wander . . . over towards the cliffs beneath the house. Aunt Margaret says he comes to get sea air, and that he's always walking about the gardens. Will you come?'

I couldn't help but smile. 'We shouldn't,' I said. 'But we might try.'

Chapter Nineteen

THE KING'S SHILLING

We were up and out of bed the moment that Aunt Margaret started raking the cinders from the fire. We'd finished our collecting by noon and scarce got the patience to eat our bread and cheese before we were offering to go seaweed picking.

'But yer father's gone to Whitby again,' Mam sighed, distracted. 'He's seeking news o' Sir Rupert. I thought I'd let yer have a bit of time off and go walking up to meet him. You could help him carry some of the goods that he's to buy for Uncle Robert.'

I hesitated, unsure what to say, for we'd usually been keen to go walking away from the works to meet Father. These visits to Whitby upset him, for there was never any sign of Sir Rupert and I knew that the errands that he ran for Uncle Robert brought home to him how penniless and dependent we were.

But there was no stopping Polly. 'We promised that we'd help old Betty,' she lied readily. Betty the seaweed burner had given us a basket of eggs just that morning.

'Aye well, you'd best go in that case,' Mam sighed. 'For we must do all we can to help. We've nowt to repay folks with but our bent backs.'

We went scrambling over the rocks with our baskets on our backs and for a little while we did pick seaweed, fast as we could. But once our baskets were half filled, we headed for the steep slope that lay beneath the terraced, walled gardens of the hall. We marched about beneath them until we were exhausted. There was no sign above us of any old man; the glimpses we got of the gardens looked neat and cared for even in April, but quite deserted. At last we flopped down on the grass, with the high garden wall at our backs, a bit of early spring sunshine warm on our faces.

'It can't be true, anyway,' I sighed, frustrated by our fruitless search.

'Nothing goes right for us,' Polly complained.

'Nay,' I agreed. ''Tis the curse I'd say. It must be the curse.'

'Well then, why does the curse fall only on us and not all alum workers? Why are we more cursed than Aunt Margaret and Uncle Robert?'

I shook my head and sighed.

'I'm sick of doing things Aunt Margaret's way,' Polly

admitted. 'Put your clogs to the side of the hearth! Rake out the cinders! Now collect the ashes! Feed the hens a bit o' grit!'

'Hush!' I told her. I knew that this was ungrateful but I did understand just what she meant. These days at Peak seemed somehow to be getting more difficult than ever, we never could forget that it was their home and their food that we ate. Mam was snappy and Father got quieter every day.

'I wish we were back at Burning Mountain,' I sighed.

'What?' Polly screeched. 'You want to live in a pile of mud and stones, with nowt to eat and nowhere to even work.'

'Yes,' I said. 'I think I'd rather.'

Polly pushed her hand through my arm and leant her head on my shoulder. 'So would I,' she murmured.

We both leant back against the wall then and somehow in the warm spring sunshine we nodded off to sleep. I woke later with a jolt to find that the sun had started to sink towards the west. I opened my eyes and couldn't think where I was for a moment, or why I could see a face hanging far above me but upside down. I gasped and then sat up. As I twisted round to look up at the sturdy walls of the garden above us, I realised somebody was looking directly down on us from above. It was indeed the face of an old man, but not moving at all, standing still as a statue.

'Polly, Polly,' I whispered, nudging her.

She sighed, yawned and opened her eyes. 'I was

dreaming that I saw the king,' she murmured.

'I think perhaps you did,' I hissed.

Suddenly she was wide awake and on her feet. We both stood looking upwards. The face looked steadily back at us. The man was old, with rather bulging eyes and he wore a black hat and cloak; well wrapped up for such a fine spring afternoon.

'Say something,' Polly whispered.

My mind went blank. What should we say to somebody that we thought might be the king? 'Curtsey,' I hissed.

We both picked up our skirts and curtsied, bending deeply down to the ground and then rising up again. Still the face never moved. 'Is it a statue?' I murmured.

'Not sure,' Polly said. I was beginning to feel that we never should have come, but Polly seemed to get a sudden inspiration.

'We'll sing his song,' she said.

'What?'

'You know,' she said. Then she pulled herself up very tall, took a deep breath and started singing:

> *'God save our gracious King,*
> *Long live our noble King,*
> *God save our King.'*

Still the face didn't move or change, but I could think of nothing else to do, so I joined in.

'Send him victorious
Happy and glorious,
Long to reign over us,
God save our King.'

There was a moment of silence when we finished, but then suddenly the face above us was wreathed in smiles, head nodding, hands clapping. We smiled up at him delighted and curtseyed again. When he stopped clapping we shuffled backwards a little way, knowing that you should never turn your back on the king. But as we still watched him, our hearts thumping in our chests, we saw that his hand was outstretched over the top of the wall. Two silver coins came tumbling down from above, landing at our feet. We pounced on them immediately, snatching up one each.

Then a gale of wild laughter came from the old man as we stood there, clutching the coins.

'Now you've taken the king's shilling! What what!' he bellowed, still howling with laughter.

We both dropped our coins as though they were red hot.

'What have we done!' Polly went white. 'We've gone and taken the king's shilling. Have we got ourselves impressed?'

'Nay, surely not,' I said. 'They'd not want lasses in the navy.'

'No – no, they wouldn't,' Polly agreed, relieved.

When we looked up again the face had vanished and

all was silent. We stood there waiting for a while, but never saw the face again.

'Did we dream that?' I muttered.

'The shillings are still here on the ground,' said Polly.

'A shilling is a shilling,' I said. 'And Father could do with two shillings very much.'

We picked up our coins. Polly bit hers. 'Perhaps these king's shillings are different, they might bring us luck,' she said.

As we went back to Aunt Margaret's in the growing dark, I couldn't stop myself trembling a little. 'Was it him?' Polly kept asking. 'Was it really him?'

'I don't know,' was all that I could reply.

But as we drew close the sound of merriment inside made us stop and smile at each other. 'Father's back,' I said. 'Is that him laughing?'

'Aye,' said Polly. 'That's his laugh all right.'

I smiled at that. 'I've not heard him laugh since Burning Mountain went down,' I said.

'What'll we say about our shillings?' Polly asked. 'Will they be angry with us?'

'They might,' I agreed. 'But Father needs 'em bad, we must give 'em to him. Shall we say Betty paid us?'

Polly had run out of ideas. 'She'd never give us that much.'

But just at that moment there was another wild burst of laughter from the house-place and it was certainly Father's laugh again. 'Has he been drinking?' I asked fearfully, wondering if despair had driven my father to do such a thing.

'Nay, not Father,' Polly was shocked. 'He'd never spend Uncle Robert's money on ale.'

We heard Mam laughing too then and knew that Father couldn't be drunk. Curiosity got the better of us and we just went in.

Father was sitting at the table and he had got a mug of ale in his hand. Uncle Robert was raising his mug to him and Mam and Margaret were both cheerfully raising mugs to their lips.

'What is it?' we asked. Had they all gone mad with the worry of it all?

'Here lasses, come and give us a kiss,' Mam cried, banging down her mug and rushing at us both. 'We're off back . . . back to Burning Mountain.'

'What!'

'How?' We couldn't believe what they were saying.

'Aye, it's true,' Mam hugged us. 'Sir Rupert's back in Whitby and he's paid a bit o' what he owes us. He's heard how yer father led workers t' safety that terrible night and wishes him to take charge of starting up the alum workings again. Father's acting manager instead o' Douthwaite. What d'yer think o' that?'

We stared open mouthed at this good fortune. It was too much to happen all in one day and we just couldn't speak.

'Why bless 'em,' Aunt Margaret cried. 'Look at their faces. Now, lasses, have yer lost yer tongues?'

Mam stroked my cheek. 'All our troubles are over,' she said.

'But . . . when shall we go?' I gasped.

'In t' morning,' Mam's face was pink with excitement. 'Sir Rupert's paid the carter to take us there.'

'But where can we live?' Polly's eyes were suddenly full of doubt and I knew that she saw the tumbling walls of our cottage again.

'New cottages will be built,' said Father, 'but 'til that be done, we'll live in Whingate Hall.'

'What?' I turned to Polly and her mouth dropped open, then suddenly she was gasping and laughing with delight. 'Lady Nan, Lady Nanny Goat,' she cried, kissing me over and over again.

'Sir Rupert's to have a fine new house built for him, much further back from the cliff edge,' said Father. 'And don't get too excited, lasses, for Whingate Hall'll not be as it was. It's standing right there on the cliff edge now, but they believe it's secure for a while.'

But Polly and I would not listen to his cautions, we were wild with excitement and grabbed each other and danced about Aunt Margaret's house-place. 'I said these shillings would be lucky shillings,' Polly howled.

'What shillings is this?' Mam asked.

We stopped our jigging then and handed over our coins to Father. It didn't seem to matter now, whether we'd be in trouble or not.

'We sang for the old man and he threw us a shilling each,' I told them. Such a thing must be unimportant

133

compared to the news that we were to go back to our home.

'He said we'd taken the king's shilling,' Polly added. 'And he laughed at us.'

Suddenly Uncle Robert started laughing. 'They took the king's shilling,' he roared, pointing at us. 'They took the king's shilling!' Everybody else joined in, screaming with laughter until you'd have thought we were all going mad.

Chapter Twenty

RETURN TO BURNING MOUNTAIN

We couldn't sleep much that night and we were all awake and bustling about in candlelight before the sun rose.

'Well, at least we've no packing to fret about,' Mam joked. 'That's one good thing to be said for having nowt but the clothes y' stand up in.'

'Now that's not quite true,' Aunt Margaret insisted. 'There's a basket of eggs that I've set aside and two laying hens packed into a crate. Robert insists that you take the young nanny; she's due to give birth soon, so that will start you off afresh and there'll soon be milk. Why . . . what is it?'

Tears had sprung to all our eyes and Mam lurched towards her sister-in-law, hugging her fiercely. 'What ever would we'er done wi'out you?'

As soon as I could get to her I went to hug my aunt as well. I couldn't find the right words to say, but clung to her tightly in silence, remembering how bitterly we'd complained about her yesterday.

'Now that's enough o' that,' she spoke with warm common sense. 'There's too much to do for us to be larking about like this. I daresay y'd do the same for us, should we be shuffled into the sea, and mebbe that day will come.'

'Lady Hilda save you from it!' Mam spoke with vehemence.

The carrier's cart arrived soon after sun-up and we were bundled inside with the goat and hens and bumping on our way over the cliff tops towards Whitby Town. We stopped in Whitby to buy picks and shovels and to meet up with Annie and her sons. Hester had heard the news that we were returning home and she came running down Kirkgate to the Inn Yard to greet us, her arms piled high with clothing. There were new aprons for us and Mam, and a strong pair of fustian breeches for Father. Rachel, Hester and her daughters had been stitching all through the winter months for us.

There were hugs and greetings again when Annie turned up with her son to join us. I hated the painful way Henry dragged his leg. With many waves and cries of gratitude to the fisher wives we rumbled away from Whitby and on towards Burning Mountain, Annie and her sons following behind us in another cart. There were no complaints when we all got out to walk up Lythe

Bank. As we scrambled back into the cart for the last bit of the journey, my stomach pulled itself tight with longing for the sight of Burning Mountain.

From the distance the first glimpse of our home was puzzling. 'What place is this?' I asked.

Mam shook her head and Father stared ahead in silence.

'This is Burning Mounting,' Jack Carter told us.

'But where . . . ?' Polly stammered.

'Look,' said Mam, pointing ahead uncertainly. 'Is that Whingate Hall?'

We stared in disbelief. It was Whingate Hall, we could tell that by the shape of the house and the six chimneys, but this Whingate Hall stood so very close to the cliff edge that no sign of wall or garden remained.

'I forgot,' I whispered, feeling frightened by the strangeness of it all. 'I forgot where the gardens had gone.'

'Aye,' Mam shrugged her shoulders. 'Over the edge,' she said.

Father shook his head. 'I knew t' would be bad,' he whispered. 'But . . . I didn't think . . .'

'Never mind,' Mam came in with determination. 'We are back and this is our home and we shall damned well make a good fist of it. I'm not turning back!'

As we drew closer we began to realise that Whingate Hall was not at all the place that it once had been. It had gone through the worst weather without fires or cleaning or care of any kind and much of it was ruined. We got down from the cart and stumbled forwards, stiff-legged. Though the stone façade was still very fine-looking, the windows were broken and thick clumps of grass had seeded themselves on the great flight of steps. Through force of habit we wandered around the side of the house looking for the back door. I remembered from before the warmth of the kitchen with its great fireplace and bread ovens and game-birds turning on the spit.

We stood back as Father came forwards with the keys that Sir Rupert had given him. He glanced at Mam, unsure what to do. 'Should we go in the front?'

'No,' Mam told him. 'The back's further away from the cliff, that's got t' be better, and maybe we'll feel more comfortable in t' servants rooms.'

So after a few false tries Father managed to turn the key in the rusted lock, and we all crowded in after him. Of course there was no fire or gleaming brass grate, we knew not to expect that, but the sight of desolation inside the place was still shocking.

'I should've known,' Father whispered, trying to calm himself. 'Should've expected it.'

Sir Rupert had sent his servants to strip the place. Every scrap of decent furniture had gone; all that was left was a broken upturned table in the corner of the kitchen and two chairs with broken legs. Everything was covered in thick grey mud and dust. It was freezing cold and damp. Most of the windows were broken and a fine sea breeze was whooshing through.

We followed Father in silence, nobody spoke and we

wandered from room to room, remembering the glimpses that we'd had in the past of this once fine house. Every room was filthy and destroyed; the great expanses of the ballroom and the entrance hall seemed worse for the very hugeness of the wreckage that was there.

'Tha wouldn't want to dance here now, Lady Nan,' Polly murmured.

Without a word we all turned and wandered back to the kitchen. Father sat down on the back doorstep, careless of all the mess. He stared ahead in blank despair, still saying nothing. Mam went to sit beside him taking tight hold of his hand.

'I was flattered,' he murmured. 'I was so damned pleased and flattered when Sir Rupert wished me manager. What a fool I was! I didn't think what I'd be manager of. A sea o' rubble and ruin.'

Mam just held him tightly, her determination seemed to have seeped away again and she could find nothing to say.

We left them there.

'I want to look at Alum Row,' I whispered, trying hard to stop my chin from trembling. I took Polly's arm and we wandered away around the side of the house, going as far as we dared so that we could look down upon the wreckage and mud that had once been our real home.

The mess beneath us was dreadful, crumbled walls, and smashed chimneys were deep in shale and mud. All the carefully built brick alum culverts and wooden channels were cracked and useless. We stared miserably down at it all.

'It was better at Aunt Margaret's,' Polly sighed.

'Aye,' I whispered. 'That's truth!'

Then as we stood there the sun came out from behind a patch of cloud and a lark started to sing, rising up from the heather warbling cheerfully. Despite the destruction, my spirits rose a little and I looked again and saw it differently. The sea was still the deepest dark blue and the grass fresh and green, the whin-flowers just coming into bloom made golden patches in amongst the mess.

'This *is* still our home,' I said.

'Aye it is,' Polly agreed.

We'd looked out on to those gorgeous spring colours every year since we could remember.

Polly sighed. 'The whins are still here for us and look – look down there! Can you see what I can see?' she cried, grabbing my arm excitedly. 'There's food here after all.'

I looked where she was pointing and the small bud of happiness that I'd felt seemed to grow inside me. Close to the rubble-dump of our old cottages we could see a clearly marked-off square of fresh green growth.

'Our cabbages!' I cried. 'Cabbages and kale.'

It was strange that such a small thing should make us feel so much better, but it did. The powerful landslip had destroyed our homes and the works from top to bottom, but still Father's careful autumn plantings were pushing their way up through the shaley soil.

Then another movement far below caught our eye.

Someone was picking a way through the mud, slowly climbing up the steep messy cliff-side towards us. As we watched them come closer, we saw that it wasn't just one person, but several. They were fisherwomen, we could tell from their frilled bonnets; they came striding up the slope, their arms laden with baskets and bags. Then the woman who led them looked up at us and started waving.

'Lyddy . . . it's Lyddy!' I cried.

We turned and ran straight back to the house. Father hadn't moved, though Mam and Annie had carried a mud-caked wooden bucket to the pump. 'There's water at least,' she was saying.

'Mam, Mam,' we cried. 'Lyddy Welford's marching up the cliff side with a besom over her shoulder and a bucket in her hand. There's half o' Sandwick Bay coming with her.'

Mam stopped her pumping and Father looked up at us, puzzled. He rose to his feet and at once they all followed us round the side of the house.

The women were much closer now and we could see that they carried cooking pots, loaves of bread, warm patched quilts and goodness knows what else. Behind them marched a train of fishermen, carrying shovels and spades.

'Bless 'em!' Mam murmured. 'Bless 'em!'

Chapter Twenty-one

IN ACTION AGAIN

There was little time for greetings, for Lyddy and her friends walked straight into Whingate kitchen and set about fixing the mess right away. Father was bewildered and Mam full of gratitude.

'Bless y' Lyddy, but you can't spare time to work up here, you've got your bait to gather and lines to fix.'

'That can be set aside for just one day,' Lyddy told us. 'We heard Sir Rupert'd sent for you, though how he thinks you'll manage here I don't know. There'll be no fishing done tonight; our fellows've come up here to help thee get started. Now then, Thomas, they'll do whatever they can to start the workings off again.'

Father looked amazed. 'We can't let you do it,' he said shaking his head in disbelief.

Francis Welford was a tall, broad fisherman who you wouldn't want to argue with. He pointed to Polly and me. 'If it were not for these lasses o' yourn and the warning that they brought us, half o' Sandwick Bay would be far away on a man o' war by now. We don't forget a thing like that.'

Father turned to us and suddenly his eyes were full of tears. 'That were the best day's work you ever did, my lasses,' he said. 'I'm so proud of you.'

I'd never seen him look at us quite like that before.

'Take these fish-faces away with yer,' Lyddy laughed. 'Leave us women to sort out here. This'll not last long, Thomas, so make the most of it. Take these fellows away and put them to work!'

'You're going to work with us?' Henry Knaggs looked stunned.

'You can't shovel, lad, not with that leg,' Annie interrupted.

'No,' Father spoke with his usual determination again. 'But he can tell these lads what to do all right!'

'Come on then, Alum Master,' Francis Welford would not be put off. 'Tell us where to start, man!'

'A clamp,' said Father faintly. 'We should find brushwood for kindling and build a clamp. I think there'll be enough loose alum shale to start us off.'

'Have we plenty o' shovels?' asked Francis.

'Aye,' Father acknowledged.

'Then let us get going, man, for we've no time to waste.'

Mam sent us girls out to scavenge coal and wood, while Lyddy and her friends started on the kitchen. If fisherwives set about doing something, they do it good and proper and they do it fast. When we returned, dragging half-filled sacks of coal and kindling, things looked very different. Whingate kitchen walls were scrubbed, the stone paved floor was scoured and the fireplace and ovens had been raked out and scraped clean.

'Now that's just what we need, lasses,' Lyddy grabbed our bags and soon had a fire going that warmed the oven and the bake-stone. A good fish stew was soon bubbling away on the reckon and the smell of it made me realise how exhausted and hungry I was.

'How am I going to get the hang of using these fancy ovens?' Mam wondered.

'Oh, I can show you well enough,' Lyddy insisted. 'Did I never tell how I was scullery-maid here when I was nobbut a lass?'

'You worked here? Never!' Mam gasped.

'Not for long,' Lyddy laughed. 'Bait-gathering suited me a deal better than scouring pans, I found that out soon enough, but I've not forgotten how to rake this thing out and set the fire.'

They left us in the evening with full bellies and mattresses to sleep on. We all slept together in the warm kitchen, and bare though it was, it was blissful to have such space after the crowding at Aunt Margaret's.

'Fresh stuffed mattresses and fresh hope too,' said

Father cheerfully. His eyes were drooping with weariness, but there was a new energetic glint there. 'Aye,' said Mam. 'It's going t' be hard work and no mistake, but we can do it. I know we can. You get those workings going and me and Annie'll make a home for us in this crumbled shell.'

'Can we make the ballroom fine?' I asked, memories of Sir Rupert's daughters still refusing to go away.

Both mam and Father laughed at me, sighing and shaking their heads.

'I wouldn't mind tripping up and down in that ballroom, lass,' Annie told me. 'I'd need a fine strapping lad to partner me though.'

We laughed again at the thought of Annie doing that.

The following weeks were hard and bitter work, but at least we didn't have to go off collecting urine, for that would only be needed for the finishing work, and it would be a long time before there'd be lead pans of alum liquor boiling again. Father and the men were busy digging steeping-pits, while some of the lads fuelled the one clamp that we'd got going, and set to work on another one. Father made Henry his assistant and, despite his troublesome leg, he seemed to be everywhere that he was needed, giving out information and advice.

'I used to hate those stinking clamps,' Polly said, standing hands on hips staring up at them. 'Now I love to see the smoke curling up puthering all around. We're really Burning Mountain again.'

I knew just what she meant.

Some of the old alum workers who'd not found proper work since the landslip heard of our return and started coming back to join us. They arrived crammed into carts, skinny and desperate, some with nowt but the clothes on their backs that they'd worn on that dreadful day. We made them as welcome as we could and helped them to clean out and repair the old sitting rooms and living rooms. Whingate Hall was slowly inhabited again, growing like a bees' nest, with busy workers buzzing in and out. We'd done well to claim the kitchen and Mam set about baking bread and oatcakes for all, exchanging the food for work and favours. She even scrubbed and mended some of the broken utensils that had been left in the old dairy, ready to start making goat's cheese. Annie brewed ale in the sitting room, scoured buckets and flagons all standing about and a fine strong smell of fermenting barley arose. We soon started to call it Annie's Alehouse.

Sir Rupert sent stone breakers to hack up big chunks of stone and spread it to make us a decent new road. Carpenters and bricklayers arrived by the cartload, with timber and bricks, all paid for by Sir Rupert. They set to work on a new boiler house and smithy, for the work sheds must be built before anything else. Barrowmen and pickmen came daily, walking over from Lythe.

Every afternoon Mam sent us down the cliff-side scavenging. At first we didn't want to do it, but soon began to find that there was joy in the small bits and pieces that we collected. We gathered coal and wood, and harvested the cabbages and kale from Father's half-buried plot. We managed to capture a few scraggy chickens that had somehow survived the winter. We dug out dirty alum crystals from shallow pits, that could be washed and sold locally. We sent a good parcel to Hester and Rachel as we'd promised. Sometimes we walked to Sandwick Bay and returned with parcels of fish heads and tails to make a good strengthening broth.

One afternoon we were digging away when we heard the wickering snort of a horse.

'What's that?' I stared about us, but couldn't see any riders.

'I know that bray,' Polly said. 'That's no horse.'

She stood up and clicked her fingers. 'Come on, mokey, come on, mokey!' she cried and to our great delight an answering wicker came again and Patience emerged, looking very puzzled, from behind a large whin-bush.

'Oh no,' we groaned. 'Not her again. How ever are we going to catch her?'

But Patience came straight to us, standing obediently still, nuzzling at our hands as she'd never done before. I took off my apron and tied the strings around her like a halter, while she stood there letting us stroke her sides. Her coat was matted and grazed, thick with mud; her ribs stood out above her shrunken belly.

'She's glad to be caught,' Polly stroked her neck.

Another treasure that we found was Mam's old

spinning wheel. It was buried deep in spent alum shale, and it took us two weeks to get it out, working for a good while each day, digging and scraping carefully round it. We didn't say anything to Mam, then one day we appeared in Whingate Hall yard with it and you should have seen her face, she didn't know whether to laugh or cry. Spokes were smashed and the wood was dented, but Father mended it up and we soon had it polished and in working order.

'Now then,' said Mam, smiling and delighted. 'All we need is a fleece and I shall be in action again.'

Chapter Twenty-two

A BIRTHDAY SURPRISE

The weeks flew by so hard we worked, and soon my birthday drew near once again.

'I can't believe it,' I said to Polly as we sat in the sun on the kitchen doorstep. 'It were only a year ago that I sat up there picking berries, looking down on Whingate Hall, wishing that I lived here. Now I do and I wish I were safe back in Alum Row.'

'Aye,' Polly replied with feeling. 'And I wished to go away over the sea, and I've had enough o' that too.'

'I doubt Mam will give us the afternoon off this year,' I sighed.

'No,' Polly agreed thoughtfully. 'But . . . maybe . . .'

'Maybe what?' I asked.

'Never you mind,' Polly told me firmly, scrambling to

her feet and going inside. 'You stay here and mind yer own business if you want a birthday treat!'

I started to get up to follow her, but then smiled and sat down again. Maybe she was going to try to persuade Mam to let us have the day off after all. I shouldn't interfere with that.

My birthday dawned and nothing was said about a holiday, so I sighed a little to myself as I carried on my usual work, scavenging coals down on the cliff-side. Polly sat beside me staring out to sea while I grubbed about in the shale.

'You're not picking up much,' I told her sharply. 'Father says they're needing more coal every day now, and they'll not be able to set up the new boiling pans without it.'

'Huh!' Polly grinned, then suddenly she was scrambling to her feet. 'I'm on the look-out for coal,' she said. 'I've got a much better way to get it, and I think I'm succeeding. Look up and see for theesen!'

I turned around thinking that she was teasing me, but then I saw sails, far out to sea, heading towards Burning Mountain.

'Can it be . . . ?' I gasped.

'Aye,' Polly grinned. *The Primrose.*'

'But how . . . ?'

'This is yer birthday treat,' Polly laughed. 'I've been keeping it secret . . . we all have. Captain Camplin managed to get a good cargo o' coal and they took it to Peak, but Uncle Robert's insisted that they bring on just a bit here to help us get the pans going. The carter brought us news and we kept it to ourssens so you'd have a fine birthday surprise. Joseph and Tommy are coming to celebrate. Look, they're all expecting *The Primrose*!'

I turned back amazed towards Whingate Hall and saw that Father was leading Patience down the hill, followed by the other six mules that Sir Rupert had sent to occupy the new stables. Mam and Annie and many of the other workers followed, clambering down the slope. I left my bag of scavenged coals and set off too, trying to follow where the old pathway had once been. Polly skidded along behind me, and soon we ran out onto the scar. I stared about us then in dismay. 'How can they get here?' I asked. The landslip had covered the channel that once cut through the rocky scars.

'Father says they'll manage,' Polly would do nothing but smile.

They did manage, but with difficulty. *The Primrose* had to anchor out in deep water, bringing loads of coal to the beach in their two small rowing boats. Then the mules were loaded up to carry it back and forth up the hill. Everyone helped and by dusk we'd managed the last load and a decent stack of coal stood beside the new and grow-ing walls of the boiler house.

Both Joseph and Tommy kissed me and wished me happy birthday. They were full of the frightening adventures they'd had with Captain Camplin, just miss-ing the press-gang at every turn. Joseph had a split ear where a rope had caught him unawares and Tommy had a bullet graze in his leg from a press-ganger's gun.

'You'll not be going again then?' Mam asked hopefully.

'We will,' they both spoke at once and showed the handful of shillings that Captain Camplin had paid them with.

Back at Whingate, a delicious smell of baking drifted from Mam's ovens. Annie came out of the ballroom and closed the damaged door quickly behind her. 'Not yet!' she snapped.

'Not yet?' I puzzled.

'Come with me,' Polly snatched my hand and pulled me into the sitting room. 'We've to dress for dinner.'

'What?'

'Take that apron off,' she ordered.

I obeyed and saw that she'd made a lovely wreath of wild flowers for me, with bluebells and campions all twined together with ivy, and Mam had stitched a fine new linen pinafore for me, dyed golden by the gorse flowers. I rushed to put them on.

'Now you're a real Lady Nan,' Polly laughed.

I kissed her. 'I can't believe what a grand day I'm having,' I said, and my eyes were full of tears that came from happiness.

'It's not finished yet,' she told me, leading the way to the ballroom. 'Are you ready now?' she shouted.

'Aye! Aye!' many voices called.

Polly flung open the ballroom doors and such a sight met my eyes. The room was swept and clean, with a fire crackling in the broken hearth. The walls were decorated with sweet scented gorse flowers, gleaming golden in the light of many flickering candles. The broken shutters and cracked glass had been removed and the warm summer's night drifted inside.

Everyone clapped and cheered for me, and Tommy came forward bowing and holding out his hand. 'Will m'lady dance?' he begged.

I nodded. I couldn't speak. Henry Knaggs struck up a tune on his fiddle and I forgot my mud-caked feet and my patched and mended skirt and danced joyfully round Whingate ballroom with him.

'Now's my chance,' cried Annie. She snatched hold of Joseph who looked startled for just a moment but then bowed and offered her his hand as everyone else joined in.

I sat up on the cliff top with Polly and Father beside me, watching a small black dot disappearing into the distance. *The Primrose* was going on her way once more, taking our Joseph and Tommy with her.

I sighed for I'd miss them both so much, but my birthday celebrations had left a great warm glow inside me that I knew would be there for a long, long time.

'Aye, lasses,' said Father, his voice deep with satisfaction. 'Listen to the busy sounds of picks and shovels, then look down there. I never thought we'd see that sight again – burning clamps, dark red steeping-pits and a fine new boiler house almost ready to be used.'

'It's grand,' I told him. 'And you've done it all.'

'I couldn't have done it without you two,' he said and leant over kissing first me, then Polly. I sighed again with joy, but — as we sat there in the sun a bad thought came into my mind that made me sigh yet again and it wasn't with joy this time.

'Father?' I asked. 'When y' get yer new boiling pans going, will me an' Polly have t' be the Collecting Ladies again?'

Father smiled, and then he started laughing loudly so that we looked startled at him.

'What?' I cried. 'What's funny?'

'Bless you, Nan,' he said, calming down at last. 'What would you say if I said you'd never have to collect stale urine again?'

'What? Never in my life?'

'Never ever again,' he said firmly.

'Well, I'd say it were a better birthday present than any I could possibly have.'

'Well, it's true,' he said and my spirits soared. 'Robert's made clear to me the best ways o' using kelp instead o' urine, but there's still trouble finding the stuff. We've nowhere near enough down on these scars, even if the pickers worked day and night at it!'

I frowned, but Father was still smiling. 'Don't fret,' he said. 'I've been talking to Camplin and he says he's seen boatloads of it coming from far up north in the Shetland Isles.'

'So can we get it from there?'

'Aye. Camplin's agreed t' fetch one load o' coal, then his next trip will be a load of kelp. He swears they're swimming in the stuff up there and will sell it cheap, glad to get it taken away. Now then, does that make my lasses happy?'

'It does,' Polly told him. 'I'd say, "God bless them up in the Shetland Isles!"'

'Aye,' I added. 'And God bless Captain Camplin too!'

BURNING MOUNTAIN AND ITS ALUM WORKS are imaginary as are the main characters in the story; however many such works were situated along the North East Coast between Ravenscar and Saltburn.

Peak Works really existed and the remains of the workings can still be seen on the cliff-side, beneath Peak Hall – now the Raven Hall Hotel, Ravenscar. That George III spent time there recovering from his illnesses is local mythology. There seems to be no proof that it really happened, but the daughter of Captain William Childs, owner of the Hall and the alum works, was indeed married to one of the Willis family of doctors to whom the care of George III was given.

Some other incidents in the story reflect real events that took place, though not all in the same year. In 1830 the workers' settlement and the Alum Works at Kettleness were swept into the sea by a cliff fall. The workers were rescued by an Alum Boat and taken to Whitby.

John Tindale's *Owlers, Hoverers and Revenue Men*, describes a serious riot that took place in Whitby in 1784 when a mob attacked the press-gang's headquarters and pulled it down. One man, William Atkinson, was charged with aiding and abetting and was hanged at York in 1790.

*

The alum shale lies in the 'Upper Blue Lias', beneath a layer of earth and ironstone, known as 'dogger head'. The miners had to remove this layer to get at the grey alum slate. This was dug out, creating a semi-circular shaped quarry, then taken in barrows to a flat ledge where it was piled up into a heap on top of burning brushwood, to form the clamps. These clamps were coated with clay and burned steadily for at least three months, giving off sulphurous fumes. The burnt slate turned to a reddish-yellow and was reduced to about half of its original size.

This roasted shale was then barrowed to steeping pits, dug close-by on the sloping cliff-side, for ease of transport. Water was pumped in and left for three days, then the water carrying the dissolved chemical known as liquor was drawn off and carried down the cliff-side in wooden gutters to the boiler house. Here, with previously reduced liquor called 'mothers' being', it was boiled in lead pans to concentrate the solution for twenty-four hours.

Urine or kelp lees were then added, as a source of ammonia, making crystals form. The crystals were often dissolved again and at this point the success of the work depended very much on the judgement and experience of the workers. When the required density was reached, the liquor was run off from the pans into 'roaching casks', great wooden butts constructed so as to be easily taken apart. The liquor was left to cool and crystallize for eight to ten days. At the right time the hoops and staves were removed, and white alum crystals found inside. This is a very basic and simple description of what was a compli-cated and fascinating process. The workers at the time did not understand the chemical process and had to work by experience, trial and error.   T.T.

www.theresatomlinson.com

157

PART TWO

The Flither Pickers

Dedicated to the fishing families of the North-East Coast

Chapter One

I bent my head down and pushed slowly forward into the wind, high on Caedmon's Cliff. Down below I could see Mam and the other flither pickers, out on Sneaton scaur.

I waved and she looked up at us. I dragged my hand back sharp. I shouldn't have made her see us. She'd be mad with me for bringing our Billy out, so early and in such a high wind.

Mam ran towards us, then stopped. I could see her face gone white. Something wrong.

'Liza Welford. Get our Billy!'

That was my sister Irene shouting at me. She'd come up behind Mam. I'd forgotten Billy as I waved and now I turned to see him balancing on the curved cliff edge that crumbles a bit each day, with a steep drop down to the rocks.

'Billy,' I yelled. He flinched as I caught his hand and dragged him back.

'You devil,' I screamed and clouted him over the ear. 'You've scared our mam.'

He started to howl and pull away but I kept tight hold of him, while I turned to look back down below.

I saw that the women had gathered round a hunched figure; that was Mam. Irene pushed them aside, making a way through. At last Mam got up, her face still white. She kept looking up at us.

'Get him back home, you silly lass,' Irene shouted.

Mam picked up her bucket and went back to work, searching out the best limpets.

I pulled our sobbing Billy along, down the steps, over the causeway, up the staith and back to our cottage.

'I'll be for it 'cause of you,' I said. I kept pinching his hand, I was so angry. I pushed him through our doorway, clapping my hand over his mouth.

'Now shut your noise. We mustn't wake Gran, or we'll have Grandpa Welford fretting again.'

He looked up at me, silent now, his shoulders shuddering. I took my hand away and pushed my fingers through his curls, fair and soft, like I wished mine were. It was myself I was mad with, not him. I should have taken better care. 'Specially with the family so feared, and Grandma Esther lying in bed sick.

I heard Grandpa Welford's stumping footsteps on the stairs.

'Is that you, our Liza? Fetch a cup of water, will you? Your grandma's wanting to drink.'

I took Grandma's favourite blue-flowered china cup from the dresser and carried it out to the pump beyond our yard. Welford's Yard, it's called. My family had lived there for so many years that the cottages that sprang up around had taken our name too.

I jumped as the water splashed over the edge and wasted into the ground. Grandma would have scolded me for that.

'Never take it for granted,' she'd say. 'Good clean spring water we've got. Never waste it. Better water than in any yard in Sandwick Bay.'

I carried the cup back inside. A hard cold lump stuck in my throat; it was thinking of my gran that brought that lump. Her fast tongue, her fierce blue eyes, the way she picked up what you were thinking before you'd spoken. Now she lay abed, getting weaker every day.

Old Miriam, the herb woman, had been called first. She'd given Gran potions, but shaken her head. Then Grandpa Welford and Daniel, my dad, had talked together and sent for the doctor from Whitby. That cost; we all knew it must be bad.

The doctor left a bottle of pills and fresh hope, but Grandma got worse. Old Miriam came often now. She brought her potions, but she still shook her head.

'For the pain,' she said.

We knew what Miriam meant: 'for the pain, not for the cure'.

I carried the water upstairs and Grandpa opened the door at the top.

'Give your gran a drink, child.'

His voice was gruff . . . he hadn't called me 'child' for a year or so, but then he patted my shoulder and stumped stiff-legged downstairs.

I thought she was asleep, so still she lay, her head propped on two pillows. I went to the stool beside the bed, as quiet as I could, but she caught my movement and her eyelids flickered. I raised her head and helped her drink. Only a sip she managed, then lay back.

'Thanks Liza, that's better . . . best water in Sandwick Bay that is . . . never waste it, my lass.'

I'd have sworn she knew I'd just splashed it all over our yard.

'Sit awhile,' she begged.

I didn't need asking twice, for I'd rather sit with Gran than be minding our Billy, or being sent off for driftwood, or going to school.

'You should be at school, child.'

I shook my head. 'I'll not be going today.'

'Your mother'll be vexed.'

'Nay, she's not bothered these last weeks. She's been glad to have me by to mind our Billy. Oh . . .' I could have bitten my tongue off, for it was Grandma's sickness that had brought that need. It'd been she and

164

Grandpa who'd kept an eye on Billy till the last week or two.

'Nay lass, don't look so grim. I know why your mam let's you be home, but it'll not be for long. I'll soon be gone and your grandpa'll look to Billy again.'

I couldn't bear to think how it'd be without her.

'Don't,' I whispered. 'There's only you that I can tell all to.'

'Aye, and that's not right. You should take more notice of your mam.'

I nodded my head and thought how many times Gran had said that. 'Take notice of your mam,' she'd say. 'She's a good woman, better than you know.'

But it was my gran I'd clung to. Gran had looked after me right from being small, for Mam'd been working at the bait-gathering, and fixing the lines and selling fish. Gran was warm and lively, quick with her tongue, quick with a slap, and always a tale to tell, while Mam was a quiet, distant sort of woman.

'She were clever,' said Gran, catching my hand to make me take notice. 'Could have been clever if she'd had the chance, but there weren't these board schools then, and she married our Dan . . . so young.'

'But I'm not like her,' I said.

'Your teacher says you're clever. She's taken a lot of trouble with you, has Miss Hindmarch.'

'But I'm not wanting schooling. I want to be going with Mam, down on the scaur, doing the work, fetching bait for my dad's lines. Our Irene goes; why not me?'

'No choice.' Gran shook her head. 'Irene had no choice. Your mam was so weak after Billy. Someone had to fetch the bait and fix the lines. Your dad still had to go with the tide.'

'I know,' I said. 'I know.' I'd heard it all often enough, how it was different for me, with my brother gone off to fight in that foreign war. They didn't need me for the flither picking. I could go to school, get some learning, maybe get to be a pupil teacher if I worked real hard.

Gran coughed and drew a painful shuddering breath. 'Lucky to have the choice, my lass.'

I nodded and sat there silent, gritting my teeth against the tears.

I heard my name called and a commotion down below. The flither pickers were back.

Gran had fallen asleep. I hated myself; I'd made her talk too much. I crept from the room and went to keep our Billy happy and out of the way, rolling his marbles in the corner of the yard.

Irene was there, getting herself ready to start to shell the limpets, or flithers as we call them. Mam always got back later as she walked the long way round, over the bridge, never crossing the causeway with the others.

Irene glowered at me. Now I'd get it.

'You know nowt, our Liza. Don't you ever take Billy up on them cliffs again.'

'I caught him back,' I said. 'I never let him go so I couldn't catch him back.'

I thought she was going to hit me, so fierce and white she went, but Mam walked into the yard and stared at us.

'What's up?'

Irene shook her head. 'Nowt . . . but I've caught my thumb again.'

Mam sat down beside her and I watched as they worked. They shelled the limpets and mussels, caving and skaning, as we say, putting them to soak and swell in buckets of cold water while they cleaned the lines, picking off the little bits of old bait. They set about fixing the shellfish to the sharp hooks, hundreds of hooks to each line, coiling the line carefully in its special basket, or skep, as they worked. An hour it took to bait each line. Strong hands they both had, flicking fast, but scarred hands . . . Irene's worse than Mam's. I remembered what my gran had said: how I was lucky to have the choice.

When they'd finished Mam went off to the bakehouse, taking her dough. Irene took up her knitting, giving me angry looks. She seemed full of sharp looks and sharp words, not like herself at all. I supposed she was upset about Grandma, as we all were in our own ways. Suddenly she got to her feet and thrust her knitting at me.

'None of your sloppy stitches now.' Then, clutching at her stomach, she ran off to our privy at the back.

I looked at the gansey growing fast from her needles. My dad was always needing leggins or cap or gansey to keep him from freezing out at sea.

I sat down. I tried to do a row or two, but my fingers

were clumsy beside Irene's. Still, it was something I had to learn – our own Sandwick stitches, with the waves and herring-bone, though even our knitting had a nasty side to it, for if my dad should be drowned and his body washed far away, at least with our pattern on his gansey they'd know he was a Sandwick man.

Chapter Two

The tide turned late that afternoon. Dad had been to look at the sea and he'd given my mam the nod. That meant they were off.

Billy and me went down to the beach with Mam and Irene walking in front, both with coiled lines in their skeps balanced on their heads. We went to give a hand pushing the coble out, for we have no other way to launch our boats in Sandwick Bay. Even our heavy lifeboat, the *Francis Welford*, has to be dragged over the sand and pushed right out into the sea.

Aunt Hannah Welford and Mary our cousin were there and we all helped push out my dad and Uncle Frank in our fine coble, *Sneaton Lass*. John Ruswarp was going off in the *Lily Belle* with his younger brother

Sam and Mrs Ruswarp was there to push them out.

Their dad had been drowned five years back and John had taken over his father's boat though he were only fifteen at the time. My dad had helped him learn the work. There'd been three great lads all of an age, all learning together. There was John Ruswarp, our Frank and my cousin Ned Welford. Always laughing and teasing they were. They'd carry me on their shoulders and bring me liquorice from Whitby . . . now there was only John Ruswarp still in Sandwick Bay.

They'd gone out together one night, all three, though my dad had warned that the sea was too rough. There'd been a storm and my cousin Ned was drowned. Our Frank changed after that; he seemed feared of going out himself. He said it was getting so that the fishing was not worthwhile, what with the new fangled trawlers draining the sea of the fry.

Then the war in South Africa had come and there'd been a call for volunteers. Our Frank went off to Scarborough and joined the Green Howards. My dad was broken-hearted about it. He thought nowt to being a soldier.

'If he thinks it's hard working the boats, he'll find it harder where he's going,' he said. Dad never mentioned Frank's name these days, but he picked up all the news he could from South Africa, and lately John Ruswarp had talked about following our Frank.

John was twenty and a handsome-looking fellow, but that day Irene didn't run over to him as she usually did.

She didn't even seem to look his way and it was fat Nelly Wright that was hanging round his boat, casting spiteful looks our way and talking at the top of her voice.

We stood on the beach and watched the boats out, then turned back to the village. Mam and Hannah walked up the beach together. Irene and Mary, who were the same age, followed close behind, heads bent together, whispering. They left me out, as though I were a child, left me with Billy tagging at my wet skirts. Mrs Ruswarp came puffing up behind me.

'Here's your friend,' she said, pointing up at the staith.

It was her daughter Mary Jane, waving and hallooing, fresh from school.

'Now then Liza, not at school again?' She ran over the shingle and took my arm.

I shook my head. 'Y' see I'm not, daft ha'p'orth.'

'Is your gran real bad then?'

I nodded and we walked on together.

'Miss Hindmarch was asking after you today, saying that it were a pity if you fell behind.'

I shrugged my shoulders. I couldn't care less if I never went to school again.

'I heard tell,' said Mary Jane, 'that some of the younger lads at Whitby were wagging off school and the kid-catcher chased them all the way down to the harbour. So they stripped off all their clothes and ran straight into the water.'

'They never did.'

'Stripped naked they did and kid-catcher, he was furious, but you can be sure he wasn't for getting himself wet. He left them there and turned back into town, looking for others.'

'Well, there's a trick,' I said.

'Yes, but I've not told you all. Those lads hadn't come out of the water before this picture chap who makes photographs comes staggering down to the front with his boxes and props, and he shouts to them, "Stay where you are lads and I'll give you a penny."'

'A penny to share?'

'No, a penny apiece. He set up his photographing things and made a picture of them – there in the water, stripped naked. A penny apiece he gave them and they say they're down there every day since, hoping he'll be back.'

'They'd not set kid-catcher on me,' I said. 'Not this far from Whitby and me a great lass, old enough to be working with me mam.'

'No,' said Mary Jane. 'They'd not bother with a lass, but Miss Hindmarch, she says a lass as clever as you should be at school. Best pupil she thinks you are, and *I* wish you'd come back for I can't work my 'rithmetic without you to help me.'

I went to sit with Gran when I got back. Just sat there quiet beside her while she slept. Her breathing was faint, I thought it gone, but then she opened her eyes and took my hand.

'Glad you're here,' she said. 'Something . . . must tell.'

I bent close for her voice was weak.

'William,' she said.

'William? You mean our Billy?'

She shook her head and tried again. 'William Archer.'

I'd not heard of William Archer, but Archer was a name I knew well enough. It was Mam's name before she was married.

'She called . . . she called Billy after him.'

'Don't talk now, Gran. Rest.'

'No,' she said, all agitated. 'Must tell. I was there, I saw. She's feared . . . more than you know.'

Her breath came difficult. I lifted the cup to her lips and helped her drink. She lay back on the pillows, her mouth working soundlessly.

'Rest, Gran,' I said. 'Tell me in the morning and I'll listen well,' but she was already asleep, exhausted with her effort.

It was late that night that I was woken from a deep sleep. Mam was shaking me. 'Get up lass and fetch Miriam, for your gran is took real bad.'

I got up from the mattress that I shared with Irene, knuckling the sleep from my eyes. Mam wrapped my shawl around me and pushed me to the ladder that led down from our loft. I stumbled down our stairs, my heart thudding, and out onto the top staith, down to Miriam's cottage.

She opened quickly to my knocking. 'So it's time.'

There was no surprise. She picked up her basket and followed me.

Gran died in the early hours. Miriam sent us downstairs while she did the laying out. I sat at our kitchen table and couldn't stop shaking. Irene put her arms around me, hugging me close . . . my kind big sister again.

Mam kept calling up the stairs where Grandpa sat. He wouldn't move from the top step, not for all Mam's persuading. He sat up there with his head in his hands and wouldn't come down.

I hated that black bonnet; it smelt of lavender and death.

'You'll wear it for respect,' said Mam.

Black silk it was, made in our special Sandwick way from a yard of silk with five pleats measured across the top and a double frill round the bottom. The frill was supposed to stop the water from the fish baskets dripping on your neck, but nobody would carry fish on a black silk bonnet. It was special, for funerals, and we had plenty of them. I shook it out and tied it beneath my chin, swallowing hard.

'I'll wear it for Gran,' I said.

Daniel, my dad, missed the tide for two days. When he returned from the sea and found his mother dead, he sat by the fire and wept.

Mam hadn't cried; I don't think she'd found time for there'd been so much to do. Irene was quiet, shut off in a world of her own, but she'd roused herself to go out with me and Mary, bidding our relations and neighbours to come to the funeral. That's always the job of young women in our bay.

Grandpa was the one we all worried about. Such a fine man my grandpa was, real respected in our community. He'd been the lifeboat cox like his father Francis, who our lifeboat's named for. Grandpa has saved so many lives, taking out our heavy boat that's so difficult to launch. Folk still talk about the day that Grandpa went out three times in that dreadful storm that sank the Whitby lifeboat. Our boat survived, though the crew exhausted themselves and one man died of pneumonia. Grandpa's leg was crushed; he's dragged it ever since. My grandpa, who was our hero, wouldn't speak to anyone after Grandma's death. He shrank into himself . . . shrunk small and grey and lost.

I'd got no tears but I knew they were there, welling up tight inside. After the funeral Irene walked off with John Ruswarp, who'd been waiting for her outside the church. I was surprised Mam didn't call her back to help with the funeral dinner. So it was me who did most of the helping. I did my best and worked hard to see that all our guests got plenty, for it was part of showing respect for the dead one, giving a good feast after the service. But when the plates were cleared and the talking and drinking began, I slipped away.

I went down to the beach, for I knew I'd have a good

cry and I didn't want them to see. I sat on Plosher Rock, as Mary Jane and me call it, after the big five-man cobles that go from Whitby Harbour. I pulled the silk bonnet from my head and held it on my lap as I stared out to sea. The tears came slow and choking at first, then pouring freely, bringing relief. I picked up the bonnet from my lap and set it carefully on the dry rock. I'd be in trouble if I soaked it, for it must be wrapped up with lavender and put away for the next funeral.

It was only as calm came that I thought of the night that Grandma'd died and remembered with a sudden catch of breath that she'd wished to tell me something . . . something about young William Archer.

Chapter Three

It was all quiet when I got back and I found Irene standing at the table in the corner of the yard, back in her working dress and apron. She saw my red eyes and swollen face.

'You must put it behind you, lass,' she said, quite kind. 'Go change your dress; there's a line needs mucking. Dad's gone to rest, for he must go with the tide tonight.'

I changed my clothes and went to help. Irene was talkative but I could see that she was still upset. Hannah and Mary had brought bait for us early that morning and we'd the worst job to do now, for we'd baited lines that Dad had not been able to use, so the bait had gone foul. Mucking we called it, and a muckier job there never could be. We hated mucking but it had to be done.

Irene's hands shook as she pulled the scraps of stinking bait from the barbs, working slow, for her. I looked from her hands to her face, and she caught that glance. She dropped the line and lifted the backs of her hands to her eyes. Quiet tears ran down her cheeks, tears that she couldn't wipe for her hands were slimed with mouldy bait.

I was shocked. I couldn't think when I'd last seen her cry.

'Is it Gran?'

She shook her head. 'Not just Gran. You'll know soon enough . . . so I'll say now. I'm to have a child.'

I blinked. I couldn't believe what she was saying.

'Aye, you'll be shocked,' she said. 'But you don't know yet how strong it can be, that feeling . . . that feeling when you're sweet on a lad.'

I couldn't think what to say and she wiped her hands on her torn apron, searching for a clean corner to dry her eyes.

'Is . . . is it John Ruswarp?'

'Aye, him. Him who wants to be joining the Army, wants to be off fighting, so far away.'

I pulled myself together then. I remembered how she'd been sick and running to the privy.

'I should have known,' I said. 'I should have guessed, a great girl like me. I've thought of nothing but Gran.'

'Nay, how should you know such things? You're nobbut a bairn and you stay that way, our Liza.'

I went and put my arms round her, hugging her tight, frightened for her.

'I fear 'tis the worst to come,' she said. 'Mam knows and she's to tell Dad.'

'What does Mam say?'

'She says I'm a fool, but I'm not the first and she'll take my side. Best get Dad told, she says, even though he's so sad for Gran. Best get our troubles over, though I dread what he'll have to say.'

We stood there quiet, but then Irene seemed to brace herself.

'Now then, our Liza, this won't do. We're forgetting the lines. We must get these done or we'll have trouble indeed.'

We returned to our work, but it was different. She was working slow, her hands shaking still, and I worked really hard for once, trying to take the lead. I took the line.

'I'll coil,' I said, flicking the baited hooks aside as carefully as I could, thinking that I must learn to do this better. Irene'd find it hard in the coming months. They'll be needing me, I thought.

We finished the lines and Mam went upstairs to wake Dad for the tide and we heard him shouting.

'She's told him,' said Irene, her eyes filling with tears.

When Mam came down she sent us both out with Billy.

'Away with you,' she said. 'Take Billy away up to the heather. Hannah and Mary'll help get them off. He'll be different in the morning. He likes John Ruswarp more than most.'

*

We walked up the hillside past the old chapel, Billy running ahead. I felt strange with Irene, as though she were someone I didn't really know. I was scared for her, but pleased that she'd told me so much. Treating me like a woman for once. I couldn't help thinking about her and John Ruswarp, what they must have done . . . up there on the hillside, I guessed, where all the couples walk in summer. I knew about that – well, some of the girls at school talked about nothing else. I thought it sounded horrible and I told Mary Jane that I wasn't ever going to let any man do that to me.

I kept thinking about Irene having a bairn, too. I'd be real frightened of that; that was another thing they talked about at school. I couldn't forget how Rachel Danby had told how her sister had screamed so loud they'd all been sent out into the yard and they could still hear her screaming from there.

I remembered our Billy being born. It had been a long and difficult birth, but I never heard a scream or any sound from Mam, though I'd been at home all the time. I was sitting on Grandpa's knee, sniffing at his pipe and poking fresh tobacco into it, when Grandma Esther came to tell us that Billy was born.

Even though I was so small I knew that Mam was very poorly for a long time afterwards and Miriam had said that there'd be no more bairns for Mam.

Now it was going to happen to Irene and she didn't seem to be worrying about that part of it. She was just unhappy about what Dad would have to say and John wanting to go off to join the fighting.

She told me that John wanted them to be wed. He'd always wanted that, but he still wished to go off to South Africa like Frank. He wanted to make something of himself . . . so he said.

We sat down near the bank top where the heather begins, watching Billy jumping and hiding in thick purple clumps. We pulled our shawls tight, for though there was a bright sun, we were well into autumn and a chilly wind blew.

'That Nelly Wright,' said Irene. 'She'll have something to say when she hears. Such a wag-tongued gossip she is and she's sweet on John herself. She'll be mouthing it all the way to Whitby, she will.'

'Nay,' I said. 'Who cares what fat Nelly says? She'd better not say owt about my sister when I'm there.'

Irene smiled and squeezed my hand. 'You're a grand sister, our Liza,' she said.

Irene had brought her knitting for no time should be wasted and Irene could knit without looking at her hands. She stared out across the bay, her fingers working of their own accord. She was a fine young woman and I could see why John might think her bonny. Even in her working clothes she looked good, with her pink cheeks and clear skin and her hair done in the new fashion that she took such trouble with, curling her fringe in rags each week. She had a little plaited bun at the back and a thick fringe brushed forwards in shiny brown curls, like the new Queen Alexandra. Irene's hair was the same colour as mine. It was only Billy who'd got the fair curls we both wanted.

I asked Irene about William Archer. I told her how Gran had wanted me to know. I wouldn't have asked her before, but she seemed so much more my friend that day.

'Do you know owt of a William Archer?'

'Do you mean that little lad who was Mam's brother?'

'Ah, that must be him,' I said. 'Gran wanted to tell me about him, but it was the night she died. She never got it said and I didn't know what she meant.'

'I don't know much about him,' said Irene. 'Just that he was drowned and Mam was with him and it upset her so much that she'll not cross the causeway. That's why she goes the long way round.'

'Gran was telling me that I should take more notice of Mam. Gran was always telling me that.'

'Aye, so you should. There's not every mother would take her daughter's side, like Mam is with me. Aunt Hannah would know about that little lad William, though. Her and Mam have always been close. I dare say Aunt Hannah would have been there at the time.'

We were silent for a while, Billy still happily playing in the heather behind us.

'There they go,' I said, pointing down to the beach. We couldn't see very clear, but we could tell which was our boat, the *Sneaton Lass*, and could see Mam and Dad, both with skeps on their heads. We saw John Ruswarp go down with his mam and it looked like Mary Jane with them. She'd not been to school because of the funeral.

Dad went over to John, but we couldn't tell what went on. Time passed and they were still together on the beach, though the other cobles were out. Irene's knitting went faster and faster.

'Oh dear,' she said. 'There's a to-do, I know there is. Would Dad hit him, do you think?'

'Nay,' I said. 'John's that much bigger than Dad.'

Irene laughed and I joined in. We giggled together, but Irene laughed on after I'd stopped ... wild laughing, then suddenly it turned to desperate sobbing that frightened me. I put my arms round her and Billy came to stare at us. I didn't know what to do. I thought of Grandma Esther and missed her bitterly. She'd have known what to say and what to do.

'It's all right,' said Irene, pushing me away and smiling wet-faced at Billy. 'It's all right, our Billy,' she said, pulling him onto her knee while I fished around for the knitting she'd dropped, trying to save the stitches.

We sat on, staring down at the jumbled red roofs of our village. The cottages are crammed tight together on the steep bankside, so that kitchens often overlook their neighbours' bedroom window and we all know each other's business ... it can't be helped. We sat silent, watching the smoke puthering out of the chimneys and the washing flapping on the lines.

At last we saw that John had gone off in his boat and Dad and Uncle Frank were following.

'Now then, our Billy,' said Irene, 'it's time we got you home.'

Mam was laying out left-overs from the funeral dinner when we got back.

'Good,' she said. 'You're here. You can eat up these bits for your supper. Go wash your hands Billy, then sit up at the table.'

I couldn't believe it was only that morning that we'd been in our funeral clothes; so much had happened that day. Irene and I stood silent, not knowing how to put the question.

'Now don't stand there like ninnies. Get set down.'

'But Mam,' said Irene. 'What's been said?'

'It wasn't so much saying as shouting,' said Mam, 'but that's for the best, I think. It was Mrs Ruswarp I was sorry for, her knowing nowt about it and she was so shamed when she realised. Hannah and I walked back with her, though, and told her all and I think she feels better now. Mary Jane was listening too, her eyes wide and her ears flapping. I've never seen John so eager to be off, shouting at his mother and her not understanding. Their Sam knew what was up all right.

'Never mind . . . I think it's over. He'll have calmed down, will your dad, by the time he's had a night out there. So get yourselves set down and make the most of a decent meal. Your gran wouldn't like to see it wasted.'

Chapter Four

Dad waited for John on the top staith when he got back the next morning. Mam had been right. They sat together for a while talking quiet and friendly.

When Dad got back to our cottage, he kissed Irene and hugged her and told her she was a silly lass. He'd talked to Uncle Frank while he was out and thought a lot about Esther, his mam, and he'd come to think that it was fine, that a new life should be coming when one so loved had just gone. He said he'd rather she married John Ruswarp than any other, though she could have waited for chapel first. Still, we'd make the best of it and he'd talk to John about the Army and try to get him to change his mind and stay.

*

I met Mary Jane down on the beach and we went arm in arm to our special rock. Mary Jane was full of it.

'Well fancy our John and your Irene! Fancy them going and doing that. I couldn't believe my ears when I heard all that shouting going on. Eeeh, our dad was vexed, and the whole village heard about it. Weren't you surprised?'

'Well . . . our Irene had told me,' I said. 'So I knew there'd be a to-do.'

'I'll like to be the auntie though,' said Mary Jane.

'But it's me as will be the auntie.'

'Oh . . .' said Mary Jane, frowning with working it out. 'So you will, for Irene's your sister, but John's my brother so I'll be the auntie, too.'

'We'll both be aunties,' I said. 'Both aunties to the same bairn. That makes us like relations, you and me.'

We liked the thought of that and we sat there planning the things we'd do. The best aunties in the world we would be.

Along the beach came Nelly Wright and her little gang of friends. Older than us they were and all of them had been bait-gatherers for a year or so. Some of the lasses were kind enough if you saw them by themselves or with their mams, but when they all got together with Nelly Wright as ringleader, a real rough noisy lot they were.

'I've not seen your Irene today,' Nelly shouted. 'I hear she's got the belly ache, the belly ache that don't go away.'

They all shrieked with laughter and shoved at each other with their elbows.

I jumped down from my rock so angry I'd forgotten to be scared.

'Don't you speak about my sister. She's better than the lot of you.'

They fell about laughing again.

'Can you hear the flither squeaking?' yelled Nelly. Then she pointed at Mary Jane who'd come and thrust her arm through mine. 'Aye, and look at that saucy face. Saucy like her brother she is. You wouldn't believe the tales I could tell about that lad . . . though I'm not so low as to let him give me the belly ache.'

They slapped each other on the backs, still shaking with their laughing, and turned to walk on up the beach.

I stuck my tongue out at their backs and Mary Jane, she followed behind at a safe distance, holding her skirt out behind her, waving it from side to side, imitating fat Nelly's wobbly walk.

We went back to Plosher Rock, giggling ourselves now. We weren't going to let them spoil us being aunties, whatever they might say.

'I wish our John wouldn't go on about joining the Army though,' said Mary Jane. 'I can't bear the thought of him going off to the war. He might get himself killed, then the poor bairn'd have no dad.'

'Aye,' I agreed with her. 'I do miss our Frank. It were grand that day when we went over to Scarborough to wave them off.' It was such a to-do. Folk were throwing flowers and bands were playing and everyone was singing and shouting. They looked so smart in their uniforms and folk were saying how volunteers had never before gone off like that to fight with the Regulars. It was so lovely, but then suddenly they were gone and we've heard nowt since, only snippets of news that my dad picks up in Whitby and we don't know whether our Frank's alive or dead. We heard that some of the lads came back last August, but never a word have we heard of Frank.

There seemed to be a bit of a commotion up in the village. A group of lads came walking down by the staith following a man, a gentleman almost, but loaded up with boxes and bits and pieces. The lads were carrying things, too. There were folded sticks and an umbrella with black material draped at the sides.

'Well I never,' said Mary Jane. 'I do believe it's him.'

'Whatever do you mean?'

'It's him . . . the picture man, the one I told you about.'

'Oooh . . . are you sure it's him?'

'Who else could it be?'

We watched as they walked along the staith to Old Miriam's cottage. We couldn't hear what was going on, but it was clear enough. He wished to make a picture of Miriam. We could tell how pleased she was, flustered and smiling and brushing down her skirt. It took a long time to get the camera fixed, but the picture man had the lads all quiet and good and running at his beck and call.

Miriam sat up straight and smart, like the squire's

lady herself, but the picture man didn't seem to be in any hurry to get his photograph done. He talked on and on to Miriam, and we'd got a fine view of it all up on our rock. At last, when Miriam picked up her knitting and leaned back in her chair chatting . . . suddenly the picture was being made.

We watched them packing everything up ready to leave and we were just going to get down from our rock to follow the procession of lads when the picture man looked our way. He stopped for a moment and held his hand up to shade his eyes, then he started to walk towards us. Our mouths dropped open; straight towards us he came. Mary Jane looked behind to see if there was someone else . . . but there was no one. We looked at each other scared for there was no doubt but he was coming over to us. I was that shocked it fair took my breath away, but there he was standing before our rock, bowing slightly and lifting his hat, the gang of lads waiting farther back.

'You make a fine picture up there on the rock, young ladies. I'd be pleased to make a picture of you.'

We stared, then Mary Jane giggled and I couldn't help it; I was giggling too, looking back at this slim man, quite tall with a kind smile and fine bushy beard.

'Do I have your permission, young ladies?'

We giggled again and nodded. 'Can if you like.'

Again he took a long time setting his camera up. He talked to us as he worked, asking our names and did we live in the bay.

He set up three spindly legs, fastened together, then

fixed his camera box on top. A bit wobbly it looked, balanced on the shingle, and he had the lads looking round for a flat-topped stone to fix beneath the back leg. At last it was fixed, but then he had to move the whole contraption farther back and find another stone. At last he seemed satisfied and stayed beneath the cape saying, 'That's good . . . that's good.'

He had to bend his long legs to get himself to the right height.

'You can't see much in there, can you?' asked Mary Jane, grown bold.

'I can see you fine young ladies,' he said. 'I see you fine, but upside-down.'

We both laughed at that and the laughing made me cheeky. I leant right over, propping up my head with my hand. 'Why should we not sit like this then?'

'You goose,' said Mary Jane.

'Stay just like that,' came the picture man's voice.

So bursting with sauciness, but frozen still, we had our picture made.

'That's done,' he said, appearing from under the cape.

'But that was daft,' I said.

'Aye, a bit of fun, but I think a good picture. I'll send a copy for your mothers if you tell me where you live.'

We did more than tell him, we walked back up the beach with him and showed him our cottages. He spoke all polite to Mam, treating her like a lady. Mam was all shamed with her apron dirty from the skaning and her hands all slimed.

We walked up the hill with him, helping to carry his boxes . . . up to the pony and trap waiting at the top. He asked us if we went to school and Mary Jane told him how Miss Hindmarch wished me back there.

'Is that not Miss Cicely Hindmarch?' he asked.

'Yes indeed,' said Mary Jane.

'I'm acquainted with Miss Hindmarch,' he said. 'A good teacher and a clever woman. If Miss Hindmarch thinks well of you, you must be a smart girl.'

Mary Jane nudged me hard.

'Perhaps you should return to school,' he said.

'Nay, learning's got nowt to do with the likes of me.'

He looked thoughtful for a moment and I thought I'd been rude, but he smiled and lifted his hat. He loaded up the trap with his boxes and went on his way.

'He never gave us any pennies,' said Mary Jane.

Chapter Five

Mam was packing a parcel of fish-heads wrapped in cloth when I got back.

'When you've finished with having your head turned, you can run an errand for me. Take these over to poor Annie Lythe. Tell her I'm sorry it's only the heads.'

Poor Annie Lythe, as everyone called her, had lost her husband: drowned at sea, the familiar way. Annie had six children all younger than me and we knew she was having a struggle to raise them, but she managed to keep them out of the workhouse somehow. She took in washing and we all gave what we could to help. It wasn't like charity; it was just 'the right thing to do', for we all knew that the next family orphaned could be ours. Mam usually sent a decent fish. If it was fish-heads for Annie

Lythe, then it would be fish-head stew for us. With the bad weather starting, Dad'd not be able to get out every time and we'd be mucking the lines.

Annie's cottage was next to Aunt Hannah's and I saw Hannah and Mary sat out at the back baiting lines as I passed. I remembered how Irene had said that Aunt Hannah was the one to ask if I wanted to know more about William, Mam's young brother. But Aunt Hannah has a bit of a sharp tongue and I hurried on to Annie's.

To find Annie, you had to fight your way through sheets and petticoats and frilly drawers all hanging from lines across the yard. She was turning the poss stick in her dolly tub, her sleeves rolled high and her muscles straining, her small kitchen filled with steam.

'Thank your mam kindly,' she said, seeing my parcel.

''Fraid it's only fish-heads,' I told her.

'I know the catches have been bad so it's most kind of her,' insisted Annie.

Her two youngest girls came and stood before me, tugging at my skirt.

'Nay, I've got no liquorice today,' I said, wishing that I'd saved a bit when Dad brought some from Whitby last week. Their dresses were clean but worn and holed. Annie had little time to spare from her laundry work to see to her own girls' clothes.

'I heard about your Irene's trouble,' said Annie. 'Tell her that I wish her well, will you? When you know how easy life is lost, you value a new life coming.'

I thanked her and said goodbye. It's funny, I thought.

Funny how it's often those that has least that manages to be kindest.

I dawdled by Aunt Hannah's door, wanting to speak to her, but I needed my courage for Aunt Hannah won't suffer fools. She's not quiet like our mam; she always has plenty to say.

'Well, Liza,' said Hannah when she spied me, 'you're here at the right time. Get yourself sat down and coil this line, for Mary's to go to Walter Snaith's to fetch our new skeps. You'll earn yourself a cup of tea then.'

At least you didn't need an invitation with Hannah.

I sat and helped, but I couldn't think how to ask what I wanted till Hannah herself showed me the way.

'You should be getting back to school, Liza,' she said. 'That'd please your mam, now that Poor Esther's gone.'

'Why . . . I would,' I said, 'but with Grandpa taken to his bed, there's none to see to Billy but me.'

'Aye, there's some as would have Billy down on the beach while the picking's done, but not Martha.'

'Grandma Esther wanted me to know,' I said, grabbing at my chance.

'Whatever do you mean? Speak sense, lass. What did Esther want you to know?'

I swallowed hard and tried again. 'Esther wanted to tell me about young William Archer, but it was the night she died and she never got it said.'

'Aah,' said Hannah, quite soft for her. 'Esther wanted

to tell you that, did she? That's what you're here for. Well, Esther did usually know what's best and we should respect her wishes.'

I nodded, uncomfortable, while Hannah inspected me.

'I'm not sure as you shouldn't ask your mam . . . but maybe it's easier for someone else to say. I'll tell you what I can.'

'I know William Archer was Mam's young brother,' I said. 'And I know he was drowned, but then we've all had family drowned haven't we, like . . .'

'Aye, like our Ned. True enough, but it's usually in bad weather or a storm and you dread it, but you half expect it. William Archer, he was drowned on a sunny spring afternoon, the sea as calm as you could wish. We were nearby, but we never saw owt amiss . . . not till it was too late.'

'You were there then, Aunt Hannah?'

'Oh aye, I was there.' Her face went sad and she spoke so quiet I could hardly believe it was my aunt.

'There was me, Esther and old Mrs Lythe – that's Annie's mother-in-law. There was your mam's mother Katherine Archer, too, and we were all fetching the flithers. I'd just started to help with it and I felt jealous of Martha, your mam, her being that bit younger than me and her still being treated like a child. She was left to splash about near the causeway with little William. She'd been told to take care of him, mind.'

It felt strange to think of my mam being a young lass

and having to look to her young brother, like I did for Billy.

'It was Esther who saw it first,' said Hannah. '"What's up with your Martha?" she said. Katherine looked . . . well we all looked and there she was lying face-down near the causeway, close to the water's edge and the tide going out, for we'd not been picking long. She wasn't shouting or making any sound, but she was kicking and punching at the sand.'

I shuddered when I heard that. I couldn't imagine my mam behaving so odd.

'"She's lost that lad," said Katherine. "She's let him run off up the staith." We wandered over to her. We weren't in any hurry, but when we got close we saw that she was in a right state, slavering and biting at the sand. Katherine went and pulled her to her feet. "Where's the lad?" she asked. "Has he run off?" Martha didn't answer, just kept opening and shutting her mouth, but she pointed to the sea. Well, then we did worry. Katherine slapped your mam hard across the face. "Where's the lad?" she asked again and at last poor Martha spoke. "In the sea."'

I'd stopped my work on Mary's line and Aunt Hannah never even noticed, so tense her face had gone.

'We stared out to sea,' she said, 'but there was nowt and it looked so calm we couldn't believe that the lad was in there. Katherine, she suddenly made up her mind to take no chances. She put down her swill and walked straight into the sea — clothes, boots and all — and once she'd done it we all seemed to think that she was right.

We followed her and we looked and looked. We went out as deep as we dared, but we found nothing. Even then we weren't sure. We made Katherine come back in. We told her not to worry, we said he'd come running down the staith before long. We stopped our picking; the men'd have to stay at home that night, for a young lad's life means more than a good catch.

'We took Katherine home and searched the village. Martha was forgotten. Where she went, I don't know, but it was Miriam who brought her home that night. Nobody held her to blame – it was the sea – but I think she blamed herself and as far as I know your mam has never crossed the causeway since.'

'But how had William gone?'

'We've never really known, but drowned he was and his body washed up at Sandsend. We could only think that he must have been caught in one of those currents. You can never trust the sea . . . it takes those it wants.'

I sat frozen, staring at my aunt, trying to take in all she'd said. Seeing my mam as a child and her so frightened that she'd near gone mad.

'Esther was right,' said Hannah, more her usual self. 'It's best that you know. Don't mock your mam when she goes traipsing over the bridge or fussing over Billy, and think how she manages to get herself down on that beach, working to feed you bairns.'

I nodded. I was chilled right through and I needed Hannah's hot sweet tea to warm me again, but Hannah wasn't one to let you sit and stew.

'Seeing as you're here and Mary's not back, you can come down to the beach with me and your Uncle Frank. Take that wreath from Mary's peg and get that skep fixed.'

My aunt went inside for Uncle Frank and I reached the padded band down and pulled it round my head. I lifted the skep I'd been working on and got it comfortably settled in its place. I was glad to be having a job to do, after what I'd heard, and at least Aunt Hannah treated me like I was useful.

Chapter Six

As the weeks went by and the sun shone lower in the sky, the winds blew cold and our lives settled into the hard pattern that each winter brings. The men had to use the longer lines and go farther out. That meant more bait to be fetched and the weather worse for doing it.

Mam and Hannah made some visits up the Cleveland coast to sell fish to the steelworkers' families. They had done this before, keeping back as much fish as they could carry from the dealer who waited above the staith with his donkey carts. It was a real tramp for them, carrying the fish baskets on their heads padded with wreaths, but they could make a bit of extra money that way, before the worst weather set in. They were getting the reputation of being sharp business women.

The flither pickers began to talk of a trek. This was something they often had to do during the winter months, but now they thought it best to get it done whilst it was still autumn, before the worst weather came.

There was such a great amount of flither picking and mussel picking done in our bay that the shellfish would become few, and small at that. So the women would organise a trek. They'd set off with a great load of sacks and swills and walk away down the coast in search of a right good supply. They had to go past Whitby, ignoring the limpets there, for they were needed by the Whitby pickers and a large supply they needed too. So our Sandwick women had to go to the scaur way past Whitby and a good fifteen miles that was. It was all a bit of a fuss and a palaver; they had to find relations or friends to stay overnight with in Whitby.

We'd send the donkey carts over the cliffs to carry the flithers back. Then the women would be up early the next morning and walking back to get the caving and skaning done, so's not to lose another day's fishing.

'Can't I come with you this time?' I begged Mam, when she and Hannah were making their plans.

'Nay,' said Mam. 'A trek's no outing and you'll stay to see to Billy and your grandpa . . . though I wish you might be back in school once your grandpa is himself again.'

I sighed and opened my mouth to make more arguments, but I caught Aunt Hannah looking at me, so I shut my mouth and went out onto the staith.

I didn't want to be getting back to school at all, but I hated Grandpa being sick. Mam talked to Hannah about it and I could tell she was worried. The thing was that you couldn't really say what was wrong. He lay in bed all day and refused to eat most of the food that we carried up to him. Even Billy couldn't rouse him. Miriam said there was nothing to be done. She said that he was suffering from grief and that had to run its course. We should leave him be, she said, and he'd come back to us in his own good time. But the weeks went by and he kept to his bed.

I sat out there on the top staith, remembering how happy I'd been when I was a little girl. Grandma Esther would wrap me up warm in my bonnet and shawl and I'd go out with Grandpa in all but the worst of weather and we'd sit up there on the top staith. We never sat alone, for every person passing would stop to speak. Sometimes we'd be surrounded by a great gang of children, listening to Grandpa's stories. I was so proud to be sat up there on Grandpa's knee, so proud to be his grandchild. He'd tell stories of shipwrecks, of smuggling, of our lifeboats and the different coxswains, the rescues that he'd made himself, but my favourite story came from a time way back: the story of Simon Wise.

Grandpa would tell how a mysterious stranger had come from the forests over Pickering way and his name, so he said, was Simon Wise. He'd taken to fishing and had gone out one night with an old fisherman who'd befriended him. That night they'd been attacked by a

French ship, a man-o'-war. Simon Wise had told his friend not to be afraid and he'd taken up his bow and arrow and shot every Frenchman that tried to board the small boat. The last few members of the crew surrendered and asked Simon Wise aboard. It turned out to be a pirate ship, loaded with stolen gold that the pirates offered to Simon Wise in payment for their lives, but he sent the pirates on their way, telling them not to pick on small fishing boats again, and gave away all the gold to the poor fisher-folk of the coast. He then returned to the forest he came from and later became known in other parts of the country as the outlaw Robin Hood.

Mam, Dad and Mrs Ruswarp were making plans for Irene's wedding. It was to be as soon as we could get it arranged, keeping a bit of decency, as Dad said, for the banns to be read up in Mulgrave Chapel. So we'd got the date fixed for late November and, although it was to be a rushed do, my dad insisted that we'd make it a fine wedding and hold our heads high. We'd have all the traditional fun and frills: a reception in the village hall and dancing late into the night, and of course we'd have John Ruswarp's coble hauled up on the beach to be decorated with flags and bunting and paper flowers. Mam said she wanted to get the trek done first, then we'd have an outing to Whitby to buy the stuff for Irene's wedding. Mary Jane and me were to be bridesmaids. Mam said two were enough in the circumstances, instead of the usual six.

*

I got up early on the morning of the trek and Billy and me walked along the beach to set them on their way. When we reached Caedmon's Cliff, Mam sent us back.

'And you see you get Billy back safe,' she said. 'The tide's on the turn so don't dawdle.'

I didn't argue as I once might have done. 'Yes, Mam,' I answered meek enough, and after we'd watched them trudge away beneath the cliffs I took his hand and I did take care, for after what Hannah had told me I could see why Mam had taken fright when I let Billy wander on the cliffs. I'd thought a bit more about our Billy, too. He was a fine little brother really and I wouldn't be without him. We played follow-my-leader as we went back to the village and I let him be the leader. I even enjoyed seeing him so delighted when he made me crawl on all fours over the scaur and walk backwards, twice round Plosher Rock.

It was quiet in the village for most of the women had gone on the trek, leaving only the young and the old, and the men still resting, having got back from the sea in the early hours. Billy and me sat on the top staith where Grandpa used to sit.

Old Walter Snaith came and sat with us for a while, working away at one of his baskets. Walter made all the baskets we needed for our work: swills for collecting flithers, skeps for the long lines and big fish-baskets, too. He asked after my grandpa and said that it was a sad thing indeed. He'd known Grandpa well; they'd been lads together.

Walter finished his basket and got up to go. He was to take the donkey carts over the cliffs to fetch the bait that was gathered. He said he must round up some of the lads to help him. I wished I could have gone too, but I was needed at home, so I sat tight.

Miriam came out into her front to get a bit of sun while she did her knitting. Miriam had no husband and no son, but every spare moment she was knitting away at a gansey. It was never for a particular person, just a medium-sized gansey for whoever needed it most. Miriam did all the things that any mother did, though she'd no children of her own. It was as though the whole village were her children. Old or young, she mothered us all; I can't think how we'd have managed without her.

She did well enough living by herself and though she wasn't rich, she didn't lack for anything either. Sometimes we paid her for her simples and her nursing care, but if folk were short they'd pay her with fish or by helping with repairs to her neat cottage on the front. However poor, none were turned away from her door.

I watched her knitting in the sun and wondered if I dare ask her about William and the dreadful thing that had happened. There was nobody else around and I could see that she wasn't busy for once. Still I was reluctant; you didn't call on Miriam unless something was up – sickness or childbirth or death. You didn't call to pass the time of day, but the strange thing was that Miriam looked up and beckoned me.

I went over to her gate.

'Well, Liza Welford, so you're left to mind your Billy.'

She continued with her knitting while she spoke, bony fingers working fast, not needing to look at what she did – like all the women in our bay.

'Aye,' I answered. 'We've set them on their way.'

I couldn't think when I'd looked close at Miriam before, she never stopped still long enough as a rule. Fine wrinkles creased her forehead and cheeks. Her hair worn thin and silver was tucked neatly beneath her blue cotton Sandwick bonnet. Light grey eyes peered sharp at me through small gold-rimmed spectacles.

'You'll be missing your Esther, I dare say?'

'Aye,' I repeated it with a sigh.

'She were right fond of you,' said Miriam, 'and you'll miss her sore, but you must treasure what you remember and that way you'll still have her.'

I nodded. She was right, but there was something more I needed to ask.

'That night,' I said. 'That night when Grandma Esther died, she tried to tell me something. It was about my mam. She tried to tell how Mam's young brother William Archer was drowned.'

Miriam's head jerked up and the wrinkles in her forehead gathered tighter still, but she nodded me to have my say.

'Well . . . she never got it said, but I've asked Aunt Hannah and she's told me what a terrible thing it was and how it'd upset my mam, but she didn't know what happened when they went off looking. She said it was you who brought Mam back.'

'So I did and there's no mystery as to where she was. She was here in my cottage till late that night, though as for what went on . . . that's between her and me.'

Miriam folded her knitting and got up from her chair. I thought she was sending me off. I thought I'd pried where I shouldn't. I was ready to go but Miriam pointed to Billy, who'd been slinging pebbles against her wall.

'Fetch your Billy through to my garden, then you may take a drink of tea with me.'

Chapter Seven

It was a special treat to go into Miriam's garden and Billy came willingly enough. It spread a long way up onto the hillside from the back of her cottage; the biggest garden in the village, packed with herbs and flowers. There was lavender to crush and sniff, and liquorice root to clean and chew. I led Billy through Miriam's kitchen that was hung with bunches of herbs drying for the winter use. I would have liked to go out with him, but there were more important things to worry about.

Miriam put on her kettle and made me sit. A proper visitor I was and I wasn't used to it. She brought our tea and sat beside her fire, thoughtful for a moment, then she spoke.

'I'll tell what I think I should, though I'll not tell

all. No one will ever know it all but your mam and me.'

I nodded, feeling the importance of what she said.

'It's a long way back now, but it's one of those days that stick in your memory. You'd like to forget it, but you can't. I was here, busy with something – I can't think what. I knew there'd been a commotion on the beach. I didn't go out, knew I'd hear soon enough if I was needed. I looked out once, I recall, and saw Martha down there by herself, but I thought nowt of that. Then I glanced out a while later and there she was in exactly the same spot. She'd never moved. The second time I looked something bothered me, something about the stillness of her, and I decided to go down.

'I passed someone on the way and I heard that William was lost and that they were all searching for him. When I got closer to Martha, I really took fright. I could see that she'd not moved, not one speck, and the sea was up to her knees . . . her face blank, like a person dead. I ran and took hold of her, but she was stiff and cold, staring out to sea, and her just a young girl like you.'

When Miriam told me that I bit my lips hard to keep back the tears. I knew I was being told something very secret. I must treat it with respect.

'I could tell what had happened,' said Miriam. 'I knew when I saw her face that William had drowned and that what she wanted was to rush into the sea and follow him, but fear stopped her. So there she stood, letting the sea come up. She couldn't go to meet it, but she couldn't resign herself to living either. Aye,' said Miriam, tapping me on the arm, 'you let the tears fall, for it was a thing no young girl should have to face.'

I did as she said; I let the tears fall and wept for my mam and her brother. When I'd dried my eyes and calmed myself, Miriam finished her telling.

'I got her to move, though it was difficult, but I got her back up here and she stayed with me for the rest of the day. Outside they were searching for William, but I knew it was in vain. William was beyond help, it was Martha who needed me. We talked and talked and I'll not say all, but a struggle took place and by the time night came, Martha had somehow gotten the strength to go on with her life. It was with grim determination though and she was never a child again, not after that.

'Now Liza,' she said, putting her hands on my shoulders to make me really take notice, 'I've said what I thought right and what Esther in her wisdom wanted you to know, but the time will come when you must speak to your mam. That would be for the best.'

It left me quiet and sad, almost wishing I'd never asked. I thanked her and called our Billy in from the garden.

I thought about my talk with Miriam all night and couldn't sleep. I didn't think I'd ever be able to speak to Mam about what happened. Mam's hard shell was as strong as the flithers. You could never break through that.

I got up early next morning and by the time Mam and Irene arrived back from spending the night with cousin Rachel in Whitby, I'd polished the fireplace and side oven and covered the table with oilskins, for it was too cold to get the baiting done outside that day. We disliked that, for it meant our only living room cluttered and mucky with it all, but we'd no choice. I'd filled the buckets ready to soak the shelled limpets and mussels and got the skeps out, with two lines all cleaned and a kettle boiling ready to make their tea.

Mam and Irene were tired, but they smiled real surprised when they saw the work I'd done.

'I do believe our Liza's growing up,' said Mam. That was compliment enough from her.

I made tea and we all gathered round the table to start shelling. I was needed to help as they'd such a load to do and the next day's supply was to be kept fresh by changing the water and fetching seaweed to cover the bucket tops.

There came a knock at the door and I went to open it. A young postboy held out a parcel addressed to me. He touched his cap and pushed the parcel into my arms.

'Special delivery, miss. I'm to wait on a reply – a message for the picture man in Whitby.'

Mam and Irene came to see what was up.

'Well fancy,' said Irene. 'Fancy our Liza getting a parcel. Get it opened, lass.'

My hands shook as I fiddled with the string. It was tightly knotted, but we couldn't cut it, for it was a good useful bit of string. At last Mam wiped her hands down her apron and took it from me. Her strong fingers quickly teased the knot apart and a beautiful new book was discovered, bound with green linen and stamped with gold lettering. A real treasure, this. I picked it up and read out loud: '*In Exchange For A Soul* by Mary Linskill.'

Mam looked at me, pleased and wondering. 'He's sent you a book, Liza. He must have thought you a clever lass.'

'Nay,' I said. 'It's that gossiping Mary Jane. She told him how Miss Hindmarch wishes me back in school.'

Irene stroked the clean new cover. 'Oh Liza . . . it's beautiful. There's nobody in the bay has a book like it.'

Mam held up a handwritten sheet for me to read.

'See what it says here, Liza, for this lad's waiting to take a reply.'

I read it carefully to myself.

'Come on, Liza,' said Irene. 'Tell us what it says.'

'You'll never believe,' I said. 'He invites Miss Liza Welford and Miss Mary Jane Ruswarp, along with any members of their families, to visit his photographic studio in Whitby. We're to view our picture, which is enlarged and on display as it has won a prize in a national photographic competition.'

'Never,' said Mam.

'What,' said Irene. 'A picture of them two cheeky things! I cannot think that's right.'

'Well, it's true enough,' I said, though I could hardly think it myself, that scared and excited I felt. 'He says we may go next Saturday if that's to our convenience and he'll provide a pony and trap for our transportation. Well Mam, what do you say to that?'

Mam was speechless, but she eventually believed it and we sent the postboy back with the message that we'd be pleased to go.

I couldn't really settle down to the caving after that. Dad came to help, as he'd not been out during the night and we needed all the help we could get. When he heard the news, he was that tickled he kept looking at me and saying. 'Well, our Liza, a prize-winning picture? Well, our Liza, who's a fine lady now?' He laughed and smiled as he hadn't done since Grandma Esther died.

No matter how I tried I couldn't concentrate on the shelling and Mam let me off. She let me run down to the Ruswarps' with the news, for I was bursting to tell and she said she'd get on better without me.

Mary Jane threw herself on the floor, laughing and laughing, till Mrs Ruswarp got worried. It was only when I showed the letter that she calmed down and they both believed me.

We talked of nothing else that week and made such preparations for our outing. Mam with her canny ways insisted that we should make it our shopping day for the wedding and save ourselves the expense of another trip. As the transport was to be provided we could all go – Mam, Dad, Irene, Mrs Ruswarp, Mary Jane and me. We'd been worried about Grandpa, but as usual Miriam came to our rescue. She said she'd look after Billy and take Grandpa his meals. We were excited and it was only the thought of Grandpa's unhappiness that marred our pleasure.

We'd tried so hard to cheer him and get him to take interest again, but nothing roused him. Not Irene's wedding, not our prize picture, not the coming bairn.

I kept my book in our loft in a fine woven basket that Grandma Esther had made for me one Eastertide. I'd never had a book. There were books at school, but they were worn and had to be shared and only for use in school time. Then we had our family bible, our family record of births and deaths, which Dad kept in a special chest. This beautiful bound book was quite different, a special book of my own. No one in the bay had such a thing. I don't think I'd ever have tried to read it if it wasn't that the picture man had written a special message inside it.

The first night that I had it, I carried my candle up to bed and looked again at my new treasure. I opened the cover and saw the picture man's writing. I thought, fancy doing that. Fancy writing in a brand new book, on such a fresh white page. It said: *For Liza, hoping that within these pages she will discover that learning can be for her*. I was puzzled, I didn't know what it meant. I remembered how I'd told him 'learning had nowt to do with me', then worried that I'd been rude. Still, rudeness or not, it had brought me this book. He means me to read it, I thought, I'd have to be very careful if I were to read it. I wouldn't have to dirty these crisp pages or mark the cover. I'd have to scrub my hands real well if I were to read it.

I turned the pages delicately, past the Contents and on to the story. I glanced at each page as I passed, then stopped. I stared at the title of Chapter Two: *A North Yorkshire Fisher Maiden*. Fisher maidens, I thought. Why, who'd put them in a book? I looked down the page and began to read.

A group of tall, handsome fisher-girls who were down by the edge of the tide — such girls as you would hardly see anywhere else in England for strength and straightness, for roundness of form and bright, fresh healthfulness of countenance.

Why, I thought, it's about girls like us ... like me or Irene or Mary Jane.

I read on and found more to interest me. It was about a fisher-girl called Barbara Burdas, who'd two young men both loving her, one of them a fisherman named David Andoe and the other was Hartas Theyn, a rather shabby squire's son.

I turned back to the beginning and started to read it properly. I'd never read anything like it before. It was a love story but very sad, with things going wrong. Dreadful things happened to Barbara Burdas, but then such things happened in our own bay, I knew that well enough. I read and read until my candle guttered and Irene came grumbling up to bed, fishing around in the dark.

Chapter Eight

We all dressed smart on the Saturday morning, scrubbed clean and wearing our Sunday best. Mam and Irene in their silk bonnets and me and Mary Jane laced tight in our best boots. The pony and trap arrived on time and we climbed in chatting and smiling at the treat of it all.

John Ruswarp came to set us off on our way. He'd have liked to be coming but wasn't allowed, for he mustn't see the stuffs for our wedding clothes – bad luck that would be. John ran beside us as the trap set off. He ran till he could keep up no more, with Irene waving and blushing till he was out of sight.

We enjoyed the drive into Whitby, passing through villages we knew well, holding our heads high, giggling as folk turned to watch, wondering what was up.

Whitby was always busy on a Saturday, what with the street traders and the market and the ladies and gentlemen buying their goods. We went straight to the photographic studios, for we couldn't wait to see our picture. The studio had a double shop front, new and grand, with flowers and plants arranged in the windows and flower designs on the glass, with dark velvet curtains behind.

We went in and stood shy and uncomfortable in the waiting room, staring at the leather upholstery and rich drapes. A lady sat there with her child and its nurse, all dressed very fine. The lady wore a cream dress with lace and tucks and a row of bows to show off her tiny waist. The nurse was dressed in black and white, but the best silk. I felt sorry for the baby; its fat cheeks bulged and it fretted and peered from beneath a bonnet that was so bedecked with lace and frills that the poor bairn could hardly see.

I tried not to stare, but that was hard for I wanted to remember it all. The lady fetched out a tiny lace handkerchief when we came in. She held it to her nose, turning her head to whisper to the nurse as if she thought us most inferior – and us all scrubbed and in our finery.

I was glad when the picture man came through to us and greeted us real pleased and polite, ignoring the lady with her miserable child. He invited us upstairs to another room and there on the wall in a carved wooden frame hung the picture of me and Mary Jane. At the sight of it we lost all shyness and talked and laughed. The picture was so full of life, you'd think we could've jumped up at any moment and splashed away into the sea.

The picture man said that he was very proud that we'd won him a prize in such an important competition. He brought out two smaller prints of our picture that he'd set in neat frames and he gave them to us to hang on the wall at home.

Mam said as how it was so kind of the picture man to have sent me such a lovely book.

'But did you read it, young lady?' he asked.

Well, once he'd got me going on that, I talked on and on, telling how I'd read it once and then read it again. How I'd told the story to Mary Jane and then how Mam and Irene had let me sit up late each night, reading the story out loud to them and how we'd all thought the story wonderful and sad and how we felt flat now that we were getting near to the end, and thinking we'd have to start at the beginning again.

'I thought it might be just the thing,' he said. 'Do you know of Mary Linskill, the lady who wrote the story? A Whitby lady she was, though sadly she died a few years back.'

'Whitby?' I said. 'Did she really live in Whitby? Did you know her?' The picture man smiled at my surprise. 'I did indeed,' he said.

Mam and Dad and the others stood quiet and smiling, letting me chatter on and on about my wonderful book. The picture man was pleased, I could tell, pleased that he'd found something that had given such pleasure and interest.

'I have to make a photograph of a baby now,' he said, 'but when I've done, I could show you where Mary lived and tell you more about her.'

I was delighted at that, but Mam said though it was most kind, he shouldn't waste his valuable time.

No, he insisted, he'd enjoy doing that, so we arranged to meet him in the market place at noon.

Mam explained that we'd shopping to do for Irene's wedding. The picture man congratulated Irene, making her blush, then he said he'd like to make a studio portrait of her, for she'd a very fine face. That made her blush even more.

We swept through the waiting room, our noses in the air.

'They'll see our picture when they go through,' Mary Jane whispered.

Our bridesmaids' shopping was soon done. We got fine white silk for our dresses, with lace to stitch at the necks; a yard of blue velvet ribbon each for our sashes and new white stockings to go with our white boots.

'We'll be fine as any lady,' said Mary Jane.

Irene couldn't make up her mind about the stuff for her dress, so we left her with Mam and Mrs Ruswarp and went with Dad to the market place. We loved going to look at the stalls and Dad let us sit up at the counter of Jacksons, beneath the cheerful striped awnings. We both had a dainty glass dishful of hokey-pokey ice cream, a rare treat that froze our tongues and made our teeth ache as we crunched the tiny slivers of ice.

Dad was in a fine mood, calling out to his Whitby friends that he hadn't seen for a time, passing on the latest gossip, telling everyone about our prize-winning photograph and worrying over the news from South Africa. There were rumours of sickness and fever and our lads suffering from poor rations. Many folk were saying that they ought to be brought back home.

When we all met up again, Irene had found the material she liked, and ribbons and lace to make it bonny. The picture man found us by the fish stall that belonged to Hannah Smith, who we all called Trickey. Mrs Smith had a reputation of being able to sell fish to anyone, so crafty and clever she was.

'You shouldn't stand talking too long to Mrs Smith,' said the picture man, 'she'll talk you into buying a haddock to take back to Sandwick Bay.'

We followed the picture man up to Church Street, then off to the right through one of the dark alleys that open into a yard, Blackburn's Yard, just as small and cramped as our own.

'She never lived here?' I said. 'Not that lady who wrote the story?'

'Yes,' said the picture man. He pointed out a small cottage. 'This is where she was born and this,' he said, pointing to a rather newer cottage, 'this is where the family moved to later.'

'But was she not rich and clever?' I asked.

'She was clever enough, but she was never rich.'

'Is that so?' said Mam. 'She wrote that lovely book, but never had money?'

'Her father was one of the constables,' said the picture man. 'A respectable working man. Sometimes, when he took female prisoners, he would keep them in the cottage with his family. Mary had the job of carrying the food to them. I think she often heard their sad stories. A strange start in life, I should think.'

Mam nodded her head. 'Strange indeed.'

'But how did she get to write her stories?' I asked.

'Ah well, young lady, she went to school. Her mam was keen for her to do that, so she went to school and she worked real hard.'

'Where did she go to school?' I asked.

'Here, in Whitby, a school like yours no doubt, though I don't believe she had anyone as kind as Miss Hindmarch for her teacher.'

'But when did she write her stories?'

'Ah, that was later. She worked as a milliner at first . . . then she became a governess and spent many years away from Whitby. It was in her middle years that she returned to Whitby and set about earning her living from writing her stories. After her father died she tried to keep her mother and sister with what she earned. Those were very hard times for Mary.'

'Did she not earn money from her books?'

'Not at first. Often she became so short of money that

there was little food in the house. Mary would dread her friends visiting, for she had nothing to offer them. Sometimes she could not walk out for she'd no boots to wear.'

That shocked me, for no visitor at our cottage would ever go short of food and though a fisher-girl like me might go barefoot on the sand, no decent person could walk through town without boots.

'Her friends lost patience with her at times,' he said, though he smiled as he remembered it. 'They thought she was mad to be trying to write, when she could have earned a respectable living as a governess. That would have been more seemly, more ladylike.'

The picture man laughed and I could tell that he admired Mary's stubbornness. 'Mary was determined,' he said, 'and she succeeded in the end.'

'So she did get to be rich?' said Mam.

'She never really did. She managed to buy a house up in Springvale, on the smart side, and she lived there with her mother, but it was not long before she died. It is only now that her books are selling well. It seems sad that Mary never lived to enjoy it.'

We all stood quiet, struck by the shame of it all.

'But now, young lady,' said the picture man, 'I have another gift that I hope you will all enjoy.'

From his pocket he took another book, just as beautifully bound as the first. My mouth dropped open and my hands went out.

'Well,' said Irene. 'Two books, two books. I've never heard the like.'

'*The Haven Under The Hill*,' I read from the stamped gold title letters. 'It's by Mary, too. Oh I can't wait to start to read.'

Mam and Dad were overwhelmed and they couldn't thank him enough. I forgot my manners and opened the book, pointing out words to Mary Jane. 'Why, it's about Whitby, this is. It tells about Hild and Caedmon and the old street Haggerlythe.'

I'd been so excited, the time had flown by and we'd had to find the pony and trap and set off back to Sandwick Bay.

We were tired after our busy day, though we were laughing and chattering and I clutched tight to my precious book. A chill wind came off the sea and the sinking sun painted patterns over the hills and valleys. When we reached the top of our steep bank, we fell silent. There was John Ruswarp waiting for us by the stile, where the heather begins. There was another young man with him, a man I didn't recognise, tall and thin and sunburnt, dressed in Army clothes.

We stared, but Mam climbed down from the trap. She stretched up her hands to the strange young man, touching his cheek.

'Our Frank,' she said.

Chapter Nine

I couldn't believe it was our Frank. I don't know how Mam recognised him straight off like that. It was more than eighteen months since he'd gone off to the fighting, but I would never have thought a lad could change so much in that time.

He'd always been strong and healthy, had our Frank, with his blue eyes and ruddy cheeks. Well built he'd been, with good muscles. It had been no effort to him to heave a coble up onto the sands, or swing a little lass up into the air. This man was pitifully thin, his cheeks sallow beneath the sunburn and his thick golden hair bleached white and sparse.

John came to help Irene down from the trap. I think he'd been shocked when Frank turned up knocking at the

Ruswarps' door, after he'd got no reply from our cottage. Irene went up to Frank and hugged him, the tears pouring down her face.

'Our Frank . . . our Frank,' she said.

It was Dad who voiced what was on all our minds. He followed Irene down and took Frank by the hand when Mam moved back, then he clapped his arm round Frank's shoulder, hugging the thin trembling body to his chest.

'Eeeh lad . . . what ails? Are you hurt?'

Frank clung to my dad for a moment as though he were a bairn, but then he pulled back, showing us he'd still got some pride.

'I've been sick, that's all. I've had the fever like a lot of them, but I'm better now. Nay,' he said, coming over to me, 'this grand lady is never our Liza? Have you not a kiss for your brother?'

I had felt shy, him looking so different and all, but it was his own cheeky way of talking and I threw my arms around him, though I didn't like the bony feel of his shoulders beneath the army jacket.

'I cannot swing you up onto my shoulder, such a fine grown lady you are,' he said, and though they laughed, Mam's lips tightened and I knew she thought that he'd not have the strength to do it either.

We let the pony and trap go back to Whitby and we all walked down the steep hill to Sandwick, carrying our parcels. We'd much to tell Frank, both happy and sad, and we talked till late at night.

Frank only had a few days' leave, then he had to get back to Scarborough where he was billeted. He'd not been able to come back in August with the others as he'd been so ill. He made light of his sickness but the weakness and fits of trembling that came over him told us that he'd been very ill indeed. There was a great deal of talking done, but most of it was on our side. Try as he might, Dad could not get Frank to tell what he'd been doing, away at the war. Once Mam tried to get him to say, but all he'd answer was that he was shamed to speak of it, and begged her not to ask.

Frank spent much of his time sitting beside Grandpa's bed. I don't think they did much talking, but they seemed to have a quiet understanding. Billy ran to hide whenever Frank looked his way.

The night before Frank was due to return, Irene came up late to bed. She'd been sitting out on the top staith with Frank and John, all talking softly together, though Mam kept saying that they'd be getting chilled. Irene lay beside me quietly sobbing; I could feel the heaving of her shoulders and hear the catch of her breath.

'What is it?' I asked.

''Tis nowt,' she said. 'Nowt, but Frank has talked John into giving up his plans for the Army.'

'What? Are you not glad of that? You didn't want him going off?'

'Oh I'm glad all right. I'm that relieved I can't say how much, but it's what Frank said that's shaken me. It's bad out there, where the fighting is, much worse than I thought. Frank says he's shamed to speak of it to Mam and Dad, but he managed to tell John, for he couldn't bear to let John follow him.'

'Well,' I said. 'All that fighting and killing must be dreadful, but why is he so shamed? Soldiers are supposed to fight, aren't they?'

'Aye, but Frank says it's the women and children involved in it all that he cannot feel right about. He says they've found many a farmhouse with the men away fighting and they've turned out the mother and her bairns and they've had orders to burn the place to the ground. They've burnt everything – their food, their clothes – and left them with nowt but what they stand in.'

'Nay,' I said, 'but what happens to them?'

'He says they're herded away into camps, where they live in tents, cramped together, sleeping on the ground. They've nowt to drink but fever-ridden water. They cannot keep themselves clean and they've very little food. They're dying in those camps, he says, mothers and bairns, dying like flies.'

I was silent then, I knew why he was shamed. I couldn't see how a decent lad like our Frank could be part of all that, then I realised that since he'd volunteered himself he'd no choice but to do it or be killed.

We all went up to the top of the bank to set Frank on his way, but we were quiet. His homecoming hadn't been the happy one we'd wanted. Mam clung to him when it was time to go and Dad told him that his lines would still be waiting, and then we had to let him be on his way.

I sat on Plosher Rock, staring out to sea, watching the wake of the boats till they vanished. Nearby, the waves burst white and fizzing, lapping at the driftwood beyond my feet. Far out, the swell was dark blue, patterned like mackerel skin with the lighter blue of the sky. All heaving gently in a quiet breathing rhythm . . . just a light stirring here and there, a hint of the power beneath.

The low sun warmed my back and apart from the guilt of knowing there was work to be done and the unspoken chiding that'd come from Mam, I was happy. Content to sit for the moment.

The weeks had passed and we were well into November, though the weather had stayed fine for that time of year. Irene's dress was ready and beautiful, hanging from the beam in our loft. My dress just needed the lace and frill, and we'd been to chapel to hear the banns being read. Mam and Mrs Ruswarp had been sitting up late into the night, getting all the stitching done, while I read to them from *The Haven Under The Hill*. We all enjoyed the story just as much as the first one and I often thought about the Whitby woman who'd written it. Irene was happy and looking forward; she was even looking forward to her baby being born, though I couldn't be understanding that. Still, I loved the thought of being an auntie . . . I had such plans: I'd make little presents, I'd carve a boat out of wood, the way I'd seen Grandpa do it.

I sat there thinking about it all, but then noticed the sky changing. Grey clouds heavy with rain came over from the horizon, heading inland, though the sun still shone through, sharp and red, in spiky rays. The clouds came over very sudden and it went dark and cold. I saw red flecks of the sun's reflection in the nearest waves. I shuddered. Flecked with blood, I thought. Great spots of rain began to fall as I ran home thinking of my dad out there on the sea.

It was late that night that the storm really broke. I couldn't remember another storm like it. Mam had sent me and Irene up to bed but we couldn't sleep, what with worrying about Dad and John who were both out in it all. We heard footsteps passing to and fro beneath our window and a lot of shouting going on. At last we heard our own door slam hard, caught in the wind . . . we knew Mam had gone out.

'I'll not lie abed in this,' said Irene and she was up and pulling on her frock that was so tight now and wrapping her shawl criss-cross, to fasten at the back. I couldn't stop her so I helped her, then dressed myself as well. I followed her down the ladder, past Billy rolling around in Mam's bed. He jumped out when he saw us and pattered downstairs behind us, his thin legs bare beneath his white shirt.

'Get back, get back,' we told him, but he followed and we couldn't make him stay.

The blast was so strong, we couldn't get the door open at first, then when we did, it slammed back so sharp our Billy screamed. He wasn't caught by it, just scared, and I got hold of him, suddenly scared myself. Mam came running up and pushed us back inside. She was soaked and her hair all snarzly. I thought she'd shout at us for coming out, but the tense, low voice she spoke with frightened me more.

'We'll have to get the boat out,' she said. 'We must help fetch the men. Irene, you run to the Pickerings.' Liza, keep Billy here . . . keep him safe for me.'

Then she was gone and Irene after her with the door banging and banging till I caught it on the sneck. Billy was white and shivering so I took him back upstairs and crept into Mam's bed beside him. I cuddled up and he fell asleep. I couldn't sleep though and I wondered about Grandpa – surely he couldn't be sleeping through all this commotion. I got up and made some tea and carried a cup into him. He lay on his back, staring wide-eyed at the ceiling. I put the cup beside him.

'There's a terrible storm, Grandpa. They're wanting to get the boat out.'

He never moved or spoke and I went back to Billy. I sat full-dressed on the edge of Mam's bed. I hated sitting there, I wanted to be out and seeing what was going on. Then Irene came back, puffing and blowing, stamping frantic up our stairs, straight into Grandpa's room.

'You must come,' she cried. 'You must come. We've no men, they're all out there, beyond the bay, and they cannot bring the boats in.'

I followed her into his room. She ran round his bed, pulling at the blankets, her hair streaming water, sprinkling wet over the sheets.

'They'll be lost if you don't come.' But Grandpa stared blank at her.

Then Mam came flying up the stairs as drenched as Irene.

'I cannot move him,' Irene's voice rose. 'I cannot make him come.'

Mam stood at the foot of his bed and spoke again in that strained, quiet voice.

'We cannot launch the boat without you be coxswain. Get out of your bed, Isaac Welford, and think what your Esther would have said.'

I'd never heard Mam speak so sharp to him before and I caught my breath at it, but Grandpa looked at Mam and I could tell he'd understood and listened to what she'd said.

'Who is there to crew?'

'There's Walter Snaith and his grandson, there's John Pickering and old Tom Danby and a gang of lads all willing to row, but there's none as knows the sandbanks and the rocks, there's none as can guide her out but you.'

Still Grandpa shook his head. 'Nay. They're only old fellas and young lads and it'll take every one of them. There's none left to launch her.'

'We can launch her,' said Irene. 'Us women can do the launching.'

Grandpa shook his head again. 'Women? It takes strong men to launch that boat. Aye, and plenty of 'em.'

'Hannah knows what to do. She's helped before.'

'Nay, we've never had women in those racks. Ye'd not stand a chance.'

Irene covered her face with her hands, near despairing.

Mam spoke firm again. 'Now listen you here, Isaac Welford. If you can be coxswain and those lads can man her, then we can launch her.'

At last Grandpa seemed to gather himself together. A spark of his old self gleamed in his face and he laughed out loud.

'All right, my lass, all right. If you lot can launch her, then we will man her. Now get me out of this bed.'

He held up his arms and Mam and Irene grabbed hold and pulled him out. Mam picked up his gansey from the dresser and eased it over his nightshirt.

'Fetch Dan's spare, Liza, and his oilskins, too.'

I ran back to Mam's room and fetched my dad's gear and watched as they got Grandpa dressed. He was shaky and stiff-legged – he'd not been out of his bed for weeks – but he bellowed questions at Mam and she answered fast and clear. Then off they went, Grandpa stumping down our stairs, and I turned back to Billy.

He was awake and out of bed and I wasn't going to stay at home, not now. I got Billy's coat and wrapped him up good and warm, pushing on his boots. 'You stay by me,' I said. 'You stay by me whatever happens.'

Billy nodded, his eyes wide and round.

Chapter Ten

The wind was so strong that it was hard to breathe at first and I nearly turned round and went back inside. Such a rush there was, folk shouting and surging like a great wave down to the boathouse. I grabbed our Billy tight and we became part of the wave, down the staith and onto the beach we went.

They'd already got the lights out, big cans with a paraffin light that we call ducks. They'd carried them down the lifeboat ramp where they lit up the beach.

The sun was just beginning to show and a dim grey light lit the sea. The sea as I'd never seen it before. Our bay was filled with white foam, seething like a boiling cauldron, the white only broken by grey breakers that turned black as they burst, sending creamy spray flying high into the sky. I turned my head sharp, catching rain-bow flashes from the corners of my eyes, and far out were glimpses of dark shapes that vanished, then reappeared: our small fishing fleet, so tossed that you couldn't see them clear.

Billy pulled my hand, pointing and shouting with delight. I turned to see them pulling open the doors of the lifeboat house and the great shining prow of our lifeboat gleaming in the light of the ducks. Our lifeboat that we loved, even worshipped – the spirit of our village, as near a holy thing as we could have.

The boat was full of young lads and the boathouse full of women. Mam helped Grandpa up the ladder and she and Hannah half-lifted, half-threw him into the stern. Some of the lads who'd come to row were swamped in their dads' oilskins, but the scratch crew were all in place. Grandpa gave the signal to Walter Snaith who fired the warning pistol. Mam and Hannah and the other women gathered round the winch, as many as could find a place to hold, and Irene let lose the safety chain. Slowly, bit by bit and jerking to the side, the boat was lowered onto its carriage, then steered out onto the ramp.

'Away ... let her away,' shouted Grandpa and our great boat rumbled down the slipway, coming to rest steady on its carriage on the sand.

Then came the launchers' hardest part. The women formed up in the launching racks, two by two, ready to push her out to the sea. Hannah stood at the front shouting instructions and I saw that Mary Jane had gone to pull on the ropes with other girls and lads.

'Right,' I said to Billy. 'We're needed.'

I ran, pulling Billy with me, and grabbed the rope beside Mary Jane.

'You get that rope and you pull hard,' I yelled at him.

I saw Mam in one of the racks, straining with the weight, then Irene slotted herself in behind. I could see that bothered Mam, she was worrying about Irene and her bairn, but strong arms pulled Irene from the rack and a great powerful body took her place. It was Nelly Wright and I could have hugged her. Irene didn't stay to argue, but went to push at the back.

The women strained, but the boat didn't move.

'I'll call,' shouted Hannah. 'One, two and away. One, two and away.'

I think every person in our bay was there, everyone who could stand. I saw Mary Jane's granny and Old Miriam hauling on the ropes, and Annie Lythe, who'd no family to save, was there with her oldest lad, pulling and heaving with the rest. At last the carriage shifted a bit and a cheer went up from the lads above. Once it started it moved slow but steady across the sand till we neared the water's edge.

We dropped our ropes then and ran to push at the back. I lost Billy at that moment, but I didn't stop to think, just ran and pushed with the others, pushed for all I was worth. The women in the racks trudged out into the waves.

I hardly noticed when we first reached the sea. My skirts were so drenched and cold that the water made no difference, but when we got further out I knew all right, for a wicked underswell pulled at me, trying to pluck my feet from under my legs. It caught me and I fell; the freezing salt waves punched me in the face. I was left wallowing as the others went on. Such a rage of anger rose in me that I dragged myself upright, shouting and screaming abuse – abuse at the sea, shaking my fists, tears bursting from my eyes.

Then I stopped. Pushing ahead was Mam, past her waist in the swirling mass. My mam, who was so feared of the sea that she couldn't cross a causeway, couldn't bear to wet her toes. I didn't know how she was doing it, wading out like that. And what of Irene, following on behind, with that little baby growing inside her, the one I'd be an auntie for. I remembered Billy; that was my job. If Billy got lost or hurt it'd be my fault. I turned back to look for him.

Billy was hiding beside the lifeboat ramp and he'd found his friend Jackie Lythe. I suppose they thought they'd got a bit of shelter from the wind, but they were both shivering down there.

'Get 'em up and make 'em run.' It was Miriam, who stood beside me pointing her bony finger at the two lads. 'Get 'em out. They can run with the ropes now. They're coming away from the racks and we'll all be needed again.'

So I made Billy and Jackie go back down the beach. Mam and Irene and the others were coming towards us through the waves. Two of the lads climbed over the sides of the boat and untied the launching ropes, flinging them down to Hannah below.

We all had to get ready now for the last big haul. The ropes had to be dragged along the beach either way and tugged real sharp, to catapult the lifeboat from its carriage, forward into the sea. We all waited on Grandpa's signal, for he had to choose just the right moment – when a wave had gone, but before the next one came.

'Away now . . . away,' came the cry. We took hold and pulled and shouted, till we were running fast.

'Away now. Away!' we yelled, as though the strength of our voices would add to the weight on the ropes. Billy hauled away, just in front of me. He was running so fast I swear his feet never touched the ground, but swung to and fro. I didn't see that I was running into a rock and I fell hard, rolling quick to the side, for I knew I'd be trampled if I didn't shift.

I rolled on the sand as the cry changed.

'She's off.' The rope fell slack and the boat plunged forward into the waves, the oars pulling back, not quite together but strong enough to move her, dipping sharp, up and down.

It was Billy who found me then. I heard his voice. 'Liza, Liza,' and I shouted back at him.

'I thought you'd got squashed,' he said.

'I'm worse than squashed,' I said. 'Pull me up. We must find our mam.'

I wasn't the only one who'd fallen; there were women helping each other up and rubbing knees and shins, all along the beach. We gathered together by the ducks. They gave little heat, but they seemed to give a bit of comfort. Hannah said that the bairns and the old ones should all go home, as there was no more we could do, but none would go. We huddled together, watching the heavy boat that looked so fragile now, swinging up and down and out of sight. Giving us a glimpse, then nowt.

Mam rubbed Irene's hands. 'Get yourself back,' she said. 'Get yourself back and into your bed.'

'I'll not . . . not till they're fetched.'

'They're doing grand,' said Mam. 'Who'd have thought those lads could row like that? They look to have reached the bank and be getting through.'

We all looked, narrowing our eyes. The bank was the dangerous shallows at the mouth of our bay.

'There's none but Isaac Welford could have taken them through,' said Hannah.

We waited helpless and dreary, but still no one would go home. Now we'd done our work and the effort was over, the freezing cold and wet made itself felt. The children began their shivering.

'Jump up and down,' said Miriam. 'Ye'll catch your deaths if ye stand there gawping. You show them, Liza, and you, Mary Jane. Jump about and clap your hands.'

We tried, but we were too cold to get going properly.

'Ye must,' said Miriam. 'Ye'll freeze solid else. Ye'll turn into breakwaters, everyone of you, stuck for ever ont' beach.'

So we laughed and tried again. Mary Jane started chanting a skipping rhyme:

> *'Souther wind souther,*
> *Bring father home to mother.'*

'That's it, lass,' Miriam said. 'They all know that,' and she joined in, jumping up and down, her sodden skirts flapping round her skinny legs:

> *'Souther wind souther,*
> *Bring father home to mother.'*

Soon we were all at it, jumping to the rhythm, clapping hands, shouting as loud as we could. We went on to another rhyme:

> *'Northern sea, silver sea,*
> *Bring my daddy back to me,*
> *Hush the waves and still the sea,*
> *And bring my daddy back to me.'*

All the mams joined in, bellowing it out faster and faster, and it warmed us and cheered us, till the cry went up.

'They're coming back!'

We stopped our jumping and ran to the water's edge, but we could see nothing clear. We waited in silence then, watching and screwing up our eyes. I thought I saw a moving shape, then it vanished, then I saw it again.

At last we could see that a small boat, tossing fiercely, was heading steadily for the shore. Then we saw another behind it.

'The cobles!' shouted Hannah, and a great cheer went up.

We couldn't see the lifeboat, but the small boats, taking courage from the lifeboat's presence, were coming in one by one. When the lifeboat did at last come into view there was more cheering and clapping of hands, but Mam and me stood next to Hannah.

'What is it?' said Mam. She knew Hannah of old.

Hannah shook her head. 'There's not all there should be.'

As the cobles came in we spread out along the beach to help drag them up. I kept looking for Dad, but I couldn't see him. When the lifeboat neared the shore we saw that it pulled a coble fastened by a line, and another upturned hull dragged behind that. I pulled at Mam's arm.

'Look,' I said. 'It's Dad's boat tied up behind. It's the *Sneaton Lass*.'

Mam didn't move. The women gathered together to help get the boat out of the water. Irene came with Mrs Ruswarp and Mary Jane following.

'We cannot see the *Lily Belle*,' Irene said. Then she

followed Mam's gaze to the upturned hull dragged behind our *Sneaton Lass*.

'No,' she whispered. 'No.'

Mam seemed to shake herself and put her arms round Irene. 'You'll see. He'll be in the lifeboat, him and your dad. There's a line fastened. We'll find them in the boat.'

We went down to help carry the ropes up to the winch. The men and lads were jumping over the sides into the shallows and the ones who'd fetched their cobles in came to help. The lifeboat was hauled back out of the water a deal more easy than she'd gone in.

We saw Dad inside the boat, but we couldn't see John. Uncle Frank was there and Sam Ruswarp; that made me think that John must be there too. Dad jumped over the edge and splashed towards us, but as he came near we saw that his face was grim and he slowed as though he didn't wish to reach us. He looked at Irene and Mrs Ruswarp, shaking his head.

'I'm sorry, lass,' he said.

Sam Ruswarp came up behind them, hanging back from his mam as though shamed. But Mrs Ruswarp threw her arms round him and Mary Jane clung to them both.

Irene stared at Dad.

'Nay, nay . . . I've seen him. Look, he's there,' she said, pointing to the lifeboat. 'He's there in the boat. I saw his gansey. I know it well. I knitted it myself, the waves and herring-bone . . . I'd know it anywhere.' She made to run towards the boat, but Dad caught her. He made her turn away from the sea, pushing her up the beach.

'He's gone lass, he's gone.'

I stood there, cold and wet forgotten, watching them go, Mrs Ruswarp and Mary Jane following slowly with their Sam.

A choking sound behind me made me turn. There was Mam bent double vomiting and Billy clutching frightened to her skirt. I ran to her and was shocked to feel the violent trembling that cut through her body. I couldn't think what else to do but hold her tight and press my hand against her forehead, as she'd done for me when I was sick as a bairn.

The retching stopped, but she still shook. Billy stared white-faced. He'd never seen his strong, quiet mam like this before and nor had I. It made me realise then that it had been no easy thing for her to go ploughing out into the sea, and of all people I should have known it.

'Come now, Mam,' I said. 'We must get us home.'

She nodded and let me lead her back, as though she were a child and I the mam. Billy followed, still holding tight to her skirt.

Just outside our cottage she stopped.

'I'm fine now Liza. I'm myself again. I must look to Irene and we must be thankful that our dad is spared.'

'Yes Mam,' I said, taking my arm away and letting her and Billy go in first. She was back to being in charge of us all again.

Chapter Eleven

Dad stayed at home the next night, even though the storm had eased. Our cottage was hushed. Even Billy was quiet, sitting on Dad's knee, watching for Mam's anxious face as she toiled up and down stairs carrying boiling water for Miriam's simples. Our Irene had a fever. Dad sat by the fire all the next day, staring into the grate. He should have been tired, but he couldn't sleep. Grandpa came down to sit with him and they talked in soft voices, saying the same things over and over again.

'I thought I had him,' Dad would say. 'I threw him a line and he fastened it. I thought they were safe, but then over they went, with a sudden cutting wave ... right sudden, and over went the *Lily Belle*. I hauled young Sam out, no trouble, but I couldn't get hold of John. He was so close, just an arm's length, no more. Just an arm's length and I could have had him.'

'Aye,' said Grandpa. 'It's always the same. You blame yourself when you shouldn't. I've seen more men go down than I can bear to think of and always you say, "if I'd done this, if I'd done that". You should not blame yourself. The sea takes those it wants.'

'Aye, it does. But it grieves me so that it should take him. Like a son he was. I taught him all I know and now he's gone, leaving my poor lass like that.'

Grandpa spoke very gentle. 'He carried the stones you know ... so Sam says. Pockets full of dogger, he says. They'd have pulled him straight down. You'd not have got him out ... weighted like that.'

It made me shudder when I heard that, but I shouldn't have been surprised. There's plenty of the fishermen carry the stones, though it wasn't talked about much. They live in fear of a long struggling death if they're thrown overboard, so they don't learn to swim – don't learn on purpose – and they carry heavy stones in their pockets so as to make sure they'll sink straight down. Sam Ruswarp is one of the few who can swim, but I never knew about John.

I hated to think of John with his pockets full of dogger. He must have gone off up the coast deliberate like, looking for the heavy, egg-shaped ironstones that we call dogger, for they're only found where the Cleveland iron seam meets the sea.

Dad shook his head. 'He never let on to me. All those

times he went out with me and he never let on that he carried the stones. He must have been more feared than I knew.'

They'd sit in silence then, Dad stroking Billy's hair, holding him close as though he daren't be letting him go. Then after a while it would all start again. Dad blaming himself and going over all that had happened and Grandpa saying what he could to comfort him.

They'd put Irene in Mam's bed and Miriam was nursing her. I wanted to go up to see her, but Mam said not.

'Soon,' she said. 'You can see her soon, but leave her to Miriam just now. We must get her to rest real well or . . .'

'What?' I said. 'Or what? What more can happen now?'

Mam bit her lip. 'I fear she could lose the bairn. She should not have been out last night, soaked and freezing and pushing at that heavy boat. I couldn't seem to stop her.'

'There's nowt could have stopped her, Mam,' I said. I sat at our table lonely and useless. I wanted to do something. I wanted to be with Mary Jane, to whisper with her as we did when things went wrong, but this time I couldn't do that for Mary Jane's brother was drowned and it must be worse for her than me. So I sat on, miserable and sad.

It was late in the afternoon when there came a knock at the door. I opened it to find Mary Jane there with her mother. Mary Jane looked scared.

'It's Mam,' she said. 'She will not settle, but she must

see Irene. I didn't know what to do for the best,' and she burst into tears.

I pulled them both inside and Mam came to see what the noise was. Mrs Ruswarp came into the kitchen, calm but determined. 'I want to see the lass, that's all. I need to see the lass.'

Mam hesitated for a moment, then nodded her head. 'Of course you must.' She led the way upstairs.

I took Mary Jane to sit with me. I put my arms round her and she leaned against my shoulder. We sat there watching Dad and Grandpa, listening to them still, but I felt better after that. I had my job, I was looking after Mary Jane.

It was growing dark when Mam came down with Miriam.

'We're leaving them two together,' said Miriam. 'Best thing for them both, and the fever's less.'

'Now, Mary Jane,' said Mam. 'You must get some sleep. Up into our loft you go with Liza.'

We passed Mam's bed on the way up and I went to kiss Irene. Mrs Ruswarp was sitting by the bed, holding her hand ... not talking, just sitting, and Irene was peaceful and resting. I knew then that she would get better, though it might take a long time.

Mam woke us early next morning in her usual brisk way. She sent Mary Jane down to her mother, for Mrs Ruswarp was preparing to return to her cottage.

'What of Irene?' I asked.

'Irene'll do fine,' said Mam.

'But what of the . . . ?'

'The bairn will do fine, so Miriam says, and there's no one better than Miriam for knowing those things. Now, Liza, you're to come with me and fetch the bait.'

I stared at Mam. 'I'm to go with the flither pickers?'

'Aye, just for today. Irene cannot come and I cannot manage myself, not today.'

Mam looked fit to drop. I should have noticed before. She'd have been up in the night looking after Irene, and before that she'd had no sleep for two days and a night.

'I'll go and pick instead of you, Mam.'

'Nay, you know nowt about it. Help me for a day or two, then you get yourself off to school. Grandpa says he can see to Billy.'

'Must Dad go tonight?'

'Aye he must, if the sea allows, for we've still to eat. We must pick for the Ruswarps too, for their Sam's to go with your dad. He must do the same for Sam as he did for John and poor Mrs Ruswarp must steel herself again.'

I wrapped myself up warm and laced on Irene's boots. Lad's boots they were. I fastened her quilted petticoat round me, though I had to tie it with string for her stomach had grown so much bigger than mine.

At last I was to go with the bait gatherers. I was to do the work of a proper fisherman's daughter. I clomped down our stairs, curling my toes at each step for Irene's boots slopped a bit. Mam had Irene's bucket and swill ready and a few extra sacks.

'You'll be needing Irene's mittens,' she said.

'Nay, I don't need mittens.'

We set off down to the scaur, crossing the bridge, for the tide had just turned and it still covered the causeway. Other pickers joined us on the way. There were no greetings or halloos as I knew they usually gave, just a nod or a pat and the unspoken knowing that we must get on with our lives and take from the sea as it takes from us.

Mam put out a bucket and a swill for the Ruswarps and the women dropped their contributions in.

And so I set to work, slipping my blunt knife beneath the limpets to break their hold. The first one took three attempts and I caught my thumb, but soon I thought I'd got the knack. Mussels, the finest bait, went into the swill; limpets which were more plentiful, into the bucket. I picked away for what seemed a long time, my back bent, for it wasn't worth straightening. I began to ache and straightened then, to ease myself. Mam and the others were hard at it and their buckets half-full.

I went back to work, determined to keep up. I picked and picked, but my knife kept slipping and my fingers gathered cuts that stung with the salt water and the juice that oozed from the shellfish. I found that the best flithers were low down where the tide had been, but that was the wettest, most slippery place.

I stopped again to straighten and rest. Aunt Hannah noticed; she would.

'Why lass, we've nobbut started yet.'

Mam brought Irene's mittens from her pocket. I took them quick and grateful, pulling them carefully over my sore fingers.

We picked, it seemed, for hours and hours. I felt as though I'd been out on those slippery rocks trying to fill that bucket all my life. I thought I'd never fill it, though it was heavy enough to move, as we went further and further away from our bay.

I slipped into a shallow pool and cursed at my clumsiness, for I'd soaked my thick petticoat that chafed cold and wet against my legs. I was soaked anyway, for an angry rain squall drenched us and the women picked on.

'I fear we'll be mucking the lines tomorrow,' said Hannah. 'They'll not be able to get out in this.'

'Better to be mucking than having to get that lifeboat out,' said Mam.

I could have cried with the weariness of it all. I wondered how we'd managed to get the boat out that night. We'd all been soaked and tired then, but we'd not felt it; warmed by fear we'd been. The flither picking was quite different. Grim relentless toil, going on and on, and I saw with shame that Mam and even Aunt Hannah were slipping limpets into my bucket as they passed.

I watched Mam's bent back and remembered all the times she'd fought for me to be in school, wanting me to be able to take my chance of something different. I'd have given anything to be in school at that moment.

Still we picked, and I went like one asleep, in a nightmare dream that repeats and repeats, but at last I woke to realise that we were stopping. The women were filling each other's buckets so that we could all return together. They covered the tops with spreading seaweed, for freshness mattered so much.

The walk back was a long weary drag. I was sure my arms were going to break. I kept stopping to rest and getting left behind.

Mam does this every day, I thought, even through the freezing winter months. Ahead of me the others reached the causeway and carried their heavy buckets over, making their short cut. Mam turned away, up round the bay, her usual long way round. I stopped and put my bucket down. Aunt Hannah had waited for me.

'Look,' she said pointing. 'Just look up there.'

Across the causeway, on the top staith, was Grandpa, with Billy beside him and a gang of children, all listening to Grandpa's tales.

'Now that's a sight to make you smile,' said Hannah. 'There's something good come out of that sad night.'

I wished it were me up there by Grandpa's side.

'But what of Mam?' I said. 'I never thought she'd stick to her long walk back, not after she'd gone out so far, pushing the lifeboat.'

'What?' said Hannah. 'You thought she'd cross the causeway, did you? Nay, Liza Welford, you cannot change

249

a lifetime of fear just like that. Eh, you know nowt lass,' and she turned and followed the others, leaving me standing.

I wanted to follow Aunt Hannah, and get home real quick. I dreaded the thought of the shelling and baiting that was still to be done, but that small shape, plodding steadily away from the causeway ... drew me. I picked up my bucket again and turned Mam's way, shouting her to wait for me.

She stopped, surprised.

'Wait, Mam,' I shouted. 'I want to come your way.'

She waited till I came near. 'Nay,' she said. 'You must be daft . . . but then you don't understand.'

'I do, Mam,' I said. 'I do understand. Gran tried to tell me, but she never got it said. So I asked Hannah and I asked Miriam, too. I do know about your little brother William and I'm right sorry about it.'

She frowned and bit her lip. I wanted to throw my arms round her and tell her how much I loved her, but I couldn't do that. So I did the only thing I could think to do and I wanted it right enough, what with my aching back and cut fingers.

'Mam,' I said. 'I *will* go back to school. Not till Irene's better and fit to pick again. But then, I'll go back and I'll work real hard. I will be a pupil teacher, or maybe . . .' I said, thinking of a thin lady, writing at a desk, with no boots for her feet, 'maybe I'll do something else.'

Mam's rare slow smile warmed me more than sun.

'That's made me glad,' she said.

PART THREE

The Herring Girls

Dedicated to all the herring girls, coopers, fishermen, and landladies who worked with the North Sea herring fleet.

'Bread on the waters! Like manna it was!
One hour nothing, the next enough to feed a town,
and the sky all lit up with the reflection of the shoal.'
Joe Tomlinson – North Sea fisherman

Chapter One

It was late in July; one of those days of sun and heavy showers, worse for us than steady rain. Our mam's the washerwoman and when there's sun we carry the washing up to the lines on Top Green, and when it rains we have to fetch it down again.

I went with Robbie and Alice and we pegged the first lot of clothes and linen out to dry, but even before we got back to our yard, the sky darkened and great spots of rain came pelting down on us. I shook my fist up at the grey clouds and got my eyes splotched full of rain.

'Away back and fetch the clothes in,' I said.

We set about the washing, all wet and angry, throwing the clean sheets and petticoats wildly into our baskets.

'Ger'outa my way,' I yelled, as Alice reached for the same white sheet as me.

'Great Gawk!' she screamed. 'Lanky Dory! You've stuck your elbow in my eye. See what she's done to me, Robbie!'

'Shut up! Daft lasses!' Robbie cried. 'You've forgotten Mrs Metcalfe's fine pillow case, our Dory.'

I leapt at the pillowcase, careless of the peg that held it, and as I snatched it down the fine lace edging ripped.

We went quiet then, standing there in the soaking rain.

'Mam'll play war with us,' I whispered.

I think we knew then that it would be a bad day.

Mam was bending over the dolly tub, her face and hands bright red through the steam. She groaned when she saw us back, the damp clothes heaped up in our baskets.

'It's all Lanky Dory's fault,' Alice cried. 'She never turned her boots to Whitby Abbey last night, though I kept on telling her to. She's brought this rain and she's ripped Mrs Metcalfe's best pillowcase.'

Mam pushed the wet hair away from her forehead with the back of her hand.

'Stop it,' she snapped. 'Stop teasing our Dorothy so. This rain is none of her fault and if she's ripped a pillowcase, then she shall mend it. We'll just have to grit our teeth and do the best we can. Rob, take the bairns and sit on the step with them. You big girls hang up the linen. We shall have to use the loft, I dare say.'

I whispered low to Alice as we climbed up the ladder.

'Miss Hindmarch says it's ignorant to think that turning your boots to the abbey'll bring us fine weather. Ignorant, she says.'

We spent the whole morning setting up drying lines all over our small cottage and getting crosser than ever. We ended up with a whole day's washing still wet, and in danger of getting itself dirty again. Then, at last, after midday, the sun came out properly, and we were able to carry some of the washing back up to Top Green.

By late afternoon Mam was still wringing out clothes. Old Mrs Wright had kindly stopped by for a while to turn the handle of the mangle for us, and Alice was lifting petticoats, fresh from the starch tub. The smell of fresh baked bread and fried taties drifted from our neighbours' doorways, but we went hungry.

'Lanky Dory should be doing this,' Alice grumbled. 'She's biggest and strongest, and my stomach's empty.'

I stuck my tongue out at her. She knows how I hate to be called Lanky Dory, just because I'm tall.

'Stop it!' Mam bellowed. She was red in the face, she was that vexed. 'Stop that noise, Alice, you'll feel the flat of my hand.' Then she turned to me, and managed to bring a kinder sound to her voice. 'Will you run up to the lines again, honey, and check if there's owt that's dry? I'll make us a bit of tea for when you get back.'

My shoulders drooped at the thought of the hill again, and Alice gave a nasty low laugh as I went to the door.

*

Though the paving stones and grass were soaking wet, strong sunlight warmed our twisting narrow streets and mist rose everywhere.

I checked the lines, and I found three sheets that were ready for ironing, but then I couldn't face going straight back to our Alice's piping voice and the dank fog of steam that filled our kitchen. I sat down on the edge of the green looking out towards the sea.

I only meant to stay there for a moment or two, but the warm summery wind was fresh on my face. It was peaceful up there, and I could look down onto the busy staithe, and watch the cobles coming back with the tide.

Seagulls swooped down towards the boats, mewing like cats, while the fishermen jumped out into the shallows and splashed thigh deep through the waves, to haul their cobles up onto the shingle.

Our Rob was down there on the staithe with the little ones. I knew what they were after – they'd be begging for fresh boiled crab claws.

A gang of women were gathering on the top staithe, and setting up tin baths and buckets over fires well stacked with driftwood. A cloud of steam rose above them, while the women shouted at the bairns to keep back.

Dan Welford had a good catch of crabs, I could see by the careful way that he lifted the waving claws from the wooden crib of his boat.

I made myself turn away and started to gather in the dry washing, folding it carefully to try to please my mam.

I sniffed at it and smiled; it smelt of the sea. Then as I turned to go I glanced back down to the top staithe, and I had to stare again.

Mr Welford and his wife were leaning on the wooden rail and they'd got their six-month-old grandson, Joby, in a fishing basket between them. He peeped over the top like a laughing, wriggling fish. They smiled, but they held themselves quite still. A few yards back from them, a tall man with a beard bent over a wooden box that stood on three thin legs. I knew him at once; we all knew him. He was the Whitby photographer, who tramped about the villages with his camera and his black capes and his folding camera legs. We called him the picture man.

I could see what a fine sight they made, though thick white mist rose from the sea behind them and blotted out the view of the cottages on the far side of the beck.

The picture man waved his arm and pointed, and our Rob went sliding along the rail to sit by Mrs Welford. Their Billy and our young Nan crept up on the other side. I knew that Rob'd be pleased as punch to be put into that picture. They held themselves still as can be for a moment or two, gathered around the laughing baby.

Then all at once the picture was made, and Mr and Mrs Welford were bending down to their baskets to sort out the crabs and lobsters. Our Robbie went to help them as I knew he would. He'd hang around the Welfords for hours, would Rob; anything to do with fishing and you could bet he'd be there in the thick of it.

I started back to our cottage, suddenly sad. I

understood our Robbie well enough, for I wished that I was one of the Welfords too; and part of a big fishing family.

I wanted it to be my dad, guiding his coble through the sea roads towards Sandwick staithe. I wanted it to be my dad, waving and calling out my name in his deep rumbling voice.

Our mam, Annie Lythe, hasn't always been a washer-woman, and as I'm the eldest I can remember the times when my dad came back from the sea with his lines dripping with cod and ling and haddock.

It was hard work then, for each day we'd have to fix up my dad's lines and fetch the bait, but we used to gossip and laugh with the other families while we worked. Then that terrible spring day came, when the tides were high and the sea was wild and changeable.

Dan Welford had come back at midday, rowing hard against the tide, and the rest of the cobles following, so that all the village ran down to the staithe knowing there must be trouble. They'd seen my dad and his brother Bob with their sail flapping loose and heading danger-ously close to Hobs Head rocks. They'd gone to their aid as fast as they could, but our coble smashed into the rocks and, by the time the Welfords had reached them, there was nowt to be found but splinters of broken mast by the wrecked coble and their flat fishing baskets floating in the water.

Dan Welford has always said that it takes three men to handle a coble and see to the lines. But my dad and his young brother were independent that way. Stubborn was what Mam called it.

Since that day, our mam has kept all six of us from the workhouse by rubbing and scouring at other folks' clothes. The vicar up at Hinderwell raised a bit of money and presented her with a strong iron mangle. So our cottage is filled with steam and the strong smell of Naptha soap that makes our eyes water. But we don't want the workhouse, nothing could be as bad as that.

We try not to grumble, but we don't like it much. I used to carry fish baskets down to the staithe, not washing to the lines. I'd give anything to go running to help my dad with his catch, and beg a ride up the hill on his shoulders as I used to, twisting my fingers into the stiff salty hairs of his beard.

I sighed as I reached our doorstep. My dad would not know me now for I'd grown too tall to ride on anyone's shoulders.

Though Mam had managed to make us some tea and bread and dripping, she was still very fussed and couldn't listen to the excited chatter of Rob and the bairns, who burst in with tales of being photographed. One of the lines in our yard had snapped, and freshly washed shirts and bloomers had gone down into the mud and must be washed again.

I sighed at the thought of it, but I knew she must be done in.

'Shall I scrub them for you, Mam?"

'Nay, lass,' she said, giving my hand a squeeze. 'I fear you must traipse up to Top Green again, for we've still got Mrs Metcalfe's linen up there, and Alice – you shall have to fetch more water from the spring.'

When I got up to Top Green I found the picture man there, crouching beside our washing lines, struggling to get his camera fixed up so that it pointed out to sea across the bay.

He stopped and doffed his hat as soon as I reached the lines. He was like that; treated a fishwife or even a washerwoman as if she were a lady, though he'd a bit of a chuckle in his voice.

'Am I in your way?' he asked.

I shook my head, gone all shy.

'I've been watching for that sight all week,' he said, his voice deep with pleasure and excitement. 'There they go . . . chasing the silver darlings.'

I was puzzled for a moment, but then as I looked out to sea, I understood.

Dark sails appeared on the horizon, heading out to sea from Whitby harbour. Just two or three at first, then quickly the skyline was filled with them. It was the herring fleet, sailing off to the fishing grounds where the herring shoals swim up to the surface at this time of year.

Chapter Two

I smiled, for we look forward each summer to the coming of the herring fleet. The Whitby fishermen are joined by the Scotch boats, and by others from all along the coast. They even come from Cornwall. Whitby is suddenly bursting with strangers and noise and bustle.

'Won't all that thick white mist spoil your picture?' I asked, forgetting my shyness.

The picture man smiled and shook his head.

'There's many a fine photographer would agree with you, but not me; I love that mist.' Then he sighed. 'The boats are moving too fast, they've a good wind behind them. I should have brought my new box camera that can snap a picture quick as a flash. There's more than twenty boats out there, and I've heard there's others expected. It looks as though there'll be herrings in Whitby tomorrow.'

'Aye,' I told him. 'I went last summer, and I saw it all. I saw the coopers and the dealers and the herring girls. Miss Hindmarch took me.'

'Did she now?' He smiled at me with interest. 'And what did you think of it?'

'A fine old carry on,' I told him.

He laughed. 'You're right about that.'

Miss Hindmarch is the kindest teacher in our school, and I think she was quite shocked when she found out that I'd never been to Whitby.

'What, Dory? A big girl like you and never been to Whitby?'

'Mam cannot spare me,' I whispered, suddenly shamed. The truth was I'd never been further than Hinderwell.

Miss Hindmarch called in at our cottage, and she fixed it up with Mam. She took me into Whitby on the next Saturday. It was the best day of my life.

We walked down Flowergate, and I went wild with excitement at the smells and the hubbub of the busy shops. But then I looked out across the harbour to the great abbey high above us on the clifftops and I suddenly stopped. I could do nothing but stare up at those still grey stones, set all about in green, high above the jumbled houses.

Miss Hindmarch asked me what was wrong. I couldn't think what to say to her for I've never been one for clever talk. I blinked and shook my head, then I whispered, 'I think that must be heaven up there.'

Miss Hindmarch laughed and hugged me. 'Have you ever had ice-cream?' she asked.

It was when we walked down towards the pier looking for the ice-cream stall that we saw the herring girls, and what a sight they were; bit strong lasses every one of them, standing behind great troughs piled high with silver herrings. Farlanes those troughs were called, Miss Hindmarch told me so. The girls worked like lightning, gutting the fish and slipping them into baskets behind them. Some worked as packers, snatching up the herrings from the baskets, two fish in each hand. They went so fast you couldn't see the fish clearly, or know how they did it.

They shouted, in loud roaring voices, 'One pair, two pair, three pair, four . . .'

'Tally!' another girl bellowed.

Then someone started counting all over again.

The strong-smelling fish guts fouled their oilskin aprons, and spattered their arms. I stared open-mouthed at them, such a wild and frightening lot they were. Miss Hindmarch laughed at my amazement. She shook her head.

'There's no one works like those Scottish girls,' she said.

The picture man gave up trying to make a photograph of the fast-moving fleet, and he began packing up his camera and boxes.

'That's enough for today,' he said. 'The light's fading.'

I set to helping him, and I lifted his wooden camera legs over the green, looking about for the pony and trap that I'd expected to find.

'How shall you get home?' I asked.

'Why, I shall tramp along to Hinderwell station as I usually do,' he told me. 'There's the evening train due in half an hour.'

'What? And carry all these boxes and things.'

'Oh, I expect I shall manage,' he smiled.

'I'll help you carry them down the lane,' I insisted. The picture man was well known for handing out pennies, and he did not disappoint me, for when I turned back at the end of our lane, he felt deep into his pockets and pulled out three shining pennies and a farthing. I think he'd given me all that was left in his pockets, for he turned them both out and found his return ticket at the bottom.

'Yes, that's all for today.'

I thanked him politely and he bowed to me and touched his hat.

'It is a shame that the light has gone or I might have made a photograph of you,' he said, looking down at me thoughtfully. 'Yes, that would be good. A young fisher girl sitting on the bank, watching the herring boats in the distance.'

'I fear I'm not really a fisher girl,' I said, feeling shy again. 'I'm the washerwoman's daughter. You wouldn't want a great lanky lass like me in your picture.'

'Lanky?' he said loudly. 'Who calls you lanky?'

'My sister does,' I whispered, wishing that I'd kept quiet. 'All the school children do.'

'I'd not call you lanky,' he spoke soft now. 'I'd call you tall and strong like me. I think it grand to be tall. You can see what others cannot.'

I smiled at him then, and waved as he walked on towards Hinderwell, his wooden camera legs swinging from a shoulder strap.

I sat there back on Top Green after the picture man had gone, watching the yellow flickering lights of the herring fleet and thinking of all the gutting that should be done in the morning.

Then suddenly I jumped up trembling and started grabbing dry sheets from the lines. The herring drifters in the distance had lit their riding lights. I'd sat up there staring stupidly out to sea while darkness gathered around me. Mam would go mad.

As I leapt down the steps from the green, my arms full of folded linen, I saw our Alice coming stumbling up the steep pathway.

'Oh, she'll love to see me in deep trouble,' I muttered. 'I'm coming, I'm coming,' I yelled, cursing myself for being so dreamy and daft.

But Alice did not look pleased or gloating. Her face was white and frightened. She burst into tears when she saw me.

'Oh, Dory, I've been shouting and shouting for you.

I'm that scared and I don't know what to do. Something terrible has happened to our mam.'

I stared at her, my heart thundering in my chest, and my arms so full of piled-up linen that I couldn't run without dropping it.

'Here . . . take these off me . . . take 'em quick!'

Alice knuckled the tears from her eyes and held out her arms obediently. Then we both skidded down the steep bank to our cottage as fast as we could.

The stone-flagged floor of our kitchen was awash with soapy water. The big earthenware dolly tub had tipped over and cracked and Mam lay awkwardly beside it on the floor, her hair all soaked in the dirty water. Little Nan crouched in the wet beside her, pulling at her shoulder. Polly stood by the table, staring white-faced at them both.

'Mam's fallen down with a great bang,' she sobbed. 'She won't get up and she's getting her frock all wet and dirty.'

I almost dropped the dry clean clothes I was so scared, but I made myself put them down safely on the table, for nothing vexed Mam more than clean clothes soiled again. Then I ran paddling through the mess to help her.

Mam's eyes rolled and a horrible gurgling sound came from her throat, her mouth slewed over to one side of her face.

'She cannot get up,' Alice cried. 'I've tried to pull her up, but she cannot.'

It was terrible to see my big strong mam, struggling

and helpless on the floor like that, and I looked wildly about, wondering where best to get help. Our closest neighbour was Hannah and her husband, Frank, more members of the big Welford family. We call her Aunt Hannah, but then so does half the bay, and Hannah can be very sharp spoken if you're fooling about. But I knew that this was no time to be fearing a telling off, and Hannah would always help when it was really needed.

I ran then and started hammering on her door.

'Hannah, Hannah,' I screamed. 'Please help us; Mam's took badly.'

There was no sound from inside and then I remembered that she'd still be down on the staithe, helping to sort the crabs.

I set off down the bank at full speed, until I met the Welford family slowly carrying up their laden baskets and our Robbie trailing alongside them.

Hannah stopped as soon as she saw me. 'What is it, honey?'

She spoke unusually kind as though she could see at once that I was frightened sick.

'Mam. She's fallen over and cracked our dolly tub.'

'Why, never mind, lass, we'll find her another.'

'Nay, nay. She cannot get up. She cannot even speak, and her face has . . . has shrunk to one side and it's horrible.'

Hannah thrust her basket into the arms of her daughter, Mary. Then she took hold of me and held my hands tight to make me listen well.

'Now, honey, you must be brave for your mam. Run straight down to Miriam's and bring her quick. I shall go on up to help poor Annie. Come along with me, Robbie, don't look so fearful, lad, we'll see what we can do.'

Old Miriam had been midwife, nurse and layer-out to the whole of Sandwick Bay since Mam were a little lass. It was not long before I was puffing back up the narrow cobbled path with Miriam puffing even harder beside me, clutching her basket of herbs and simples.

'Here, carry my medicines, lass,' she gasped. 'I swear I get too old for this.'

Chapter Three

But Miriam was not too old for, skinny and bent though she was, she took us in hand and sorted us out before night came. With her help and Hannah's, we got the floor wiped clean and dry and the broken pot taken out to the back. We tucked Mam up in the bedplace downstairs by the kitchen fire.

Martha Welford and her daughter, Liza, brought us a supper of fresh boiled crabmeat and bread and milk. Liza bullied my brothers and sisters up to their beds and settled them all to sleep. She's a clever big girl is Liza and Miss Hindmarch has made her pupil teacher at our school, so we're all well used to doing as Liza Welford tells us.

Miriam patiently fed our mam with spoonfuls of a

sleeping draught, and at last she slept, though her face and body still looked all wrong to me. I sat quietly by the fire watching her, while Miriam settled herself in Mam's wooden rocking chair. It seemed she'd be staying the night.

'Miriam,' I whispered at last. 'Will she die?'

Miriam shook her head firmly.

'Will she mend then?'

Miriam frowned, shaking her head again. 'That I can't say. I've seen it before, honey, and sometimes they mend and sometimes they don't.'

I sat there in silence staring into the fire and worrying.

'Now, Dorothy,' said Miriam. 'Do you remember old Jimmy Loftus who died last spring? Remember how he dragged his left leg just a little?'

'Aye?'

'Well, he was same as your mam is now, and he got better fine and lived on for years, and he was a worker, was Jimmy. You'd never have guessed there'd been anything wrong, just that little drag to the leg gave it away. Nowt to speak of.'

'I pray my mam will be like him,' I whispered.

Miriam rocked gently in Mam's chair.

'Aye,' she nodded. 'We'll both pray for that.'

I crept up to the loft and climbed into bed beside Alice, and at last I slept. Having Miriam downstairs made me feel safe, despite our trouble.

Next morning I woke quite happy, thinking that it

must have been a bad dream, but when I heard Miriam calling up our stairs for me, I knew that it was true and the fright came thundering back. I went down to find a grand breakfast of fried fishcakes waiting for us. Hannah had sent them round.

After we'd eaten, Hannah and Mary came to help us with the bairns, then Miriam told our Rob to take the little ones down to play on the staithe.

'I want to be here to help my mam,' Rob said.

'Best way to help her is to give her peace and see to the bairns,' Hannah insisted.

Rob sighed, but he did as she asked. I knew he'd rather be doing anything than watching his little brother and sisters.

I could see that all three women were tight-lipped and worried.

'Now we shall have to have a good talk,' Miriam said.

'I think Dory should stay,' said Mary, putting her arm about my shoulders. 'She's a big enough lass and it is her right.'

'I want to stay, too,' said Alice, her thin face all white and drawn.

Miriam nodded and I was glad. I crouched down beside my mam and stroked her hair. Alice came and sat close to me. She pushed her arm through mine, and for once I was really glad of her bony body pressing into my side.

Mam was awake and taking notice of all that went on, though she still could not speak. It was as though all the right side of her body had fallen asleep and would not move or work; not her arm, not her hand, not her leg.

Hannah sat down on the floor to speak to her.

'Annie,' she said. 'We are going to have to send to Whitby for the doctor.'

'Naaah, naaah!' Mam struggled to make them understand.

Miriam bent forwards. 'You must be calm, Annie, or you shall make yourself worse. 'Tis bad, what's happened to you, and I cannot put you right, but maybe the Whitby doctor can do something. We cannot know unless he come and look at you.'

It was then that I whispered aloud the thing that I knew must be troubling Mam.

'We've got no money to pay him with.'

'Aye,' Miriam sighed. 'We shall have to apply to the Guardians. I fear there's no other way.'

'But will they not send us to the workhouse?'

Mam lay quiet and helpless beside me, a tear trickled over her cheek.

'Not if we can help it,' said Hannah. She bent down and took tight hold of Mam's hand. 'I promise you this, Annie Lythe, we shall do all we can to keep you here in Sandwick Bay.'

The Doctor came that afternoon in his pony and trap, and we were all sent outside. The little ones ran down to the crab boiling pots, happy enough for the moment, not understanding as Rob and Alice and I did that if the Whitby doctor came to call it must be bad.

We trailed slowly down the bankside after them, and found them greedily poking fresh crab meat from the claws they'd been given.

Nelly Wright was stirring the boiling tubs, her fat face red and sweating.

'Here y' are Alice,' she shouted, 'and you, Dory . . . tek it then!'

Nelly, who's usually rude to everyone, was trying in her awkward way to be kind to us; thrusting steaming crabs' claws into our faces. I took it, but I'd little stomach for it. I could see sorrow in every face that turned our way. Folk smiled sadly at us, then looked away. It was clear enough; they wondered if we'd be in the workhouse within a week. I couldn't stand their pity.

'Keep your eye on the bairns,' I told Alice sharply, and before she'd a chance to complain I was running over the staithe to the beach.

I marched furiously onwards, stamping through the shingle so that it crunched beneath my feet. A warm wind blew straight off the sea into my face, soothing me a little, but still I marched on and on towards the scaur. Then suddenly I stopped; two girls sat together on the big boat-shaped rock that we call Plosher Rock.

Though I wasn't close enough to see them clearly, I knew that it would be Liza Welford and Mary Jane Ruswarp. Best friends they'd always been, and they spent any free moment they had gossiping out there. I walked on, but slowly now, for they sat close together, very still. It was not like them to be so quiet. I almost forgot my own misery as curiosity gripped me.

At last they both turned at the sound of my footsteps in the shingle. I stopped then, ready to turn and run back to the staithe, feeling that I was nosing in on something private.

But Liza grinned and swung her legs round towards me.

'It's all right, Dory. We've got to be getting back. We've just been saying our goodbyes.'

I looked from one to the other, wondering who was going. I must have looked daft for they both laughed, and jumped down from the rock.

'Did you not know?' said Mary Jane. 'This clever Miss Liza is going off to Whitby to play nursemaid to rich visitors.'

Liza dug her elbow into Mary Jane's ribs. 'She's such a jealous cat. I'm going to have a grand time. I'm to teach the children drawing and look after them, while their family's on holiday. I'm to have my own room in one of those huge smart houses, up on the West Cliff. Miss Hindmarch recommended me for the place.'

'Oh, Liza,' I whispered. 'A room all to yourself? But Liza,' I cried, my own fears crowding back in on me. 'I might never see you again.'

''Course you will,' Liza laughed, pushing her arm through mine. 'I'll be back in the autumn for school.'

'But we'll maybe not be here. Miriam says that they

must apply to the Board of Guardians to pay Mam's doctor's bill, and I dread that they may send us all off to the Whitby Union Workhouse.'

Liza stared at me, then looked over at Mary Jane. 'Surely not?'

'Eeh dear, let's hope not,' said Mary Jane, pushing her hand through my other arm.

They set off walking slowly back to the staithe, with me between them. I was cheered by their warmth; two big kind girls on either side of me, but they were both quiet.

'I doubt I'll bother going back to school,' said Mary Jane. 'Now that I'm fourteen I can work with my mam at the bait picking. I can't stay at school just to play on that organ.'

'Take no notice of her! She'll be back at school!' Liza told me cheerfully. 'Now that Miss Hindmarch is teaching her to play the hymns, you can't keep her away.'

I smiled, for Mary Jane had amazed us all, and beneath her fingers the old school organ rippled into life.

'I love to hear you play,' I told her.

'If there's just one thing I dream about,' said Mary Jane, 'it'd be to have an organ at home. I can just see it standing there in mam's front room – but they cost so much.'

When we reached the staithe, Mary Jane sighed and pulled a face at Liza. 'Well, if Liza here is off to be a fine lady, there'll be nowt to do in Sandwick Bay. I might as well go off to Whitby myself for the herring gipping.'

'What!' Liza exploded.

'Why not? I heard they'd such a good catch yesterday that they're asking for more girls. A lot of the Scotch girls have gone to Scarborough this year to suit the dealers.'

'You?' Liza laughed. 'They'd not have you! Gutting all that fish! It'd kill you!'

'I can gut fish . . . faster than you.'

Liza grinned at her. 'But not as fast as them.'

'They get good money,' said Mary Jane. 'They get as much as a nursemaid. They get more if they're fast, and the catches are good.'

'Aye, but look what they do for it.' Liza shuddered and pinched her nose.

'I thought it was only the Scotch lasses that gipped the herrings,' I said.

'Oh aye, it's mainly the Scotch lasses. They make it their living, those big tough girls. They manage to do it just about all year round. They get on the trains and off they go to wherever the fleet are.'

'But where do they come from?' I asked.

'Oh, from way up north, and they get the trains right down to Lowestoft and Yarmouth in the autumn when the herrings swim south. Nobody can work like the Scotch lasses, but then, if the curers are short-handed in Whitby, they'll take on any woman that can do the gutting, just for the Whitby season. They'll not have trouble finding them for there's plenty round here that can gut fish, in't there? And plenty that want a bit of extra money.'

'Would . . . would they take me on, d'you think? Maybe I could get some money for my mam?'

'Ey now, Dory,' Liza hugged me. 'The work they do is terrible. It'll surely not come to that.'

Chapter Four

I walked over the staithe to where Alice and the little ones were playing hopscotch.

'We can take them back now,' I told her. 'The doctor must have had his say by now. Where's our Rob?'

She nodded her head, looking down to the sea where Rob was splashing through the shallows to help pull Dan Welford's coble up onto the beach.

'Leave him be,' I said. 'He'll come back when he's ready.'

When we got back to Lythe's Yard, the doctor had gone and Miriam was busily whitening our front step.

'Ah, there you are,' she looked up from her job. 'I'm glad you're back. We've work to do.'

'Please Miriam,' I begged, 'what has the doctor said?'

'Good news, I do believe. The doctor says he thinks your mam will recover in time, but listen well to this,' she dropped her voice so that Mam shouldn't hear us. 'The doctor says that she must not be vexed or fretful, that could make her worse.'

I caught my breath. 'But how can she not be fretful when she fears the workhouse so?'

'Aye, it's hard, honey, I know. But you two lasses can help a great deal by being brave and not fussing. Tomorrow they are sending the Reverend Hawkins down to see us and, as you know, he's on the Board of Guardians.'

'Oh no,' I cried.

Alice's face crumpled and her chin shook.

'Now, that's what I mean,' Miriam told us. 'It will fret your mam to hear you weeping. We have to face up to this and all's not lost. Miss Hindmarch has sent to say that she'll come too. She knows the gentleman and she'll do her best to help. We must get this cottage spick and span so that the Reverend has nowt to complain about, and I shall offer to stay here with you to nurse your mam and see to the bairns. We must beg for just a few outside relief payments, to tide us over the worst.'

I nodded my head, seeing the sense of that, though I knew that the Board of Guardians would not willingly give outdoor relief.

'Right,' said Miriam. 'We must set to. There's all this linen to press, then we've to parcel it up and deliver it.

Alice, will you run and fetch your Rob? There's errands enough for him to do.'

Rob came to help us willingly enough, and he ran up and down our bank with parcels of clean clothes, while we black-leaded our stove and polished till it gleamed. I tried to tell him what we planned and how we meant to keep us all together with Miriam's help, but he looked miserable.

''Tis the only thing we can hope for,' I told him.

'If I had a boat,' he said, kicking the heavy iron mangle that stood in the corner of our yard, 'then I could be a fisherman, and I could keep us all.'

'Maybe one day, Robbie,' I said, for I wished the same. 'I'd fetch your bait, Robbie, and I'd clean your lines, but we've no boat and dreaming won't help us. So leave that mangle be . . . I fear we'll be needing it.'

Alice and me lay awake that night, curled comfortably together for once.

'Oh, Dory,' she whispered. 'They say that they make you strip naked and they scrub you down with nasty smelling stuff and they cut off your hair.'

'Hush,' I tried to soothe her. 'Maybe it's not as bad as people say.'

'But they make you wear tight scratchy uniforms, I know that's true, for Johnny Liverton's grandpa were born in the workhouse, and he stayed there while he were a bairn. They take the babbies from the mams, and they take the lads from the lasses. Oh, Dory, we might never see our Robbie or Jackie again! Would we be put with the twins, do you think? Would you and me be together?'

'Ssh. Don't fret so.' I held her tight and stroked her hair. I never knew how much I loved my sister till then. 'Hush now,' I whispered. 'We must not worry our mam.'

We were woken next morning by a great knocking on our door. I stumbled sleepily down the loft stairs, wondering why our Rob had not answered the knock. He'd been sent to sleep downstairs in the bedplace now that we'd got Mam settled upstairs.

Miriam came out of Mam's bedroom, yawning and half asleep, in her long white nightgown and sleeping bonnet.

'Are yer there? Are yer up?' A loud voice called, and the knocking continued.

'Whatever's going on?' Miriam sounded quite cross and muddled. 'I told young Robbie to wake me soon after dawn.'

'I know that voice,' I said, running to open the door. 'It's Nelly Wright, I'm sure of it.'

I'd guessed right. There was Nelly standing on our doorstep, smiling broadly, as though we should be pleased to see her. Almost as though we should be expecting her.

'I've just to let yer know as he's all right,' she said. 'He'll be back in October with his pay, so he says.'

'Let us know what?' Miriam snapped. 'Who shall be back?'

'Their young Robbie, of course,' said Nelly.

'Where is he?' I asked. 'He should be down here, ready to wake us and build up the fire.'

Nelly laughed as if that were the greatest joke. 'Where is he? He's halfway to Whitby by now. That's what I'm telling yer. I passed him on the road an hour since and he'd his pillowcase slung over his back, all stuffed with straw for bedding. He says he's taken half a loaf for his dinner and he's off to Whitby to go with the herring boats.'

We just stood there open-mouthed, staring at each other, then our Alice started to sob.

'Hush,' I said, remembering Mam. I clapped my hand over her mouth.

Miriam quickly came to her senses. 'Why, you daft lass,' she told Nelly. 'Why did you not stop him and bring him back?'

'Well,' Nelly shrugged her shoulders, puzzled by the fuss. 'I thought it were his own business. He's big enough, in't he? How old is he?'

'He's only eleven,' I said. 'Though he's big for his age, like me.'

'They tek 'em at eleven,' said Nelly.

'Is that right?' I asked Miriam.

She sighed. 'I believe they do, honey.'

'He'll be all right,' Nelly told us cheerfully. 'And he seems bent on fetching yer some money. Well, I've given yer't message. It's nowt to do wi' me.'

And Nelly went off down the street, carrying a

heavy pitcher of milk that slopped a little as she swayed.

We stood at our doorway, staring after her. We could think of nothing to say.

Just as we were about to go back inside, a great commotion arose down at the bottom of the bank. It seemed the whole of the Welford family were coming marching up the street. I saw Liza dressed in her Sunday best and then I remembered that she was off to Whitby to be a nursemaid.

'Liza, Liza,' I shouted, jumping down from our step and running to catch hold of her arm, 'our Rob has taken himself off to Whitby. He says he's going on a herring boat.'

'Oh never!' she cried.

'Bless the lad!' Dan Welford cried. 'I'm sorry, lass, and I do blame myself. He's been trying hard to get me to take him on with us, for we go to join in the herringing tonight. I said he were to stay here to see to his mam. I should have known he'd not take no for an answer.'

'It's not your fault, Mr Welford,' I said. 'You know our Robbie; he'll do nowt that he's told.'

'We'd all have said the same to him,' Miriam agreed. 'Will he get taken on, do you think?'

Dan Welford scratched his head. 'He might well. The catches are so good that they're all joining in. I'll keep a look out for him, young Dory. If he's in any trouble, I'll take him on my boat.'

'We'd be much obliged,' I said. Then I kissed Liza and I wished her well.

'I'll see you in October,' she told me firmly.

Chapter Five

The Reverend Hawkins and Miss Hindmarch sat at our kitchen table and sipped their tea from Hannah's best china cups. The gentleman was stout with a curling grey moustache. He wore a good black suit, and he'd put down his hat on Mam's rocking chair. Miss Hindmarch nodded smiles at him and us, and complimented Miriam on the cleanliness of the children and of the cottage.

Alice and I stood quietly side by side, our hands linked tightly together. The little ones shuffled impatiently, though I felt proud of the way that they looked; faces and hands scrubbed, their hair brushed neatly and aprons clean. Though Mam was settled in her bed upstairs, I knew she'd be lying awake, straining to catch what was said.

'Do you think perhaps the youngest children could be allowed to go outside now?' Miss Hindmarch asked the Reverend.

He nodded, and Miriam told Alice to take them out. I wanted to go running out with them down to the staithe, running away from all our troubles, but I knew that I had to stay.

There was a knock on the door and Hannah and Martha Welford both came in. They bowed their heads politely to the visitors.

The Reverend Hawkins looked a little surprised. 'Relatives only,' he said.

Hannah folded her arms and smiled. 'Aye. We're all family in Sandwick Bay, sir.'

Then our door opened quietly again and in stepped Mrs Ruswarp and old Mrs Wright and, though the clergyman looked puzzled, he didn't object again. After all, what Hannah said was true enough. Though we had no close family left, we had so many second and third cousins that we lost track of who was who.

At last the Reverend gentleman cleared his throat. He turned to Miriam. 'What you propose, dear lady, is most generous, and if poor Mrs Lythe were likely to recover her health in a week or two, the Board of Guardians could make such outdoor relief payments. But let us face it, recovery could take months or even years. Mrs Lythe would get proper attention in the hospital wing of the workhouse and the children would be taught their manners and some useful work.'

I clenched my hands together behind my back until they hurt, biting my lips to stop the tears from coming.

'I do assure you that they are all good mannered, hard-working children,' Miss Hindmarch smiled sweetly at the man. 'And they are so close to their mother since their father's death. Might it not seem a great charity to keep the family together?'

'Yes, yes,' he nodded impatiently. 'But you say the young boy has already gone off to Whitby.'

'He's gone off to earn some money for the family,' Miriam told the gentleman firmly. 'Though we're fearful for him, being only eleven years old.'

Reverend Hawkins shrugged his shoulders. 'I should say that it's commendable in the child. If there were just a little more money coming in to the home. Some prospect of earnings . . .'

Suddenly he pointed his finger in my face. 'How old are you child?'

I stammered with shock. 'I . . . I'm thirteen . . . sir.'

Miss Hindmarch was full of kind concern. 'Dorothy's a good girl, but she's never been away from home.'

My heart was thumping with fear. I could see the way things were going; I was like to be sent away from home to work. The very thought terrified me, but if it would only keep Mam and the little ones safe here, then I knew I must do it.

'She's tall and she looks strong enough,' the Reverend Hawkins insisted. 'You say she's helped her mother with the washing. She could be found a place as a laundry maid. Then we might well be in a position to consider outdoor relief payments until her wages are sent home.'

There was silence in our cramped little room. The women did not look at me. I knew they would not like the choices being offered, but they could see no way to help. I must go away and earn us some money, or we'd all be sent to the workhouse. But I was damned if I was going to be a laundry maid.

I had to gather together all the small courage that I'd got and, though my mam was brought so low that she could not speak to me, something that she'd often told me crept into my mind.

'Don't droop your head so, Dory,' she'd say. 'When you hold up your head and stand tall, there's no finer lass in all the Bay.'

So I took a deep breath and I did it. I held up my head and looked straight at Reverend Hawkins, and I said, 'Not a laundry maid, sir. I shall go to be a herring gutter.'

Again there was silence and everyone stared at me, but the clergyman smiled, and suddenly he seemed to find me most amusing. I was all muddled in my mind and could only think what strong white teeth he'd got.

'And what makes you think you'll be a herring girl and not a laundry maid?'

I knew the answer to that all right. 'My father was a fisherman, sir.'

Reverend Hawkins looked amazed, but a ripple of sighs came from the women. They understood.

I smiled. I suddenly knew how to please the man, so I spoke again. 'And another thing, sir, a herring girl earns more money if she's fast.'

He laughed at that, while the women shuffled and whispered together behind me.

'A herring girl must certainly be fast! Are you fast?'

My usual fear and shyness came flooding back.

'I . . . I will learn to be, sir.'

But Miriam came to stand by me then, snatching up my hand in hers. I think she knew that my courage had ebbed away as fast as it came.

''Tis terrible hard work for a little lass, but if Dorothy feels that she can do it, then I can certainly see to the bairns and nurse her mother while she's away.'

Miss Hindmarch looked worried at the way things were going, but the vicar turned to her shaking his head.

'It's quite ridiculous! Good-mannered did you say? The girl must be a laundry maid. It's what she's been taught.'

My heart sank heavy as ironstone.

But then Hannah came to stand on the other side of me.

'The girl can gut fish,' she said. 'I've taught her that. You said yourself, sir, she's tall and strong.'

'So I did, but, well, don't those women work in teams?'

'Aye, they do. But we shall find a team from the village. We can fix her up as one of three.'

The Reverend Hawkins face grew serious. 'Doesn't she need equipment, knives and such like?'

'We'll find her the knives that she needs.' It was Martha Welford speaking now.

The man looked up at the women. Something had changed in our small kitchen. They'd gathered around me like a warm, strong blanket. They spoke as one, with stubborn determination. I'd seen it before, often enough. They'd gang up on a man who beat his wife, or strip the trousers from a lad who courted too freely. I could not believe it, for though they must think I'd gone barmy, still they stood by me.

Hannah spoke for them all.

'If the child can face the hard work, then we shall find all that she needs.'

It wasn't till the visitors had gone that it really hit me, and I realised what I'd let myself in for. I started shaking all over so that Miriam made me sit by the fire and sip some hot sweet tea.

The women didn't fuss me.

'Aye, she's bound to feel like that,' said Hannah, in her matter-of-fact way. 'You can sit for a bit, Dory, but you can't sit for long; there's much to do. I shall go straight down to the staithe to speak to our Frank. He and Dan are making the plosher ready for the herringing.'

'Right,' said Martha. 'See if they'll hold back a hundred herrings, for we'll have to teach her to gip.'

'But I can gut a cod or a haddock,' I said, quite offended. 'Didn't Aunt Hannah tell the gentleman that I could?'

'Never mind what I told him!' said Hannah. 'Gipping

a herring is quite a different matter, and I shall have told no lie, for I will teach you to gip before you go to Whitby, and you are going to have to learn fast, my girl.'

'We'll send a message to Cousin Rachel,' said Martha. 'She sometimes lets her rooms to herring girls. She used to be fond of Annie, when we were lasses. She'd help you out, Dory, and keep a bit of an eye on you.'

'That's a grand idea,' Hannah agreed. 'But first things first. Finding a team of three is the sticky thing. 'Twould be best if we could find someone who's done it before. Your Irene would be good, but I doubt if she'd leave that bairn.'

Martha shook her head. 'I'd have the little lad, quick as a flash, she knows that, but she's besotted with the bairn.'

I got up from the fireside, for I'd my own ideas about who might make up the team, and I knew I must get busy before I got too scared and changed my mind.

'I think I might know someone who'd go wi' me.'

'Our Nelly might,' said old Mrs Wright as she set off home. 'She were on about it the other night. I'll speak to her.'

I said nothing till she and Mrs Ruswarp had gone, but I wasn't keen on going off to Whitby with their Nelly. Miriam's sharp eyes caught the look on my face.

'You could do worse than Nelly,' she told me. 'I seem to recall that Nelly's done the gipping once before, and again it were illness that caused it. Her father was laid up one summer with a bad leg, and old Mrs Wright took

Nelly off to Whitby with her. They worked all through the season, and Nelly can't have been older than you are now, Dory. She's a tough 'un, is that Nelly, and that's what you want.'

Chapter Six

I scooted down the bank as fast as I could, looking for Mary Jane, my whole body prickling with the excitement of it all. I hadn't said anything to Mrs Ruswarp about it for I didn't know what she'd think, Mary Jane being her youngest.

Alice was sitting on the staithe with our twins and Jackie. I knew I must tell her and not waste time.

'Well?' she cried. 'What have they said?'

'We're not to go in the workhouse so you can stop worrying about that. I'm to go off to Whitby to gip the herrings and earn us some money.'

'Oh no, Dory, no. You cannot do that. Not you and Robbie both gone.'

'Now stop that,' I wagged a finger in her face. 'I'll be

back when the herrings swim south in October, and Miriam will look after you till then.'

'I don't like Miriam,' she said, her chin trembling. 'She's old and snappy.'

I sighed and I put my arms about her. 'Come on, Alice. You've to be the big lass now.'

'I'm our big boy,' little Jackie spoke up cheerfully, catching what we said. 'I'm our big boy now Robbie's gone.'

'Aye,' I said, and I reached out and slapped his rump to tease him. 'You're the big boy. Tell our Alice that she must be the big girl.'

'Big girl,' he said giggling, and thumped Alice on the head.

'Big girl, big girl,' the twins echoed.

I turned serious. 'It's either Miriam or the workhouse. Which do you want Alice?'

A faint smile touched her lips. 'If that's what I've got to choose, then I want Miriam,' she whispered.

There was no sign of Mary Jane on the staithe or in the yards, and I was just wondering whether I'd have to go knocking on the Ruswarps' door when it came flooding into my mind that I knew exactly where she'd be.

I ran across the staithe and onto the sand. It was a hot afternoon, and the rocking of the waves sent glittering shots of sunlight into my eyes. I was dizzy with the regular swish and fizz of the sea, as it washed against the pebbles. The faster I tried to go, the more my feet seemed to sink into the soft dry sand. But Mary Jane was there, just where I thought she'd be; a small lonely figure sitting on Plosher Rock.

'Mary Jane! Mary Jane!' I yelled at her, waving my arms.

She looked up at once and stared at me, then she turned away disappointed. I swear she'd hoped for a moment that it was Liza Welford, come back to Sandwick Bay. I could see that she didn't feel much like bothering with me, but I'd no time for messing about.

'Please Mary Jane,' I panted, crunching through the shingle, and throwing my arms over Plosher Rock. 'Please Mary Jane, I'm begging you. Will you come with me to Whitby to gip the herrings?'

'What?' she stared at me amazed.

'Well, I am surely going,' I told her. 'It's all fixed. I've either to do that or go as a laundry maid, and I'd rather be a herring gutter. The Guardians will make outdoor relief payments for my mam if I go away to earn some money. So you see I've got to go, but now I must find myself two more to make a team of three, and fat Nelly might be one of them – but I hope not.'

The words tumbled fast from my mouth; I couldn't stop to draw breath.

Mary Jane listened to it all in shocked silence.

'You must be mad,' she said at last.

I waited by the rock, dismayed and miserable. I knew that I could not wait for long. If she would not come with me, I must get on and find another.

'Well,' I said at last. 'I thought I'd ask, after what you said yesterday. I daresay you were only teasing Liza, and never meant it. You've no need to earn money, not like me.'

I turned to go, and started back across the shingle.

'Wait!' Mary Jane called after me. She swung herself down from the rock, and ran to push her arm through mine. 'Wait a while. I do want money! I was only teasing yesterday, but now you've made me wonder. Do you think I'd earn enough to buy an organ?'

I smiled. 'If the catches are good, and we can work fast enough, then I think you might.'

'I'll be miserable here in Sandwick without Liza, and now you're going too, Dory. At least it's all go in Whitby, though I swear the work will kill us.'

'I daren't even think about it,' I told her. 'I've just got to do it.'

'Well,' said Mary Jane. 'We'd better find another to make up our team, and not Nelly Wright.'

'You'll come then?'

'I must be mad! But I'll come with you. I'd best go to tell my mam.'

Mrs Ruswarp frowned at us both, and then she sighed, but she accepted it.

'You both seem such little lasses to be going off to work like this. Still, I know that you must go, Dory love, and most folk would think that Mary Jane is quite old enough at fourteen. It's just that she's my baby, you see.'

Mary Jane kissed her mam. 'Wait till you see the money I'll fetch back wi' me. And Mam, how would you like to see a beautiful polished wood organ standing in your parlour?

Mrs Ruswarp smiled and shook her head. 'Just see that you find an older body for the third.'

We went knocking on the Welfords' door to see Irene. We didn't hold out much hope of her coming, but we thought she'd be the best one to ask; her being kind, and having done the gutting before.

'I thought she'd maybe need a bit of money for the bairn,' I whispered to Mary Jane, but she shook her head.

'You know their Frank? The one that went fighting in the war? Well, he's got himself a job up at Stockton now, working in the steelworks. He sends Irene money to help her with the lad. Our John were his friend, you know.'

I nodded silently, sorry that I'd reminded Mary Jane of her drowned brother John.

Irene opened the door with little Joby in her arms.

'I know what you want, Dory, but this bairn's right fretful and awake all night. He's starting cutting his teeth, so that I can't bear to leave him with my mam.'

Joby smiled at us, and dribbled.

'Give your auntie a kiss,' Mary Jane insisted, smacking her lips at Joby till he giggled.

Joby's father, John Ruswarp, had been Mary Jane's eldest brother, but John had died before ever Joby was born. All the village treasured the baby, for none of them could ever forget the fierce storm that had drowned his father, and the terrible struggle that they'd had to save the other men.

Irene had had a hard time getting through her pregnancy, she'd been so sick and so miserable. But then when Joby was born, she'd not stayed sad for long, for you'd never seen a bairn with a happier, funnier face. Just one look at him and you had to smile, whether you wished to or not. Irene had named him John, for his father, but the villagers had insisted on calling him John's boy, and after a while it had shortened itself to Joby.

'I don't blame you for not wanting to leave him,' I told Irene. 'I'd not want to leave him either. Mary Jane is going to come with me.'

'Eeh dear! I hope you both know what you're taking on,' she said. 'I've got something for you, though. I've gipping knives and a good wooden trunk. Come on in and have a look!'

The trunk was a proper kist box, the kind that the Scotch girls used, with its wooden shuttle drawer at the top, made specially to hold the knives, and space beneath for clothes.

'I'd think you two could share one box,' said Irene. 'It's not as though you're going right down to Yarmouth, like the Scotch girls do.'

I agreed with that for the trunk looked big to me, and I'd nothing to put in it. I'd only my best clothes and my working clothes and that was it.

We carried the kist box round to the Ruswarps'

cottage, and then we went banging on the Pickerings' door.

Bessie Pickering was one of the younger married women who'd got no children. She smiled when she saw us and asked us in. It seemed the whole village knew our business.

'I do wish you well,' she said. 'I was meaning to help with the gipping this year, but I've just come to realise that I'm expecting. I've wanted a bairn for more than three years now, so I'll not take any risks.'

We said that we were pleased for her, and we were just about to go when she lifted a great pile of cotton strips down from her sideboard.

'I've been saving flour bags all through the winter,' she said. 'I've cut them into bandage strips. You'll be needing them now, instead of me.'

I remembered then how the herring girls must bandage up their thumbs and their first two fingers to save them from the cuts. We took the cotton strips most gratefully.

Though we knocked on doors all through the afternoon, we could not find a woman who was willing and free to come gipping with us. Still, we didn't come away empty handed. We were given strong oilskin aprons, with straps that crossed at the back, old working skirts and shirts, and worn-out knitted ganseys that the fishermen wore to keep them from freezing out on the sea. There was a pot of Mrs Love's ointment for curing cuts, and a deal of sound advice to go with it.

Mary Jane and I were worn out when we got back to the Ruswarps' cottage, our arms piled high with gifts.

'Mam! You should see what we've been given,' Mary Jane called out. 'But we've still got nobody to make a third.'

Mrs Ruswarp nodded her head towards their kitchen. There standing in front of their fire place was Nelly Wright.

'Yer should have asked me,' Nelly said. 'I'll come to Whitby wi' yer. There y' are then . . . that's all right.'

Chapter Seven

It was quiet back at the cottage. Miriam had sent the three younger children off to bed and she and Alice were ironing our Sunday-best clothes. Buckets of washing were soaking out in the yard.

'More washing?' I said. I wanted to cry when I saw those buckets. 'They'll keep on sending it, won't they? What shall we do? And why have you ironed our Sunday clothes?'

Miriam smiled and shook her head. 'Don't you always press your clothes on Saturday night?'

'It can't be Saturday already,' I said.

So much had happened that I'd got my days all muddled.

'Stop fussing, Dory,' said Alice, suddenly all

grown-up. 'This is our washing. We've not had much chance to deal with it, so we've set it to soak till Monday. Miriam has sent messages telling our customers that Mam is sick and cannot take in washing for a while.'

'Oh thank you, Miriam,' I said, relieved. Suddenly I was blinking back tears. 'You're doing that much to help us and I can't see as we can ever repay it.'

Miriam waved her hands in the air. 'Now Dory, you know that I never had bairns of my own so I'm glad o' the chance to see to other folks' little 'uns.'

I nodded my head and wiped my eyes.

'Mam's wanting you,' Alice told me. 'She's made it plain enough.'

'What shall I say to her?' I looked at Miriam.

'Say nowt,' Miriam shrugged her shoulders. 'I've told her that you're off to Whitby. I don't think she likes it much, but she can still think straight; she knows there's little choice. Now up you go, she wants to see you.'

Mam was propped up on the pillows, Miriam had left an oil lamp burning low on the small cupboard beside her, so that Mam's silver hairs glowed golden against the brown ones. She looked a bit better to me.

'Oh, Mam,' I said, and I went to put my arms about her. We stayed like that for a moment my cheek against hers; she stroked my hair with her good hand. But then she pulled away.

'What is it?' I asked.

'Naah . . . naah!' Mam pointed down towards the bottom of the bed.

'What is it you want?' I asked stupidly. 'A rug? A drink? Miriam?'

'Naah . . . naah.' She tried again, and I carefully followed where she pointed.

'Dad's sea chest?'

She nodded at last, and beckoned me to bring it to her.

I grabbed the handle of the heavy chest and dragged it across the room. I lifted the lid with shaking hands. Most times Mam would not let us touch it, though we knew well what was inside. We treated those few poor things with reverence: Dad's old clothes, his Sunday-best suit, his three clay pipes all different sizes and his bowler hat.

Mam lurched to the side of the bed, trying to reach down into the trunk.

'What is it?' I asked again.

Mam couldn't seem to find what she wanted. She waved her good hand wildly in the air.

'Naah! Naah,' she cried out with rage. I was feared to see her so vexed and helpless.

'Whatever is wrong?' Miriam appeared at the top of our narrow stairs.

'I do believe she wants me to tip Dad's sea chest out.'

'Well, in that case, I should do it, honey.'

So I did, I tipped all my father's things so that they rolled out onto the bedroom floor. Mam calmed down straightaway; she went quiet and thoughtful, inspecting the stuff carefully, then at last she pointed clearly at his boots.

'Dad's sea boots?'

Mam nodded, and I picked them up. They were his best pair and they were almost unworn.

'What am I to do with them?' I looked at Miriam, puzzled.

'You're to wear them, Dory, what do y' think?' Miriam chuckled and Mam pointed to my feet.

'I'm to wear my dad's best boots?' I whispered.

'I think your mam wants that,' said Miriam. 'There's nowt better. You've to stand for hours in the muck and wet, and they'll keep you comfortable and dry. There's many a herring girl wears her dad's old sea boots. You're to have a strong decent pair that's hardly worn.'

I shook my head. 'They're too big.'

It wasn't really the size that troubled me, more that it seemed a sinful thing to wear my poor dead father's boots.

'They won't be,' Miriam said firmly. 'Not when you've three pair o' woolly socks inside 'em.'

I looked at Mam, and I could see that she tried to smile though it came out all lopsided. A tear ran down her cheek.

'Oh thank you, Mam,' I said, hugging the boots to my chest. 'I'll take good care o' them and clean them well. Now I've summat precious to put in Irene's trunk.'

Miriam made us go to Sunday school, as we usually did, and I sat quietly with Mam all Sunday afternoon.

On Monday I woke early and I dressed and went straight round to Hannah's cottage, for Hannah had promised to teach us how to gip herrings. Mary Jane was there, all sleepy and yawning.

'Is Nelly learning to gip?' I asked.

'She is not.' Mary Jane giggled. 'Fastest herring gipper in Sandwick is Nelly . . . or so she says.'

We'd got three baskets with two hundred overday herrings that Frank and Dan Welford had kept back from the dealers on Saturday, so that we could practise our gipping. It was good of them, for decent-sized herrings were selling for three shilling a hundred in Whitby.

'They've landed six lasts in Whitby this week,' said Hannah.

We were impressed at that, for it meant more than sixty thousand herrings caught in just a few days' work.

'And they're expecting more Cornishmen to arrive tonight. It's just like the old days. Fancy them Cornishmen sticking to fishing out of Whitby, when so many dealers have gone over to Scarborough.'

'Why is Scarborough so favoured now?' I asked.

'The dealers are asking for new building work to be done on Whitby harbour, but the Board hasn't the money.' Hannah shrugged her shoulders. 'So it's loyal of these Cornish chaps to stick with us. My Frank says Whitby's the place for Penzancemen, no matter what. They like the chapels, see.'

'Has Mr Welford seen owt of our Robbie?' I begged.

Hannah shook her head. 'I'm sorry, lass, but they'll be looking again today, and you must seek for him yourself.

I've asked our Frank and Dan to take you lasses round to Whitby tonight.'

'What?' said Mary Jane. 'We've not even learnt how to gut a herring yet!'

'You'll either've learnt by tonight or never,' said Hannah. 'They're telling me the curers have fixed up three teams of Whitby women. Either you go tonight or you'll have missed your chance. Our cousin, Rachel Welford, has sent to say that she's getting her downstairs room ready for you. She'll see you're all right.'

Mary Jane pulled a face, and whispered in my ear. 'Aye. She'll see us all right. Just like Hannah, she is.'

'What's that?' said Hannah. 'No time for fooling, Mary Jane, you fetch those gipping knives and those oilie aprons. We must get on.'

'Oilie aprons? While we're learning?' Mary Jane looked amazed.

'Aye . . . aprons, boots and bandages. You're like to make a worse mess now than ever, and you don't want to start it all with a bad cut. Come on! Fetch all the stuff! Spread that oilskin on my table top!'

Hannah made us bandage up our fingers carefully, and tie the knots with our teeth for, as she said, there'd be nobody to help us in Whitby, and no time to help each other. I knew then what a grand present Bessie had made us, for we'd never have been able to find the stuff and carefully cut up all those bandages ourselves.

My first attempts at gipping were useless.

'Nay, Dory, lass,' Hannah cried. 'You're bringing out good flesh. Here let me stand behind you. Start slow and get it right! You'll come into speed later.'

I gripped the plump silver-skinned fish and Hannah put her hand over mine to guide the short sharp gipping knife.

'There now, make the cut in its throat like that, then push in so. Now a quick twist to pick up the guts, then gently flick – and out they come.'

The strong smelling herring guts slopped out onto the oilskin cover.

'Is that it?' I asked. The fish stared mournfully up at me, its eyes still bright on either side of its upturned nose. It looked almost untouched, just a small neat hole in its throat.

'That's it,' said Hannah. 'So long as the gut and the gills are out. Now try yourself.'

I copied her carefully, trying to judge the right spot to push in my knife, and just the right angle to pick up the guts when I twisted. And I did judge it right, but I pulled the knife out fast and a slimy spurt of fish guts shot up into my face. The stinking guts went up my nose, and into my mouth.

Hanna snorted with laughter and Mary Jane shrieked out loud. I staggered back, spluttering and spitting. The herring guts tasted foul.

'Ugh! Dory,' yelled Mary Jane.

'Eeeh! Dory love,' cried Hannah. 'I know it's wicked to laugh. But . . . oh, your face! The guts should go in the gut tub, honey! There's a cloth behind you. Now then, come on, we'll try again.'

I wiped my face and shuddered, I couldn't stop spitting.

'It's all right you laughing,' I told Mary Jane. 'I've not seen you bring the guts out yet.'

We worked slowly all morning under Hannah's instruction, and when we'd used up almost thirty herrings, we'd begun to get the knack of hitting the right spot and bringing the guts out each time. Our arms and aprons were spattered with mess and our bandaged fingers slippery and wet, but Hannah had made us work slowly and we'd not cut ourselves.

Hannah set three baskets behind us and showed us how to judge the size of each herring, and throw the gutted fish carefully into the right basket. The smallest ones were called Matties. The medium-sized fish were called Mattiefulls, and the largest herrings were called Fulls. Hannah made us guess the size and shout it out as we gutted. If we guessed wrong, she scooped the fish out and made us do it all again. At noon she let us stop.

'I'll make us a pot of tea,' she said. 'Though there'll be no stopping for breaks in Whitby you know.'

Mary Jane slumped down onto a chair.

'Mind my decent furniture with those filthy oilies!' Hannah snapped. 'You can sit on the doorstep if you must.'

We sat on Hannah's doorstep and sipped our tea. Apart from the gentle babble of Alice and the bairns next door, the village seemed deserted. I frowned. Where had they all gone? Then suddenly it came to me.

'Is it Regatta Day?' I asked.

'Why, you great daft head,' Mary Jane laughed. 'O' course it's Regatta Day. You must be flummoxed with all your troubles, Dory.'

I nodded, and I turned to Hannah, who sat on her chair behind us. 'You've missed Whitby Regatta to teach us how to gip.'

Hannah smiled kindly and shook her head.

'I've seen plenty of regattas, honey, and I daresay I'll see plenty more.'

Mary Jane groaned, and rolled her shoulders back.

'I'm aching already,' she said. 'We must be mad! Why are we doing it?'

'Money,' I answered her quickly. 'Think of that fine organ standing in your mam's best room.'

I didn't need to remind myself how badly that money was needed.

Chapter Eight

The two Welford brothers had to row hard for the tide was against them. I clutched tight to the side of their plosher that was named the *Esther Welford*. She was one of the big five-man coble boats that the Whitby men use for chasing the herring. They'd had to come away from the regatta early, in order to row us back to Whitby before the herring fleet went off for the night.

The afternoon had passed in a whirl of fast fish gutting, and then frantic last minute packing of Irene's trunk.

I was all of a dither, and I think Mary Jane was worn out and regretting her promise to come to Whitby and work. Nelly had come up to Hannah's to watch us gip.

'Yer'll have t' work faster 'n that,' she told us. 'Ey dear, I can see as I'm going to be having to do most of t' gipping. You two'll have to take turns at packing.'

'I shouldn't think they'll complain at that,' Hannah said.

'You don't have to come with us, Nelly,' Mary Jane said, hopefully.

'I'll put up wi' yer,' said Nelly. 'I've got me box ready now.'

We'd been so busy that I couldn't think straight. I hadn't said goodbye to my mam or to Alice. It was Miriam who'd come down to the staithe and kissed me. Our Jackie and little Nan and Polly had been there waving, all cheerful and excited. I don't think they realised that they'd not be seeing me again for two months. They thought I was having a nice ride in the Welfords' plosher.

Nelly sat beside me, smiling calmly as the big coble pulled out of the bay, taking it all in her stride. She was twenty-one and she was a big woman. One of the few older lasses who'd no young man to court her. I'd always been wary of her; she'd tease the bairns and she could be right rough and loud-mouthed. You never quite knew what she'd do or what she'd say.

Mary Jane sat in the stern along with her brother, Sam, who often worked the boat with the Welford brothers. She was telling him that she'd have finished his gansey by the time the herring season was over.

'You ought to knit a gansey, Dory,' she told me. 'All the herring lasses knit ganseys.'

Knitting the warm jumpers that we call ganseys is vital work for all fishermans' wives and daughters. There's never an excuse for idle hands in our small village and the women are knitting away every spare minute of the day. Without their fine ganseys to keep out the wet and cold, our men would freeze out on the sea.

I shrugged my shoulders. 'Who should I knit for?' I asked.

'Your Robbie of course; he's a fisherman now, isn't he?'

'Aye, maybe,' I answered. 'But if I find him safe, I'll send him home.'

Nelly laughed and shook her head. 'He'll not go,' she told me. 'He'll not tek notice of his sister fussing at 'im. Not that lad. He were that determined when he spoke to me.'

I sighed. 'If he'll not go home, then I'll knit him a gansey.'

We fell quiet as we left our bay. My stomach lurched as the boat rolled with the waves. In the distance, we could see the fleet of visiting herring boats riding at anchor in the sea roads off Whitby harbour.

I smiled to myself. I remembered the delicious smell of fried herrings that had come to us as we carried our boxes down to the staithe. We'd laughed about it. The smell seemed to waft from every window and every doorway. The whole of Sandwick Bay had come back from Whitby Regatta, full of excitement at who'd won the coble race and who'd won the long boat race, to find they'd cheap fresh herrings for their tea. Hannah had sent our Jackie and Billy Welford round the houses selling the herrings that we'd gutted at a halfpenny a pair.

The sea grew choppy, and the sky darkened as though we might be in for rain.

'We're going a long way out,' I said, trying not to sound worried.

I'd not had much chance to go out in the boats since Dad died.

'Don't fret, young Dory,' Dan Welford winked at me. 'We have to follow the sea roads, so we don't catch the scaur. They're right awkward are those low lying rocks. They stretch for more than a mile, so we must go out further, just to keep ourselves clear of them.'

'I'd not want to do this every day,' I said. 'Our Robbie must be daft.'

'Aye, we're all daft,' Frank Welford said cheerfully. 'And your Robbie's another stubborn fellow, just like his father.'

There were spots of rain and the boat rocked wildly as we drew close to the Cornish boats with their double masts and lug sails. I was feeling very sick, and wondering what the men'd say if I begged them to take me back to the bay, when they turned the boat southerly to ride with the tide and we could see Whitby harbour small and flat looking and misty in the distance.

We went towards it fast then; my stomach pulling itself tight with excitement. My spirits lifted with the boat as it rode the waves towards the town.

As soon as we passed through the curved arms of the harbour, the sea grew calm, and Whitby seemed to rear itself high about us on either side of the river Esk. Smoke from the chimneys mingled with the mist.

'Oh, look at the Abbey,' I shrieked at Mary Jane. 'And St Mary's church up on the clifftop, and all those grey stone stairs.'

'Henrietta Street,' she shouted, pointing wildly at the old street that ran below St Mary's church. The small houses up there seemed lost in clouds of puthering smoke. 'See, it's got the little beach below it. That's where we're stopping.'

'I don't know what yer both yelling about,' said Nelly. 'This here's the fish quay where yer'll be working. And yer'd better get used to the smell of bloaters and red herrings, for Henrietta Street's nowt but smoke-houses.'

Cousin Rachel was waiting for us by the fish quay on Pier Road. There were no herring girls in their usual places that day as all the work had stopped for the regatta.

Rachel was a small woman, about Mam's age, with grey hair combed smooth beneath the blue cotton bonnet that all the fisherwomen wore in the summer months. She stood by the harbour rail, her arms folded over the top of a spotless white apron, She had that stony, determined look that I knew well. Most of the fishwives had that same look. You'd have a job to pull the wool over their eyes.

She gave Mary Jane a quick kiss and turned to me.

'So you're Annie Lythe's oldest lass. I knew your mam when we were young. You've more a look of your father though. Now then, Nelly! I spoke to the curer's chaps this morning and told them you were on your way, but they've fixed up two more teams and they say they don't need any more.'

'You mean we're too late?' Mary Jane looked horrified.

I couldn't bear the thought of going back to Sandwick Bay empty-handed now that we were here in Whitby.

'Can we not ask again?' I tried to make my voice sound calm, though I was desperate inside.

''Course we can,' Nelly told me. 'Yer can't expect to be taken on just like that.'

'Oh aye. We must ask again tomorrow, honey,' Rachel said kindly. 'No need to give up yet. I've heard all about your mam, and I know you need the work. The room's all cleared and ready for you, so come on back to Henrietta Street and I'll make you a bit of tea.'

We said our goodbyes to Dan and Frank, but I kept staring at the big wooden farlanes that the coopers were setting up on Pier Road, ready for the herring girls in the morning.

'Come on,' Nelly said. 'Never mind gawping at them, time for that tomorrow. Tek up my box, will yer! Rachel and Mary Jane have taken yours.'

'Can yer not hold it up a bit,' Nelly complained as we followed the others over the bridge.

I'd remembered that I should be looking out for our Robbie, and what with that and the busy streets my head turned this way and that. We went down Sandgate, and up through the market place, and along Church Street. It was full of the whirring of machines and tapping sounds that came from the busy jet workshops.

'They're doing all right,' Rachel told us. 'Ever since the old Queen lost her husband and took to wearing the black jet stones in her jewellery, business has been booming.'

We reached the bottom of Abbey stairs and went past them into Henrietta Street.

'Eeh, you can smell bloaters up here.' I laughed, my eyes watering a little.

'You'll soon get used to it,' Rachel said. 'Mr Fortune's sheds are up on the bankside, just opposite my bedroom window. I only ever take notice if he's not got fish smoking for some reason.'

Nelly's box was heavy and I was ready to drop it when Rachel stopped to open her front door. It was one of the last few cottages on the harbour side of the street, though the pathway carried on past more smoke-houses and led down to the East Pier.

The door next to Rachel's opened and a woman stuck her head out; another fisherman's wife, by her bonnet and apron. She looked at our boxes, surprised.

'Now Rachel, what's this? I thought you weren't taking Scotch lasses this year.'

'I'm not,' said Rachel. 'This lot's from Sandwick. You've seen Mary Jane before, and this'n's Annie Lythe's lass, and this'n's Nelly.'

'Have they fixed them up, then?'

'No,' said Rachel. 'They'll have to try again in the morning.'

The woman clicked her tongue and shut her door.

'That's my neighbour, Hannah Smith,' Rachel told us. 'She's known as Trickey around here. You can guess why! She's a good enough neighbour to me though. She's got eight of the Scotch girls stopping with her. You'll hear them when they come back.'

I stared at Trickey's door. Eight Scotch girls? Where did she put them all. The cottages were bigger than ours in Sandwick, but they weren't that big.

Rachel went into the narrow passage with a door to the right. She flung it open, and we saw a small bare basement room with three steps down to it.

'There you are,' Rachel said. 'I've put you in here so that you don't need to traipse through the rest of the house.'

Nelly and I followed the others in, bumping her box down the three steps.

The room was so dark and dismal that my spirits sank. It was all so very bare, nothing in but three beds, covered with worn patchwork quilts. Our living rooms at Sandwick bloomed with fine brass ornaments and

pictures and I'd expected the same. In Rachel's room the
floorboards were covered with oilcloth, and the curtains
that hung at the window, just above the street level, had
brown paper pinned carefully over them. There were no
curtains at all on the far small window that overlooked the
harbour and beach.

'I've had a good clear-out, as you can see,' Rachel told
us, as though we should be pleased. 'So now you won't
need to worry about mess.'

'Aye,' said Nelly. 'I prefer it like that,' and she
thumped herself down on the bed nearest to the street
window.

'I'll make some tea, and give you a shout,' said Rachel.
'You can come up to my kitchen today, but once you're
working I'll bring your food and drink to you. I'll want
your boots and oilies left outside of course.'

The three of us were left together. Nelly swung her legs
up onto her bed, trying it and prodding it.

'Not bad,' she decided.

Mary Jane looked across at me. I think she felt a bit
lost too.

'I knew they cleared the best furniture out,' she said. 'I
just didn't think how plain it'd leave it. We haven't even a
chair to sit on.'

'We sit on't boxes, of course!' Nelly said, disgusted at
our ignorance.

I went to peep out of the window on the harbour
side, and I got a grand view of the West Cliff and the

boats in the harbour, making ready to set off for the night.

'Can I have this bed?' I asked, going to the nearest one.

'You can,' said Nelly. 'I'm not sleeping there. I don't want the sea keeping me awake all night.'

Chapter Nine

Rachel called us up to her kitchen and I was glad to see that it was as bright and cosy as any in Sandwick Bay. She served thick slices of bread with a little butter and sweet bilberry jam.

'The bairns fetch t' berries down from the moors,' she told us. 'Then they come round knocking on doors with their hands and faces stained black and purple. They've the cheek to ask a penny a basket, but they're fine berries for jam, and my husband has a sweet tooth, so I usually buy from them.'

The food cheered me for a moment. It looked as though we'd be well fed if nothing else. Then a terrible thought came to me and I had to put down my bread and jam.

'Oh dear,' I cried, going red with the shame of it. 'If the curers won't take us on, we'll get no fixing money. I'll have nowt to pay you for my lodgings, Rachel.'

'No,' Mary Jane agreed, looking worried. 'That's true enough.'

Nelly went on eating steadily.

'Ey lass, haven't you enough to worry about?' Rachel shook her head. 'Now drink up your tea and stop getting yourself into such a bother over nowt. It's up to me to see that you get fixed up, if I'm worried about my rent money. But do you not think I'd give food and a bed to Annie Lythe's lass without payment. Now eat up and shut up afore you get me cross.'

I stared down at my plate then, feeling terrible. When I glanced back up at Mary Jane, my cheeks all hot and red, she grinned at me and winked. I picked up my bread and jam again.

'Thank you, Rachel,' I said.

We ate on in silence, till all at once a great commotion came from Trickey's cottage.

'Here they come,' Rachel told us. 'Wait for it! They've been out parading round town in their best clothes today.'

There was the tramp of feet on the stone cobbles outside, the sounds of loud voices and laughing; the floorboards started creaking and doors banged as the Scotch girls arrived back next door.

We had to smile at each other.

Mary Jane got up from the table and looked out of Rachel's kitchen window.

'Oh lor', Dory!' she squealed. 'The boats ... the boats are setting off.'

I jumped up, and ran to join her. 'Our Robbie!' I said. 'I meant to look for him and I'm too late.'

'No you're not,' Rachel told me. 'Leave these pots, and run down the path to the ladder. You can get onto the pier from here, and watch all the Whitby boats as they pass. Go on! You'll have to hurry! You can wave to the *Whitby Rose* for me.'

I ran down the path to the edge of the cliff, and I almost had to close my eyes as I walked the wooden bridge that Rachel called the ladder. It sloped down from the cliff edge to the pier, carrying me over a great space, with rocks beneath and the sea swilling back and forth as the tide turned. Mary Jane came pounding along behind me.

'Ooh . . . I don't like crossing this,' I called back to her.

'Just keep your Robbie in mind,' she shouted.

I breathed out with relief as my feet touched the solid stone slabs of the pier and hurtled on to the very end of it.

Two boats had passed already and most of the visiting fleet were already heading off to the fishing grounds.

'Oh let me see him ... please let me see him,' I whispered.

'Them's Penzancemen,' Mary Jane shouted.

'How can you tell?' I screwed up my eyes to see better.

'You can tell by the double masts, and the PZ register mark on the side. Look!' she cried, hopping up and down

322

beside me and pointing. 'The *Whitby Rose*, David Welford's plosher. He's Rachel's husband . . . wave to 'im! Here's two Fifies with their brown sails and the sloping gaff rigg at the top. This un's from Lowestoft . . . see the cloth caps that the fellers wear.'

'How do you know all that?' I asked, looking at Mary Jane with new respect.

'Our Sam's told me. He brought me last summer for the regatta. There he is . . . there he is now,' she went frantic, waving and jumping up and down.

'Where? Where?' I begged, my head turning this way and that as the local boats passed quickly through the narrow harbour mouth and out into the open sea. They'd a steady westerly wind behind them.

'There,' she yelled. 'The *Esther Welford*.'

'Oh yes,' I waved along with her at the Welford brothers and Sam Ruswarp, but I was disappointed for I'd thought for a moment that she'd seen our Robbie.

Then, as the last few boats passed out between the arms of the two piers, I did see a young lad with a familiar look to him, in the stern of a sturdy Whitby plosher.

'Robbie!' I yelled at the top of my voice.

The lad turned towards us and it was our Robbie.

I ripped off my woollen shawl and waved it wildly over my head.

'Dory! Dory!' I heard him shout. He spoke to one of the men beside him and pointed to me and waved, but the boat was moving fast away. I waved and waved till it was out of sight.

'Did you see him?' I asked Mary Jane. 'It was him, wasn't it?'

Mary Jane stared after the wake of the boats. 'Oh aye, it was your Robbie, but did you see who he was with?' Her eyes were wide with surprise. 'It was the *Louie Becket* he was on.'

'The *Louie Becket*?' I shook my head, it meant nowt to me. 'I saw a big feller with a great bushy beard?'

'Aye. He's the old lifeboat man. You know the one . . . him as was the only one saved when the Whitby boat went down.'

'Him?' I said. 'Our Robbie with the old lifeboat man?'

'Aye,' she spoke quietly, impressed. 'I think your Robbie's done all right for himself.'

We ran back up to Henrietta Street, and told Rachel how we'd seen our Robbie. She laughed when she heard that.

'I might of known,' she said. 'Wait till I tell Trickey! The old feller cannot resist the herring season. He's supposed to be retired and they've certainly retired him from his lifeboat work. He swore last summer that the herring catches were so poor, he'd not be going again.'

'Well, there's no mistaking him,' Mary Jane said. 'And there was their Robbie as large as life on his boat.'

'In that case, Dory, you can stop your fretting over Robbie,' Rachel told me. 'He couldn't be safer, and he'll be looked after, too. The old feller never had bairns of his own, and he's always had a fondness for the young 'uns.'

'Yer'll not be sending him back to Sandwick now,' said Nelly.

'No,' I said. 'I'll not even try.'

I couldn't settle down to sleep that night, what with the strangeness of the room and Nelly snoring. The swish and lap of the sea was loud by our window, though the sound of it was a comfort to me.

We got up early next morning and bandaged up our fingers, for, as Rachel said, we had to look as though we meant business. Then we went straight round to the fish quay, carrying our oilies and boots.

Rachel spoke to two of the curer's men, but one said firmly that he'd more than enough. The other looked us up and down and said that I was nowt but a bairn.

'She's a big strong lass,' said Rachel.

'Aye, but I can see by her face she's a bairn. Look now,' he said. 'If I need another team I'll consider them, but I've all I need at the moment.'

We hung around on the harbourside, watching the Scotch girls turning up for work in a noisy huddle as the boats began to arrive back, with a fair catch of gleaming herrings on board.

I looked out for Robbie, but I couldn't see him or the *Louie Becket*.

'Come on,' said Rachel. 'We'll go and get us a bite to eat, for there's nowt doing here.'

We followed her back to Henrietta Street, feeling a bit down, and sat ourselves by the fire in Rachel's kitchen.

It was warm and spotlessly clean in there. Rachel had three freshly washed aprons drying by the fireside on a strange looking wooden clothes horse with three spindly legs. I frowned at it; the washing reminded me of Mam, and there was something familiar about that clothes horse.

We sipped the hot tea that Rachel handed out to us, and we were just beginning to unwind our bandaged fingers when there was a shout from the street and hammering on Rachel's door. Trickey came pounding up the hallway stairs.

'You want to get those lasses down to Pier Road,' she shouted.

'What!' We all jumped up from our seats.

'There's a right old to-do,' she panted, trying to get her breath, her eyes wide and excited.

'What's it all about?' Rachel asked.

'There's a Scotch lass sacked for bulking!'

'Now's your chance,' Rachel cried, leaping up to grasp her shawl. 'Get your oilies and boots and run as fast as you can.'

We didn't need telling twice. We grabbed our things and pelted down through the streets to the bridge. But just as we got there, they closed the gates so that three tall masted herring boats could pass through into the upper harbour.

We cursed and swore and jostled each other and jumped up and down on the spot.

'Look over there,' Rachel cried, pointing to Pier Road.

'I can tell there's trouble from here. Listen to them Scotch lasses shrieking!'

'What is it that they've done wrong?' I asked fearfully.

'Bulking,' Rachel told me. 'It's the packer that's at fault. She's been chucking the herrings into the barrels all anyhow, then covering it up with a neat layer at the top. They can fill the barrels quicker that way, but it's not allowed. Oh no, you're sacked on the spot for bulking.'

I caught my breath. It didn't seem such a terrible thing to me.

Then as soon as the bridge was back in place, we were off running over it and down to Pier Road.

When we got close I slowed up, my heart pounding with fright. I didn't fancy taking the place of a girl who'd been sacked. All the gutters had stopped their work and they were bellowing and shouting and shaking their fists at the foreman. Their speech was so different that it was hard to understand, but their meaning was clear enough.

'Gi'er another chance, Willie!'

'Couldna ye give 'er another chance?'

'She's had all the chances she's going to get.' The man wouldn't be budged.

'Then we sh'll come wi'ye, Maggie!' Another girl shouted.

'Aye. We'll nae work for ye Willie if Maggie's sacked. We'll be off to Scarborough. They're crying oot for lassies there. We wouldna stay wi'oot ye, Maggie!'

And suddenly there were three big lassies, unfastening

their aprons and marching away from the long wooden farlanes of herrings.

Rachel was in there quick as a flash, pushing us forward. 'You said my lasses could have the next chance.'

'Aye,' the foreman sighed and scratched his head. 'So I did. I'll try them, but they'll be on their own. It's all Scotch lasses down here on Pier Road, you know. The Whitby teams are by the upper harbour.'

'We're not bothered,' Nelly said.

'Well, they'll not be fixed till I see how they work. Right, lass,' he pointed to me. 'Get behind that farlane and let me see thee gip.'

Chapter Ten

I struggled into my apron, my hands shaking horribly. I knew he'd picked on me because he thought I looked least able to do it. Quite a crowd had gathered about us.

'Look ye noo, he's teking on wee bairns,' one of the Scotch girls muttered.

'Back to yer work,' the man bellowed, and reluctantly the women turned again to their troughs.

I took the sharpest knife from my pocket and picked up a good-sized fish, trying hard to remember what Hannah had taught me. I pushed the knife in carefully and twisted it, and the guts flew out into the gut tub.

The man grunted. 'Now size?' he snapped.

'Mattiefull,' I answered him, my voice all shaky.

'What?' He put his hand to his ear.

'Mattiefull,' I said it loudly.

He nodded and pointed to the basket behind me. I slipped the fish in and snatched up another herring to gut.

Nelly pushed in beside me and set to work. Mary Jane went to pack the barrel behind us.

'That one'll have to be packed again,' the man said.

Mary Jane nodded, she began pulling the herrings out and setting them gently in a basket. The cooper went to help her.

I paused to watch Nelly for a moment and my mouth dropped open. Nelly could certainly gip, and she could gip fast. She'd done four fish while I did one.

'Stop gawping,' she muttered under her breath. 'Get gipping!'

'I'll try 'em for a week,' the foreman told Rachel. 'But that young un'll have to come into speed or she's out, and there'd better be no bulking.'

'Then I'll be needing a week's food and rent money,' said Rachel, holding out her hand to him.

The herring catch wasn't huge, but by the time we'd emptied our farlanes at the end of the day, I felt as though I'd gipped the whole of the ocean.

My back ached, my legs ached, my hands were sore and swollen and I'd gathered three cuts that stung with the salt that the coopers sprinkled onto the herrings. Mary Jane and I took turns at packing and it brought us a bit of relief, though we had to pack the fish in perfect neat layers. The foreman kept watching us and checking in case we grew careless. All the while the Scotch girls frowned at us and looked on with suspicion.

One of the young coopers was kind to us. He was a strong, broad-built lad, who lifted the barrels as though they were bairns and whispered good advice that we gratefully took. The coopers' job was to make the barrels and see that they were carefully packed, with just the right amount of salt sprinkled between the layers of herrings. Then they'd stack the filled barrels up neatly behind us for the herrings must be left to pickle for ten days.

I was so tired and hungry by midday that I thought I'd faint, and yet I knew that there was no stopping to eat or drink. I almost cried with relief at the sight of Rachel coming down Pier Road with a jug of warm broth and three bowls. It was the best broth I'd ever tasted, even though we had to take it in small quick sips while we stood at the farlanes.

Nelly gipped fast and steadily all through the day. She said little but she plodded on through the work like a donkey. I was glad to have her there with us, and I knew how right Miriam had been when she called her a tough 'un.

'Is that it?' said Mary Jane, stretching and rubbing her back.

'Aye,' said Nelly, carefully wiping her knives and putting them into her pocket.

'I thought I'd die,' said Mary Jane. 'I'm sore all over.'

'My legs won't stop wobbling,' I groaned. 'I swear I can't walk back to Henrietta Street.'

'Yer'll manage,' said Nelly. 'That were a slow day. I've seen 'em gip three times that lot.'

'We'll want you back at six in t' morning, to help wi' topping up,' the foreman told us. 'Don't you be late.'

We rinsed our hands at the pump, and then set off walking slowly back to Rachel's house, a gang of the Scotch girls following behind us.

They shouted rude remarks at our backs and most of it I couldn't understand, but it was clear that they felt bitter about us taking the place of the girls that had gone, and I was scared of them.

At last, as we reached our door, one of the girls shouted out loudly so that we couldn't ignore it.

'You lot took Maggie's job fra her, we di'nna like that, ye ken. Wee bairns taking work fra those puir lasses that need the money.'

I wanted to rush into Rachel's house and get away from them but Rachel herself opened the door. She'd clearly heard it all and she caught me by the arm.

'No,' she said. 'We've to sort this out.'

She marched up to the women, dragging me reluctantly along with her. Nelly and Mary Jane followed slowly.

'Now lasses,' she said, 'it's not as it seems. We didn't wish your Maggie sacked, but these lasses do need the money bad. We had to grab at the chance. Dory's mam is

332

sick, and cannot earn. Her father was drowned a few years back. Now you lasses know well what that means to a family.'

The girls looked down and shuffled their feet.

Rachel went on, while I hung my head. 'For this lass, it's the gipping or the workhouse. Aye and all her little brothers and sisters, too.'

I took a deep breath and lifted my head to face them. 'I didn't like to take your Maggie's job,' I said. 'I didn't like it at all.'

The Scotch girl sighed. 'Di'nna fret, hinny. I do believe ye.' She gently touched my cheek. 'We'll forget it noo,' she said.

'Aye, we'll forget it noo,' the others agreed. They went quietly into Trickey's cottage.

'They'll be all right,' Rachel said, as we turned back to her door. 'They're grand lassies really and wonderful the way they work. We don't like to fall out wi' them for they bring us good rent money each summer, and they don't ask much for it. Now,' she said, back to her usual practical self, 'oilies and boots outside and straight to your room. I'll fetch your water and your supper to you.'

Nelly flopped down on her bed in all her muck, and lay like that until Rachel appeared with washing water and cloths and a good super of fish stew.

'You surprised me, Dory!' Mary Jane grinned. 'That were brave of you to speak up to them like that. It's not like you.'

'No,' I shook my head. 'I don't know what come over

me. My fingers hurt so much I don't seem to care for owt else.'

Nelly ate fast, then flopped back onto her bed again. Though I ached with each movement, I unwound the bandages and tried to wash my hands and put Mrs Love's ointment on my cuts.

'This water's going cold, Nelly, will you not wash?' I asked.

'No point,' said Nelly and closed her eyes. 'I'll wash meself on Sunday.'

'Will you not change into your nightdress, Nelly?' Mary Jane asked, wrinkling her nose and pulling a face at me.

'Nobbut a waste o' time,' Nelly muttered, already half asleep.

We were stiff as boards next morning when Rachel looked in to wake us.

'Come on,' she called, grinning at the groans that came from us. 'Aye, you'll be stiff I daresay, but there's only one way to be rid of it.'

'What's that?' Mary Jane asked hopefully.

'Work on, hard and fast,' Rachel told her.

That second day was even more difficult than the first, for the catch was good and we had to struggle through our stiffness and try to build up speed, but by the end of the day we all walked back to Henrietta Street feeling happier.

I was pleased for I'd seen our Robbie and he was mad

with delight when he saw me gipping at the farlanes. He stood beside me for an hour or so chattering on and on about the fine time he was having fishing out of Whitby. I told him that I couldn't stop my work and he helped by pushing the herrings towards me.

'You should see them, Dory,' he shouted. 'You should see them silver darlings when we're scudding the nets. We haul them in, and they come flying at us, through the air and into the boat. They're everywhere! We're up to our knees in fish and covered in scales. And the smell, Dory! You wouldn't believe the smell!'

'Oh Robbie,' I fussed. 'Are you all right? Are you treated well?'

'Am I treated well?' he asked, a great smile on his face. 'The old feller treats me like I'm his own lad. I make the tea for them,' he said, beaming with importance. 'And I make a good plum duff, boiled up in old condensed milk tins, for they need something warm and solid to fill their bellies out there.'

'And can you do all that, Robbie?'

'Aye, I can. They've taught me how, and they never slap me if I spill. They just bellow at me and laugh.'

'Oh Robbie,' I worried. 'It seems you've grown all of a sudden.'

'Aye,' he answered me sadly. 'You've grown too, Dory. I would never have thought to see you working like this at the farlanes, and nagging at me just as if you were my mam.'

*

Mary Jane was pleased that day, for suddenly there was a face we all knew well, staring open-mouthed at us on the harbourside: Liza Welford, done up in smart nurse-maid's clothes of good grey cloth all neatly buttoned. She'd a young boy dressed in a sailor suit held firmly by the hand on one side of her, and a tiny girl in silks and ribbons on the other side.

Mary Jane grinned and shouted. 'I told you I could gip a herring, Liza Welford.'

'I cannot believe my eyes,' Liza gasped and stared at us, but the young boy pulled at her.

'Ice-cream,' he shouted. 'Want some ice-cream.'

'Just a moment, Master Rupert,' Liza spoke patiently. 'These are my friends.'

The boy looked up at us puzzled. 'Are they trades-people?' he demanded. 'Phew! They smell! Mama says I mustn't speak to tradespeople. Stop talking to them and get me ice-cream. I'll tell Mama of you!'

Liza smiled rather sadly at us and shrugged her shoulders.

'I'll be back tomorrow,' she called as the boy dragged her away.

We were glad to see her, and impressed by the elegance of her clothes, but we agreed that Liza did not seem at all happy. I'd never heard a young child speak to Liza like that. In our small school up at Bank Top, Liza Welford's word is law.

'What that one wants is a good hiding,' Nelly said.

*

336

Nelly seemed to be in an unusually cheerful mood that day. She was quite chatty to us as we staggered our way back to Henrietta Street.

'Them Scotch lasses has been fine today,' she said.

'Aye,' I smiled. 'That lass that shouted at us last night, she showed me how to drain off the pickle juice through the bunghole this morning, and she showed me how to pick the best fish for topping up the barrel. She was right kind to me and said to call her Jeanie.'

'Aye,' said Nelly, a secretive smile on her face. 'And what about that big strong chap that works as our cooper. He says his name is George. He told me that as he filled our farlane and then he called me pet.'

Mary Jane giggled. 'He comes from Blythe. They call everyone pet up that way.'

But the smile stayed there on Nelly's face.

'He called me pet,' she said. 'And he called me darling.'

Chapter Eleven

We struggled on through the next few days and by the time we'd cleared the farlanes on the Saturday night, we were dead on our feet.

'I'm gipped . . . as well as these herrings,' Mary Jane grimaced at us, stretching to ease her back.

'I don't know what you're complaining about,' said Nelly. 'All these Scotch lasses are upset at the small catches.'

Greater catches of herrings meant more money earned by us; for each team was paid by the number of barrels they managed to gut and pack. That week, I was grateful that the catches weren't huge for I couldn't have worked faster or harder than I did.

I grew to love the walk back to Rachel's cottage each

night. Though my feet and my back ached and my fingers were swollen and stinging, still the relief at the end of the day was wonderful. Rachel's generous stews and puddings tasted as good as any fancy food we could dream up and the thought of them roused my spirits.

That first Saturday night, Jeanie's team, who'd been walking behind us, shouted wildly as we reached our door.

'What is it now?' I asked Mary Jane, nervously.

'I can't tell a word they're saying.' She giggled as she wearily started to peel herself out of her smelly, crusted pinafore. 'They get so excited and they talk so fast. If they'd only calm down and talk a bit slow.'

It was Nelly that went to them. She listened frowning, then suddenly smiled back at us.

'Ceilidh?' she said. 'Aye, I know what that means.'

'What is it?' Mary Jane demanded.

'It's a bit of singing and dancing,' Nelly told us, her eyes gleaming at the thought of it. 'And the coopers are coming over to Tate Hill Pier.'

We rushed then to get out of our oilies, and kicked off our boots by Rachel's doorstep.

After we'd had our supper we made good use of the washing water that Rachel brought to us, and got ourselves as clean and tidy as we could. Then we hurried down to Tate Hill Pier.

At first we sat and listened to a band playing on the far side of the harbour. The strains of music and the steady beat of the drum came to us clearly across the calm water.

We could see the coopers gathered by the bandstand and some of the Scotch girls. They'd lodgings on Burtree Crag, on the Westside, where they rented little rooms like ours from the fishermen's wives. Most of them were packed five or six into a room, and I knew that our lodgings with Rachel were spacious beside theirs. They kept waving at us, and when the bandsmen packed away their instruments and left, the coopers and the lasses came over the bridge to join us. Two of the lads had brought their squeeze boxes and another had a mouth organ. They settled themselves on the solid stone slabs of Tate Hill Pier and began playing tunes that were familiar to us all. It wasn't long before the fishermen came leaping ashore from their boats to join in with the singing.

There were Cornishmen, Scotchmen, and the Lowestoft men in their best Norfolk jackets and cloth caps. There were others like our cooper George who'd come down from Northumberland. They chattered and sang together in their different voices, making a fine and funny mixture of sounds.

Nelly was full of cheek and asked George outright if he were married.

He shook his head and smiled.

'Are you courtin' then?' she demanded.

'Why no, pet,' he said. 'Are y' offering?'

Nelly suddenly went quiet and pink in the cheeks, while all the fellows laughed and hooted. I'd never seen Nelly look ashamed before.

It was a beautiful summer evening; still and warm. I forgot my tiredness and wished that it would go on for ever. Even the old women came out from their cottages and sat by the harbourside knitting and nodding their heads to the tunes they played. As dusk fell, lamps were lit everywhere for all the boats had crowded into the harbour for the weekend. The golden shimmer of their riding lights reflected in the water and the boats creaked gently as they rocked up and down to the wash of the waves.

Our Robbie came running down over Tate Hill sands with the old lifeboatman striding after him.

'I've found our Dory!' he yelled, and flung his arms round me. The old fellow went to gossip with Trickey and Rachel who'd brought their knitting outside.

The singing and clapping grew loud and jolly and some of the lasses got up and danced.

George held out his hand to Nelly. 'Come Nelly, dance wi' me, pet. I never meant to give offence.'

Nelly didn't need asking twice.

Soon me and Mary Jane were skipping along with them, though I don't know where the energy came from. One young Scotch girl sat alone and would not join in.

'What's up wi' her?' I nudged Mary Jane and pointed.

'She's one o' them that's come down from Stornaway,' said Mary Jane. 'See her black scarf. Jeanie told me she only speaks the gaelic.'

I stared at her. I could see from her face that she was young, no older than me. I was homesick enough, just coming down from Sandwick. I couldn't imagine what it must be like to travel so far from your home to such mucky work.

'Jeanie, Jeanie,' I called as she whirled past with one of the coopers. 'Will the Stornaway lass not dance?'

'Och, Katrina,' Jeanie shook her head. 'The poor bairn's nae left her home afore. We try oor best to look after her, but her faither has made her promise to keep herself away fra the laddies. She keeps to her word like a wee saint.'

'Poor soul!' said Mary Jane. 'Will she dance with us? We're not the laddies?'

'Ye canna do harm to try,' Jeanie nodded.

So we went and stood in front of Katrina and we held out our hands to her. At first she would not budge, but as we kept on at her, with daft bits of miming and prancing around, at last she giggled and gave in. We took both of her hands and skipped round together until she was pink-cheeked and laughing.

'How can I skip like this when my feet hurt so?' I yelled at Mary Jane.

'I can't feel my feet at all,' she grinned.

When at last we could stand no more, we flopped down by Robbie who sat with the lifeboatman.

'I wish Liza Welford were here to see all this,' said Mary Jane. 'Would they let her out on a Saturday night, do you think?'

I shook my head. I somehow didn't think that they would.

'I wonder if she can hear all this singing, up in her fine room,' I said.

Just at that moment we seemed to have more in common with a Stornaway fisherlass who couldn't even speak to us, than any of those fine English folk who stayed up there on the West Cliff.

The dancing faded out, and Jeanie stood up to sing.

'Who'll buy my fresh herrin'
they're bonny fish and wholesome farin.
Who'll buy my fresh herrin'
new pulled from the sea.
When you were sleeping on your pillows,
did you think of our poor fellows?
Darkling with the wildest billows,
pulling herrin' from the sea.

Who'll buy my fresh herrin' . . .'

She'd a lovely deep voice and we all listened quietly and clapped her when she stopped.

'We sing out there, you know,' said Robbie, his eyes bright in the oil lamp's glow.

'What, you sing at sea?'

'Oh aye,' he said, 'but singing is quite different out there, Dory. It makes me want to cry.'

'Nay, Robbie. Why should it make you cry?'

'It's the quiet of the sea all around us. First we have the fuss of shooting the nets, but then we have to settle down

343

and wait. It goes very quiet, Dory . . . too quiet, and that's when they start. One of the Cornishmen will pick out the tune on his accordion, and we listen for a bit, then one of the chaps will start to sing, and we listen again, then slowly, slowly we join in. The sound o' deep voices comes from all the distant boats and it grows and grows until the whole fleet is singing.'

'Oh Robbie,' I cried. 'It sounds beautiful.'

'Aye, it's grand,' he said, shaking his head. 'But they only sing hymns out there. I don't think it would seem right to sing owt else.'

'Oh, I wish I could hear it,' I said.

The old lifeboatman who'd been listening to us, leaned forwards and touched my arm. 'Don't you fret, little lass. You shall hear the Cornishmen singing their hymns, for I believe they've arranged to have a service on the boats tomorrow.'

Sunday was a quiet day, and even Nelly kept to her word and had a good wash, though we knew the smell of herrings still clung to us and would not be washed away however many rinses of fresh water Rachel brought. We dressed ourselves in our Sunday clothes and gathered by the harbourside to listen to the lovely sounds of the Cornishmen singing their hymns, just as the old fellow had promised. They'd carried a harmonium out onto Tate Hill Pier, and Mary Jane edged closer and closer to it. I saw her fingers twitching to the solemn rhythm of the hymns, her face lit up with pleasure.

When they'd finished, we went to help Rachel with the dinner. I'd never had such a fine meal in all my life. Rachel and her husband had invited John Jack Trevorrow, the skipper of one of the Cornish luggers who'd been coming to Whitby for many years, and us three lasses sat at the table with them in our Sunday-best clothes.

Like all the fishermen's wives, Rachel had her ornaments and brasses polished and displayed for Sunday. Her kitchen looked a treat, with the black-leaded cooking range shining like jet, and the strange wooden drying rack folded away neatly in the fire corner.

As soon as we'd finished our dinner, Rachel sent us down to John Jack's boat, the Silver Star, to carry roast beef and a jug of gravy to the four men and the young cook who made up his crew.

Mary Jane pulled faces at me.

'We're never going to get Nelly away from these Cornish lads,' she mouthed.

But she was wrong, for though the Cornish lads were full of fun and cheek, Nelly was not her usual loud-mouthed, forward self.

Later that afternoon, we set off with Jeanie's gang, marching arm-in-arm up the Abbey stairs to look down on the town from the top of the East Cliff. When we'd had our fill of the fine view from up there, we set off to parade ourselves round town; then last of all we climbed the steep hill up onto the West Cliff. All the other gipping girls did the same, and we yelled and cheered at the tops of our voices when we saw another gang of herring gutters coming towards us.

We caught a glimpse of Liza up near the Saloon Gardens with her charges. We greeted her loudly, but she seemed flustered.

'I've been told I've not to speak to you, nor any tradespeople,' she whispered, her cheeks red with the shame of it.

This was not the brave Liza Welford that we all knew. I hated to see her so timid and anxious.

The boy pulled at her arm and pinched his nose rudely. 'Mama said no speaking to stinky fish girls,' he cried. 'Get me more lemonade or I'll tell Mama.'

Liza ignored him for a moment. 'I've to take them both to the picture man's studio tomorrow,' she said. 'They're to have their portraits made.'

'It's a good job he's a patient man,' said Mary Jane. 'Even he might have a job to make that one look sweet.'

'Best go now,' said Liza.

'Did you see that?' Mary Jane spoke furiously as Liza went off towards the gardens.

'What?' I stared about us.

'He kicked her. That spoilt brat of a child kicked our Liza on purpose, and she did nothing.'

'I told you,' said Nelly. 'He needs a good clout.'

'I'd throw the lemonade right in his face!' cried Mary Jane.

*

We went to chapel with Rachel for the evening service, and found it filled with Cornishmen. Their voices swelled the singing and made it very fine. We didn't argue with Rachel when she insisted that we should get an early night, even though we knew that Monday should be a quiet day for the men would never go out fishing on a Sunday night.

Chapter Twelve

On Monday we slept till seven o'clock, then went to help the coopers sort out the barrels ready to go to the railway station. We had to open up the bung holes to drain off the salty oil and fish juices from the barrels that had stood there pining and pickling for more than a week. Then we had to top the barrels up with more herrings and pour back the pining juice till they were full and tightly packed, with a layer of perfect herrings on the top and straw to protect them.

'Ye canna get a finer handcream than the pining juice,' Jeanie told us.

She made us dabble our hands in the smelly stuff and rub it well in, though it made my cuts sting for a while. I found she was right for, as it seeped in, my skin grew soft and supple.

George pegged down the barrel lids carefully. He patted the top fondly, proud of a well-made barrel, filled and finished just right.

'They'll keep for a good twelve month now,' he said. 'It's off you go for a nice train ride, my fine fat silver darlings.'

We giggled for he sounded as though he spoke to his bairns, or even his sweetheart.

'Hey Nelly! You'd better watch out,' said Mary Jane, full of sauciness. 'This lad's in love with the little fishes.'

Monday was an easy day with no herrings arriving. There was no need to bandage up our fingers and our work was done by noon. So we went back to Henrietta Street and helped Rachel to cover all her ornaments for the week's work; then we settled to do our knitting by the harbourside, gossiping and watching the men load up the boats with food, and freshly mended nets.

The weeks fell into a hard pattern of work, though Sunday and Monday brought us some relief. I managed to come into a bit of speed, and the foreman agreed to keep us on till the season in Whitby ended. Though I managed to gip the herrings faster, I could not come near to the Scotch girls.

'Well noo,' boasted Jeanie. 'When ye've worked at the gipping as long as me, ye'll tern oot fifty or sixty herrin' a minute.'

'Aye, so you say, so you say,' said Nelly gutting steadily. But we all knew that Jeanie was not far wrong.

Frank Welford came to the farlanes looking for us. He was pleased to see that we'd got work, and he told me that all was well at home and that my mam was certainly no worse.

Sometimes we'd have an early morning visit from the picture man. He'd turn up with his new box cameras slung about his neck, and he'd be there beside the farlanes just as we were getting going, or late in the evening when we were packing up. He took snap-shot pictures of us, as he called them, while we chatted to him, though we dare not stop our work to help him with his pictures.

'You should come to take our pictures at noon when the sun's bright and we're piled high with herring,' we told him.

He smiled and shook his head. 'I've an appointment to make a picture of a bouncing baby at noon,' he said sadly, and looked at his watch and left.

The first time that he saw us, he bowed in surprise and raised his hat.

'Herring ladies from Sandwick, I believe.'

Mary Jane giggled and smiled broadly. 'Do you remember, sir, how you took my picture once, sitting on Plosher Rock along with Liza Welford? The print you gave us has pride of place on Mam's mantelpiece.'

'How could I ever forget?' he said. 'That picture won

me a medal. It was the beauty of the models that did it, of course.'

That made Mary Jane giggle even more.

The first few weeks of August seemed to pass very fast. Sometimes I'd get a great tightness in my stomach that brought a terrible homesickness. It came when I thought about my mam and Alice and the bairns, but the work was so hard that there just wasn't time to sit and fret about it, and at least I saw that our Robbie was safe and well.

It was the last week in August when the change came. The catches were down and there were a lot of anxious folk about. We all stood to lose from poor catches; the dealers, the curers, the fishermen, the coopers and the gipping girls. Then we had four terrible days, one after another, when the catch was downright poor.

Everyone was thrown into despair. The dealers were talking of giving up and moving down to Grimsby. The fishermen's wives were most upset at that; if the fleet moved south so early, the herring girls and coopers would have to follow them and they'd lose the rent money that they got as landladies. I was fearful, for I knew I'd be ashamed to go back to Sandwick Bay with such a small amount of money to show for my efforts.

'Aye. It's not like it used to be,' Rachel told me. 'It's all fading away. There were summers when I were a lass that the herrings were so plentiful we didn't need the bridge to get us across Whitby Harbour.'

I must have looked puzzled for Rachel laughed. 'We

didn't need the bridge see, there were so many boats all crowded into the harbour that you could cross the water just by stepping from boat to boat.'

'No!' said Mary Jane. 'Can that be really true?'

'I swear it's no lie,' Rachel told us. 'Folk just walked from one boat to another, especially at weekends. And there were days when the barrels of herrings were piled so high in Whitby streets that they had to put on special trains to carry them away. There were hundreds of wagonloads leaving for market every week.'

'Then why are the catches so poor now?' I asked.

'My husband swears that it's these big new steam trawlers, dredging up the herring young and making it hard for the small boats.'

Suddenly we were spending our days by the harbourside, watching the comings and goings, and the gansey that I was knitting our Robbie grew fast from my needles.

Fishermen stood around the harbour rail fretting and discussing the weather and the wind and the swimming of the shoals. The weather was hot, too hot some said. Too calm and still and heavy.

The Whitby men and those from Lowestoft were talking about fishing on Sunday to see if they could make up their losses. The Cornishmen were shocked at that and the Scotchmen didn't like it at all.

At last it was decided that the Cornishmen should hold a special prayer meeting in the Old Primitive Methodist Chapel, and it was agreed that there'd be no more talk of Sunday fishing till after the service.

We were sitting on Tate Hill Pier that evening, doing our knitting and wondering whether we should attend the service or whether it were best left to the Cornishmen, when the picture man came wandering up the beach, carrying his heavy black camera box. He walked slowly and he seemed to be looking behind the rocks and peeping into the boat sheds.

'Have yer lost summat?' Nelly shouted to him.

He looked up at us and smiled, scratching his head.

'I know it's ridiculous,' he said. 'But I've lost my legs.'

We all giggled for he looked to have a fine pair of legs to us.

He laughed with us. 'Wooden legs, camera legs.' He chuckled. 'I swear that I left them somewhere near Tate Hill Pier, one day in spring. It was a dreadful day, poured with rain, and I stashed them somewhere meaning to come back for them.'

All of a sudden it came to me in a flash that I knew exactly where the camera legs were hidden. Rachel's clotheshorse that aired her washing by the fire had always looked somehow familiar to me. Now I knew why; it was just like the folding wooden camera legs that I'd helped the picture man carry so long ago in Sandwick Bay.

My mouth dropped open and my hand flew up to cover it.

'What's wrong?' Mary Jane asked. 'You look as if you've seen a ghost!'

'I know,' I said all blushing and excited. 'I know where

your camera legs are, sir, but I don't know what Rachel will say.'

I explained it to him and he looked amused.

'A drying rack, you say?'

We all got up then, smiling about it, and we led the picture man back to Henrietta Street. Rachel herself was there, just finishing the whitening of her doorstep.

'There y' are,' she said, and she bobbed to the picture man. 'I've a kettle just boiling,' she told him. 'Won't you come in and take a cup of tea, sir. I were just making some for the lasses.'

'That's most kind of you,' he said, and we all trooped into Rachel's kitchen, and sat ourselves down. There, in front of the fire, was the strange drying rack with a couple of Rachel's petticoats slung over it to air.

The picture man clearly recognised his camera legs, and he nodded at me and smiled while Rachel made the tea. Then we all sat there, chatting on about the lack of herrings, while we sipped at our tea and waited for the picture man to mention the drying rack.

At last he got up to go and he'd still said nothing to Rachel about it. I was puzzled as to what to do when Mary Jane came to the rescue.

'Rachel,' she said. 'He don't like to tell you, but the gentleman has lost his camera legs, and there they are in front of the fire, airing your petticoats.'

'What!' Rachel went quite red and flustered.

'Pray don't upset yourself, dear lady,' the picture man said. 'I don't need them after all, and you have found such a good use for them. I'd be pleased if you'd keep them.'

'Oh heavens!' said Rachel, crossing the room and whisking her petticoats off the wooden camera legs. 'Why ever did I not realise? I found them down by Dryden's boatshed. I thought the tide had washed them up. I was sure I'd find a use for them for they're made of good strong varnished wood.'

'And you have found a use for them. As good a use as I. I'd be delighted if you'd keep them now.'

Rachel hesitated just for a moment, then she firmly folded up the camera legs and handed them to the picture man, smiling comfortably now.

'You take them back,' she said. 'For I can air my petticoats on any old piece of wood, but you need these to fix up that camera of yours.'

He took them then, and thanked her for the tea, and went off happily down Henrietta Street. We laughed when he'd gone.

'I thought he were never going to take them,' said Mary Jane.

'Ey dear,' said Nelly. 'He's a daft 'un. Fancy not wishing to tek his own belongings.'

'Not daft,' said Rachel. 'Not daft at all. He's what I call a proper gentleman.'

Chapter Thirteen

We went along with Rachel and her husband to the service, but we could not even get inside, the chapel was so crowded. We stood out on the street and joined in the singing. The Cornishmen were in good voice and we sang for all we were worth.

My eyes filled up with tears as the service finished with the hymn my dad loved best of all. I remembered how he used to bellow out the words in his deep voice at the back of our small chapel in Sandwick Bay, so that folk turned round to look at him, and Mam would stick her elbow in his side to quiet him a bit.

The powerful words and music poured out of the small chapel and filled the streets and alleyways.

Will your anchor hold in the straits of fear,
When the breakers roar and the reef is near;
While the surges rave, and the wild winds blow,
Shall the angry waves then your bark o'erflow?

We have an anchor that keeps the soul,
Steadfast and sure while the billows roll;
Fastened to the rock which cannot move,
Grounded firm and deep in the saviour's love!

As we walked back to Henrietta Street, it turned cooler and a chilly wind started to blow.

'Well, let us hope all that singing and praising does some good,' Rachel said, and I silently echoed her prayer.

David Welford sniffed at the wind. 'This breeze comes off the heather,' he said. 'A good north-westerly, I swear. Maybe these Cornishmen know what they're about.'

'Well,' said Mary Jane. 'I've never known prayers answered fast as that.'

The wind grew strong, and the town was filled with excitement. Some of the herring boats put out to sea at once, though others hesitated, fearing it might turn into a gale.

As the blast grew stronger and the sea rough, the herring drifters that were anchored out in the sea roads ran for the safety of the harbour. The tide was on the turn and it would not be long before the shallow water would make the harbour entry difficult. We wrapped our shawls around us tight, and stood up on the cliffside watching them.

'By the heck!' David Welford said. 'When these Cornishmen sing up a storm, they don't muck about.'

As dusk fell, two luggers and three of the coble boats that had bravely gone out to sea as soon as the wind rose were seen heading back through rough water.

We ran along to the cliff ladder to see them better.

Mary Jane clutched my arm. 'Dear God!' she cried. 'Look at that!'

The sea swilled through the space beneath the cliff ladder with a violent force even though the tide was going out. The luggers made the harbour safely, and the three cobles following came steadily towards the welcoming outstretched arms of the harbour. The small boats were tossed fiercely as the waves grew, it was hard going for them, we could all see that, and I clenched my fists up tight as we watched them.

'Can we not do summat!' I said.

Suddenly a rocket was fired on the far side of the harbour.

'See!' cried Rachel, pointing to the beach beyond the West Pier. 'Thomas Langlands has set the lads to launch the life boat.'

'Aye,' her husband had to shout, for the wind snatched his voice away. 'They've got a job on mind. I wonder whether to go to help. They'll be done by the time I get round there.'

'You stay put,' Rachel told him firmly. 'They've plenty

o' lads, and look – they're already off down the slipway.'

We watched from the very point where the ladder joined the cliff as they hauled the lifeboat over the sand and out into the rough sea.

The men who pulled on the ropes were up to their waists in swirling water.

'Ah,' David sighed, as the boat breasted the waves. 'They're off! He's done well, has Thomas.'

I was frightened standing out there, so near the cliff edge. The force of the wind drummed away behind us, pushing us closer to the edge at every blast, but I couldn't get back till we'd seen the cobles safely in.

The lifeboat stood by, and a cheer went up from the great crowd of watchers that had gathered as the first coble reached the safety of the harbour mouth. But almost at once a dreadful groan came from all around, for the two following cobles had been knocked sharply off-course as two cutting waves collided and rose high into the air. For a sickening moment both the boats were lost to our sight.

I cried out loud and grabbed tight hold of Mary Jane's shoulder. 'Are they over?'

'Nay,' she said. 'But they're like to be.'

Then we saw them again, both boats driven behind the great bulk of the East Pier close below us.

'The rocks!' David Welford cried. 'They'll run aground. They cannot get the lifeboat round here, too shallow by far. We'll have to drag 'em off, Rachel.'

And with that he was leaping down the precarious cliff

ladder, over the water that crashed through the gap and down to the pier.

'Fetch all them lassies from Trickey's house!' Rachel shouted to us. Then she hurried after her husband.

'I'll get them,' Nelly cried.

'Come wi' me,' Mary Jane bellowed and snatched at my arm. 'They'll be needing a great gang.' Then she turned to run down the cliff ladder after Rachel.

I heard cries, shouts, and the sound of running feet behind me. People were pounding their way up Henrietta Street and heading for the ladder; they'd seen the need for help. I was terrified, but they'd be needing plenty of us if there were any hope of dragging the boats away from the rocks and keeping the coblemen out of the wretched sea.

I stepped onto the wooden ladder and made myself move forward, though it rocked with the fierce wind. Then I froze as I looked down at the drop beneath and the sea that roared and slavered below me like an angry starving beast. I must move on, for folk were coming up fast behind me and I could be thrown over the side in the panic and rush, but the drop was so deep and the sea so wild that terror gripped me. It was Rachel that made me move. I think she'd seen that I was stuck, all iced-up with fear.

'Dory!' she cried. 'Get down here now! It's the *Louie Becket*! We need you!'

That was it! That did it! Our Robbie was on that boat. I couldn't leave Robbie to be tossed into the sea, or crushed on those rocks. I stepped forward and, though the ladder seemed to swing wildly, I stared ahead through the gloom and the gale, making myself walk on till at last I stepped out onto the solid slabs of the pier.

David Welford had managed to snatch up a rope that they'd thrown from the *Louie Becket*. He handed it to Rachel, and then went teetering on the edge of the pier to catch a rope from the second boat.

'Help me!' Rachel shouted, lurching towards the pier side, dragged by the weight of the boat and the strength of the waves.

We ran! Mary Jane grabbed at the rope and I clung onto Rachel, gripping her round the waist. I caught a glimpse of our Robbie's white face below us. He was clinging to the side of the boat.

'Never fear,' Rachel bellowed in my ear. 'I can see 'em both. The old feller has him by the braces.'

All I could do was cry out stupidly. 'It's me as stitched those braces.'

'Let's pray you stitched 'em well,' said Mary Jane.

We struggled to hang on tight for what seemed like ages, but at last when Trickey arrived with Jeanie and the other Scotch girls, we knew that we'd enough help to keep the rope safe, and we started to haul the coble towards the cured tip of the pier.

As we rounded the tip we had to be careful and listen well to David, who told us when to pull and when to stop, for we'd so many folk on the pier all heaving and hauling that we were in danger of falling into the sea ourselves.

The old lifeboatman and his men kept the *Louie Becket* clear of the stone pier with their oars. Robbie was grinning and yelling with excitement, while the plosher pitched and tossed in the darkening water. I don't think he knew what danger he was in.

When at last we had the *Louie Becket* safe inside the harbour, I ran straight up the cliff ladder without a thought and down to the sands where people had gathered to help the men out. I ran to them, careless as to whether the second coble was saved or not.

Once we'd got them safely up to Henrietta Street, Rachel and Trickey flung open their warm kitchens to the drenched fishermen. Robbie and the old feller were soon sitting by our fireside, wrapped in warm dry blankets sipping broth.

I hugged my brother, while he grinned at me.

'Oh Robbie, I was so scared.'

'Aye,' said Mary Jane. 'All she'd do was fret about your braces.'

'Now Robbie,' the old fellow chuckled, and wiped the broth from his beard. 'I've always said braces is unlucky on a fishermen, but it seems yours have saved your life.'

Though the storm carried on and the noise of the wind wouldn't let us sleep, Rachel sent us off to our beds, saying that Robbie and the old feller must stay till morning. We lay there whispering restlessly until a great crash and the sound of splintering wood sent us jumping out of our beds in the early hours. We ran to the small window near my bed and stared out through the dim light of dawn. The wind had dropped, but we could see the great mast of a ship, tilted to the side, down beyond the pier. Again a loud cracking sound was heard and the mast juddered. It was clear that another ship had run aground.

'Rachel, Rachel,' we called. 'We must go down again. There's men will need help.'

'Nay,' Rachel shouted to us, coming into our room fully dressed with a bucket in each hand. She laughed and shook her head. 'They don't need saving. Thomas Langlands and his crew have got them off and they're safe ashore. It's the ship breaking up that's banging and cracking so, and she's a collier. Now you know what that means, don't you, lasses?'

We all three smiled broadly. 'Free coal!'

'Right,' said Rachel. 'Are you fit to help us then, for they'll all be down . . . fast as you can say knife?'

We flung on our clothes and Rachel handed out buckets and baskets and sacks, but though we'd not wasted any time, we found that half of Whitby was down there by the rocks, slipping and sliding and grubbing about, up to their waists in blackened water.

All through the morning we clambered over the rocks picking up lumps of wet coal. By noon there was not a scrap of it left, though there were damp black trails all through the streets and alleyways, and folk with smeared faces, and hands and arms and aprons. Bairns carried baskets of coal through the streets to their grannies and everywhere there were smiling faces.

'They say God works in a mysterious way,' said Rachel with a laugh. 'We ask for fish and he gives us coal. Now we've hope of keeping warm next winter.'

The shiny black stuff was as good as lumps of gold, and whether the Cornishmen had sung up a storm of fishes or not, everyone was glad.

When the fleet set off that evening, there was a good crowd down on the pier to watch them go, with a steady westerly wind behind them. I stood there waving to our Robbie as he passed in the *Louie Becket*.

'Oh, I wish he wasn't going,' I said. 'Not after last night.'

Mary Jane shrugged her shoulders. 'It's their last chance,' she said. 'The dealers will surely go, if there's no better catch in the morning.'

We slept well that night, for the wind had dropped and we were exhausted with all the upset and excitement that we'd had. Next morning we were up early and waiting hopefully at the farlanes before ever there was any sign of the boats coming in.

The dealers were restlessly walking up and down Pier Road, and the coopers and gippers all there and ready to work. At last there were shouts from the pier, and the sound of cheering. Most of the folk went running off down towards the harbour mouth.

'We should stay by the farlanes and wait,' said Nelly.

'I'm not,' said Mary Jane.

'I can't wait,' I said, and hurtled off after her down

towards the pier, pushing my way through the crowd.

There was a fine sight, all the drifters heading steadily back to harbour, mobbed by gangs of hungry herring gulls that wheeled and whimpered above them. One of the Whitby ploshers led them all.

'Look,' Mary Jane yelled. 'Look it's the *Louie Becket*.'

I screamed out loud, bursting with pride, for there was our Robbie standing in the bows, up to his knees in a huge pile of gleaming herrings.

'Robbie! Robbie,' we yelled, jumping up and down.

'Look, Dory!' he shouted. 'Silver darlings! Hundreds of 'em, thousands of 'em.'

Chapter Fourteen

We had to run back fast to our farlanes then, for we'd be sacked if we were not there when the coopers came to fill them up.

It was a wild day that followed, what with dealers competing for the fish and the prices going up and up and us gipping for ever. The farlanes were piled high like I'd never seen them, and the smart visitors came down the steep pathways to gawp at us. They milled around, asking daft questions and getting in our way.

Though we were already tired by noon, there was such a spirit of rejoicing that I could not feel miserable. It was a warm sunny day and as we worked the fish seemed to fly through our hands. Glints of deep purple and blue glanced up into our eyes from the pattern of black diamonds on the herrings' backs, while the bright midday sun caught their creamy white underbellies, making them gleam with rainbow lights like mother of pearl.

'Treasure . . .' I murmured.

'Treasure all right,' Nelly agreed with me for once. 'Good as silver coins these are.'

I went into a waking dream, my hands working of their own accord, not noticing any more the strong oily smell of fish and the dark red blood of the guts that spattered my face and arms.

When dusk fell we'd still got our farlanes piled high, and the fleet had set out to try their luck once more. George and the other coopers set up oil lamps between the farlanes so that we could see as it grew dark.

It started to rain and though we got soaked to our skins, still we gipped the herrings.

'How long must we go on?' I begged Jeanie.

'We've tae work till we've done, lassie,' she told me.

It was then that exhaustion really hit me, I felt as though someone had been beating me over the shoulders, leaving me bruised and sore. I looked down and saw properly just what I stood amongst. My father's best sea boots were deep in fish guts so that I could not see them clear, my apron the same, and my arms crusted up to the elbows. Nelly stood beside me, crusted and filthy, steadily gipping away.

'Oh Jeanie,' I said. 'I cannot do it. I cannot gip another fish.'

'Ye canna stop noo, lassie,' she told me cheerfully.

'Keep going, and we'll have a bit of a sing, tae cheer us. Turn the lamps up, George!'

The warm golden glow lifted my spirits, though the sooty smuts from the smoking lamps blew into our faces. Jeanie got us singing fast and loud.

> *'Halibut for the swanky squire,*
> *Haddock for his wife,*
> *Cod is for the parson,*
> *Mackerel for long life.*
>
> *Ling is for the fishermen,*
> *Fishead stew for free,*
> *But the bonny salted herring,*
> *Is the only fish for me!'*

We all joined in, smiling and laughing. The rhythm and the tune seemed to help us and, as our voices grew loud and rough, we gipped faster than ever.

> *'Oh, we are jolly herring girls,*
> *A-salting all day through.*
> *We salt the silver darlings,*
> *And we'll do the same to you.*
>
> *Oh, we are jolly herring girls,*
> *A-gipping all day through,*
> *We gip the silver darlings,*
> *And we'll do the same to you.*

Oh, we are jolly herring girls,
A-pickling all day through.
We pickle the silver darlings,
And we'll do the same to you.'

The singing finished with wild cheers and screaming.
At last, with thick darkness gathering around the glow of
our oil lamps, we could see that we were coming to the
end and emptying our farlanes.

I can't remember the walk back to Henrietta Street,
though I seem to think that Rachel was with us. I think she
must have carried us back. What I do know is that we all
slept in our filthy clothes that night, glad of the bare rooms
and brown paper covered curtains. None of us washed till
the morning, and we didn't bother over-much then.

Next day the catches were up again, though not quite as
much of a miracle as the day before. Though we ached
and grumbled, everyone told us that the only way to get
right was to work on, and so we did. It was at noon that
day that we had a terrible bit of excitement.

The usual gang of visitors was gathering about to
watch us at work, and even the picture man had deserted
his studio to struggle through the crowd to make his
snap-shots. Then we saw Liza Welford, there with her
two charges.

'Liza! Liza!' Mary Jane shouted happily, though
she never stopped her packing. 'I thought the smelly
fisherlasses were forbidden.'

'Aye. So they are, but I don't care, I'm not missing this.'

That sounded much more like the Liza that we all knew. She stood at the back of the crowd, holding the little lass up to watch our work. The boy climbed up beside her, close to the harbour rail pulling at her and whining as usual, though I could see that Liza told him to get down.

I was glad that I paused just for a moment in my work to smile across at them, for it was then it happened and I saw it clearly. One minute the lad was there, scratching and hot in his expensive sailor suit, the next he wasn't, and all I could see was the space by the harbour rail where he'd been.

I dropped the herring that I was gutting and I screamed at the top of my voice.

'Liza! The lad! He's fallen in the water!'

George had been sprinkling our fish with salt. He looked up at me as I screamed and just for one moment he stared into my face with horror, then he turned about and I've never seen anyone move so fast. He cut straight through the pushing crowd, leaping up onto the harbour rail, and vanished from sight after the boy.

'George!' A great frightened bellow went up beside me from Nelly. Then everyone rushed to the harbour rail.

The tide was in and the water was cold and deep, but George had the lad by the collar of his suit. The child came up, choking and spouting dirty harbour water but George swam quickly to the nearest steps and they were both hauled out of the water by many willing hands. It was all over in a minute, and the big man was standing dripping on the quayside with the spluttering shivering lad in his arms.

'Liza! Where's Liza?' Mary Jane turned about, looking for her friend.

Though everyone else had stopped their work and rushed to the harbour side, Liza had not moved. She stood just where she'd been before, her face gone white as a ghost. She clutched the little lass so tightly that the bairn could scarce breathe, and she shivered as violently as though it were her, Liza Welford, as had been soaked in the water.

Mary Jane ran to her and threw her arms about her, fish guts and all.

'It's all right, love,' she told her. 'It's all right. The lad's as right as rain, just wet and fearful.'

George followed her, carrying the lad who coughed and spluttered, his lips gone rather blue.

'Show me where you're staying,' he said. 'I'll carry the lad to his home, for I'll have to stop my work to go and change.'

Liza just stared up at him, her eyes wide and wild.

'Let's get him back quickly, pet,' George touched her arm. 'Then he'll not take chill.'

Liza seemed to come to then. She nodded, and turned to show the way.

'Come now, lass, let's run.'

Mary Jane and I watched them go, reluctantly turning

back to our farlanes. It was only then that we saw that Nelly was bent double over the fish troughs, and Jeanie beside her, fishing fresh bandages from her pocket.

'What is it, Nelly?' we cried.

'The puir bairn's got a nasty cut,' Jeanie told us. 'Och, what a day we're having!'

Nelly straightened herself, but all the colour had drained from her face. Blood poured down form the base of her thumb.

''M all right,' she muttered.

Jeanie shook her head. 'I dinna call it right. Ye should go hame and get Rachel to clean it properly for ye.'

'What's happening here?' the foreman came to ask. 'Are you gipping herrings or what?'

He was answered by angry shouts and cries from all the Scotch girls.

'Can ye not see!'

'The lass has cut herself!'

'We'll work when she's taken care of and not before!'

The foreman sighed and Nelly picked up her knife.

''M all right,' she repeated, and snatched up a herring in the tightly bandaged hand and set about gutting it.

'I dinna like it,' Jeanie muttered, but she went back to her work and we all followed her.

We worked on for the rest of the day and Nelly seemed to recover well, her cheeks soon pink again. It was a long day and we gutted on through the dusk, cheered by the number of barrels we filled and the thought of the money that they'd bring.

Rachel clicked her tongue when she unwrapped Nelly's bandaged hand that night. The cut was deep and nasty, and Nelly flinched as Rachel cleaned it up and smoothed on Mrs Love's ointment.

I don't think any of us were surprised when we heard a hesitant knock on Rachel's door, quite late that night. We didn't leave our beds, we were too tired, but we heard Liza's stumbling miserable voice.

'I'm so sorry, Aunt Rachel.'

'Away inside, lass,' Rachel told her calmly. 'I know well enough what's happened. I've the bed place made up and ready for you.'

It was good to find Liza looking comfortable in her old clothes, knitting furiously by Rachel's fireside when we got back to Henrietta Street after work the next day. Rachel broke her rule and let us go up to the kitchen in all our muck just to see her for a while, though we'd to promise not to touch anything and not to sit down. Mary Jane was delighted to be back with her friend, though Liza was miserable. She kept going over it all and making herself feel worse and worse.

'How can I go back to Sandwick and tell my mam I'm sacked?' she said. 'How could I have let it happen?'

'I don't think it were really your fault,' I told her. 'I saw the lad. He wouldn't get down. He wouldn't do as he were told.'

'I shouldn't have taken him near the harbour,' Liza shook her head. 'Mam will be so shamed of me, and what will Miss Hindmarch think?'

'That lad had trouble coming to him,' said Nelly. 'He's maybe learnt summat.'

But Liza would only shake her head and sigh. 'I've lost more than half the wages I should've earned,' she said. 'Rachel says that I may stay for a day or two, but then I'll have to go home and face Mam. Do you know what they told me? That I was sacked for bringing him back, wet and smelling of fish! They didn't seem bothered about the danger, just the smell of fish!'

We could not help but smile at that, but Liza was tearful.

'How can Miss Hindmarch take me back as pupil teacher after this?'

'Why don't you write to her?' I said. 'You're good at writing, Liza.'

'That's a grand idea,' said Mary Jane. 'Write one of your beautiful letters to Miss Hindmarch and tell her all about it. It can't make things worse.'

'Aye,' said Liza, thoughtfully. 'I'll maybe try.'

The catches stayed good for the rest of the week and we worked like beasts. I think it was just the happy thought of the money that kept us going. Nelly gipped as steadily as ever, with her cut hand all bandaged up. It seemed to bother George.

'What made your knife slip, Nelly?' he asked. 'You're as grand a gipper as any I've known. Was it the shock of the little lad falling?'

'Aye,' said Nelly, blushing. 'That were it.'

Mary Jane grinned saucily at me. We both knew well what it was that had made Nelly go and cut herself, and it wasn't that spoilt little lad.

Chapter Fifteen

Towards the end of the week, we began to worry about Nelly. When Rachel tended the cut hand each night, she shook her head at the puffy swollen flesh that was revealed.

'The curer's salt won't let it heal,' she said. 'It eats into the wounds, does that salt. I don't like the look of it, Nelly. You'd do best to let the doctor see it.'

'I'm not working like this to spend my money on doctor's bills,' said Nelly.

'Why not rest for a day and let Liza go in your place.'

'She can't gip,' Nelly was stubborn. 'None of them can gip like me.'

Though she didn't look at all well, we couldn't disagree with that. None of us could gip like Nelly.

We'd another good catch on the Saturday, and I was standing up at the farlanes in the hot midday sun. Nelly worked beside me, but she'd gone very quiet.

'Are you all right, Nelly?' I asked.

Beads of sweat covered her face, and her cheeks had turned red. The look of her frightened me.

'Nelly?' I said. 'Are you sick?'

There was no answer, though she carried on gipping.

Then, all at once, the colour drained from her face and she keeled over, head first into the trough of herrings.

'George!' I shrieked, and he was there at once.

'Eh dear, eh dear . . . come on, lass!' he muttered, pulling Nelly out of the trough. She was still senseless as he heaved her up into his arms. Both of them were covered with fish scales.

He carried her over the harbour rail. 'Give her some air!' he shouted, as people fussed around, curiously. I followed, trembling with the shock of it.

Jeanie dropped her gipping knife and rushed over to us. At last Nelly seemed to revive a little, but then her whole body took to shivering violently. She couldn't seem to stand or even speak, her teeth were chattering so.

'She shouldna be here,' Jeanie said, worriedly pressing the back of her hand to Nelly's flushed cheek. 'Take her straight back to her lodgings and see she's put to bed.'

'Aye,' George agreed. 'Come on now, pet.'

He put his arm round her waist, and set off towards the bridge, half-carrying the girl.

'Can he manage?' I asked Jeanie. 'She's a big lass.'

'Well, he's a big lad,' said Mary Jane. She'd left the packing and come to see what was up. 'I shouldn't laugh.' She giggled.

'Noo, ye shouldna,' Jeanie said, turning cross. 'Ye'll noo be laughing if it's the blood poisoning, and I fear it is.'

'Oh no,' I cried. I didn't like the sound of that and my eyes filled up with tears.

'I dinna ken how ye'll manage withoot her,' Jeanie rubbed it in.

We didn't know either, but we set to work again before the foreman noticed that we were short handed, both of us gipping together and taking turns to do a bit of packing now and then. Jeanie'd been right; we couldn't make half the speed that we'd had with Nelly and I despaired at the sight of the mountain of silver fish in front of me.

'Where's George?' Mary Jane complained angrily. 'It's never taking him all this time to find Henrietta Street.'

Suddenly tears poured from my eyes, I couldn't stop them, and my hands would not stop shaking as I tried to gip.

'We can't do it!' I sobbed. 'We can't manage without Nelly!'

'Look at ye both,' Jeanie sighed, leaving her own farlane and coming to us. 'Bairns, both o' ye. Didna I say it. Dinna fret, shove up and make space for me. We canna have ye pickling these fish wi' salt tears.'

She set herself to gip our herrings at the speed of lightning.

'Oh thank you, Jeanie,' I said, knuckling the tears from my eyes and trying to get on.

She shook her head. 'I canna do it for long, lassie.'

It seemed ages before George came back, but when he did he brought Liza with him, already wrapped in Nelly's oilskin apron.

'Nelly's awful poorly,' she said. 'She's in a right state and Rachel's putting her to bed.'

'Oh, Liza,' I begged. 'Will you help us?'

'Course I will,' she said. 'But I'm not much good at gipping.'

'You soon will be,' said Mary Jane.

'Bless ye, lassie,' said Jeanie. 'Set her to do the packing, George. Now you two must gip like the wind.'

That night we found that Rachel had settled Nelly in the bed place in her kitchen, where she shivered and shook. Liza's belongings were dumped in our room.

We washed ourselves, then we went up to Rachel's kitchen to see if we could help. It was shocking to find our big strong Nelly weak as a bairn. She'd a rash on her cheeks and she was tearful, not at all herself.

'I'm sorry, lasses,' she kept saying. 'I'm so sorry.'

I'd never heard Nelly apologise to anyone. It made me feel quite sad to hear it. She seemed to go from burning hot one minute to shivering cold the next.

Rachel shook her head. 'It's as I've feared all along. The poison in that cut has got into her blood, and it's brought on a fever. She must rest and keep warm and quiet, and let me clean that cut each day. It's no good trying to gip with a wound like that.'

'So we'll have to finish the season without her?'

'Aye.' Rachel was firm about that.

'Well,' said Liza cheerfully. 'I came as a nursemaid, but it seems I'll go back as a herring girl.'

'Do you mind?' I asked her.

'Nay, Dory,' she put her arm about me. 'It's better far than going home in disgrace.'

On Sunday George came round to Henrietta Street and found us in a right taking. Sunday dinner and Sunday service was forgotten while we boiled up broth and herbs and brought bowls of fresh cooling water from the pump. None of it seemed to do any good; Nelly thrashed about in a high fever, shouting out at Rachel and calling for her mam. She stared wildly about her, knowing none of us, two hectic red patches on her cheeks.

Rachel was shaken from her usual calm. 'I'm thinking Nelly should have the doctor,' she told George. 'Though she swore she would not. She keeps crying out for her mam, and I'm wondering if we should send for old Mrs Wright.'

'Nelly shall have the doctor whether she likes it or not,' said George angrily. 'I shall fetch him, and I shall pay him too.'

'Will he come visiting on a Sunday?' I wondered, doubtfully.

'I shall make sure that he comes,' cried George.

He was back within the hour with the smart doctor who lived up on the West Cliff. The doctor was clearly annoyed to be dragged away from his Sunday dinner, but when he saw the state of Nelly, he spoke kindly and said we'd done right to call him. He sent George running round to the ice-cream man for ice to cool the fever. The doctor said it all depended on us keeping her calm and getting her to rest. He left a special mixture that he said would help.

George was the only one that Nelly would take notice of. While he sat beside her, holding her hand and murmuring gentle words, she'd be still and quiet; but as soon as he moved she'd grow wild again. Poor George sat there all night. In the morning we were relieved to find that she was sleeping peacefully and Rachel was hopeful that the worst was over.

Through the next weeks we worked on at the gipping with Liza in our team. First she did most of the packing, but gradually she began to work at the gipping, and I was very proud to find myself teaching her how to gut a herring. She picked it up quickly and, by the start of October, Liza was as fast as me and Mary Jane.

'Oh, Liza,' I said. 'We're missing school now, aren't we. It don't matter for me and Mary Jane, but what will Miss Hindmarch do without her pupil teacher? Did you write that letter?'

Liza shrugged her shoulders. 'Aye. I wrote it, but I've heard nowt. I'm sure Miss Hindmarch will have had such bad reports of me that I can never face her again.' Liza sighed and smiled. 'At least my dad has told me that he's proud to see me gipping with the other girls and he says that he's explained it all to Mam.'

Each evening George walked back to Henrietta Street with us to see Nelly. He examined the cut hand each day, saying that he'd seen many a nasty cut in his work, but few as bad as that one. Once she was up and gaining strength, Nelly would walk slowly down to Tate Hill Pier with him, and they'd sit there together, watching the busy harbour.

As the days passed, the work became more patchy and the catches dwindled. There'd be a bad day, and the drifter men would talk of moving down to Grimsby; then they'd have three days of decent fishing and they'd be cheered. All the talk was of the herring movement.

'They're taking off,' David Welford told us.

'Aye, for sure,' Rachel agreed. 'The time has come, they're taking off; they're swimming south.'

The Lowestoft men set off for East Anglian waters to chase the black noses, as they called the autumn fish that they caught down there. The Cornishmen stocked up their boats in readiness to follow them.

In the third week of October the dealers went, and the foreman told us that we'd be paid off at the end of the week. The Scotch girls were packing their kist boxes ready to take the train down to Grimsby, though some of them were going as far as Yarmouth and Lowestoft. We'd to top up the last lot of barrels on Saturday, then we were done.

When we got back to Henrietta Street on the Saturday afternoon, Rachel called us up into the kitchen, and said we'd got a visitor. There, sitting by the fireside, sipping tea from Rachel's best china, was our own Miss Hindmarch.

We were so surprised that all we could do was stare at her. She laughed and got up and kissed us all; she didn't seem to mind the smell of fish.

'I'm sorry, so sorry,' Liza stammered. 'I know I've let you down.'

'Oh no,' Miss Hindmarch told her. 'I think it's quite the other way. I got your letter and I got another letter, too. My friend the photographer wrote to me. He told me how patient you'd been with that awkward little boy, and how dreadfully the child behaved when you visited his studio. How he'd grabbed at all the photographic plates and poked his fingers into the chemical jars. No, I think it's me that let you down, Liza. The family were not at all what I'd thought, and the little boy was quite clearly pampered and spoilt. Now will you forgive me, and come back to Banktop School? I am missing my pupil teacher very much. Indeed, I cannot manage without you.'

'Of course I will,' Liza smiled happily.

Robbie came running down to Henrietta Street, all excited that he'd got his pay.

'I can't wait to get home and give it to Mam,' he told me. 'The old fellow says he's taking me back to Sandwick in the *Louie Becket*. He'll take you too, Dory, if you wish. He wants to visit Mam, he insists on it.'

'That's right kind of him,' I said.

Me and Mary Jane and Liza went to the railway station with Jeanie's gang to see them onto the Yarmouth train.

'Well noo, we're going to miss ye Yorkshire lasses, that's for sure,' said Jeanie, hugging us one by one. 'Will ye nae come doon for the herringing next year?'

'Aye. We'll come again,' we told her.

When we got back to Henrietta Street, we found George and Nelly sitting together on Rachel's step, Nelly's arm comfortably linked through his. Nelly was looking well again, due to Rachel's careful nursing.

'George is off tomorrow,' Nelly told us, smiling hugely.

'No need to look so pleased about it,' Liza said.

'But then he's coming back,' Nelly blushed.

'Oh! Do you mean . . . ?' Mary Jane for once didn't know how to ask.

'Aye,' said George. 'I'm fixed to work till Christmas, but then I'll be coming back up north. I'll be calling in at Sandwick Bay and I'm hoping that me and Nelly will be wed.'

I threw myself at Nelly then, hugging her for all I was worth. She looked surprised and pleased. I truly wanted her to be happy.

'You'll make a right couple, you two will.' Mary Jane smiled at them. 'Are we to be bridesmaids, then?'

'Can be, if yer like,' Nelly looked coy.

It wasn't easy to share out the money that we'd earned. Mary Jane and I agreed that Nelly had a right to claim more than us, as she's carried us for the first few weeks. But Nelly was full of joy and kindness.

'Fair shares, fair shares,' she insisted. 'Liza and me shall split the third between us.'

The payment that I got seemed a fortune to me, and Mary Jane had enough for a decent organ.

So the herring season came quietly to a close, and the Whitby men turned to bait their long lines once more, and braced themselves for the winter gales.

Epilogue

On a chilly afternoon in late October, we set out of Whitby harbour in two ploshers, dressed in our best clothes, heading for Sandwick Bay. I was so proud of Robbie, a proper fisherman he looked, wearing the new gansey that I'd just finished knitting in our special Sandwick pattern that we call the waves and herringbone. I went with him in the *Louie Becket*, and Liza, Nelly and Mary Jane followed in the *Esther Welford*.

I'd been worried about the journey, for when we'd come to Whitby in July, the choppy water had made me feel thoroughly sick. I'd almost wondered whether to insist on riding home in the carrier's cart, but then I reminded myself that as Father was a fisherman and I was now a herring girl, I should be shamed. I needn't have worried; the sea was calm, the water like silk, and as we turned towards our bay the sun came out from behind grey clouds and lit up a silver shining pathway before us on the water.

It seemed that half the village was expecting our arrival, for there were all the Welfords down on the staithe to greet us, and Miriam and Alice and Nelly's old mother, Mrs Wright.

'Mam, Mam,' Nelly shouted at the top of her voice. 'Mam, I'm getting wed.'

'Now, young Dory. Don't you go splashing in the water, and getting your good frock all wet,' the old lifeboatman told me kindly. He jumped into the water himself and lifted me out.

I ran to Miriam and Alice.

'Lord! I swear you're taller than ever, Lanky Dory,' Alice squealed and I hugged her tightly, happy to be called Lanky Dory once again.

'How's our mam?' I begged Miriam.

'Well, you can go and see for yourself.' Miriam laughed.

'She's there!' Robbie yelled beside me, pointing to the stone blocks that we used as seats outside the lifeboat house.

'Aye,' said Miriam. 'She's insisted on walking down the bank to greet you.'

'What? She can walk?'

'She can. But it's slow and hard work for her. Go and see.'

We both ran over the staithe to Mam, slowing a little as we got close, both of us gone suddenly shy.

'Wel . . . come home,' she said. The words came slow and halting.

'Mam,' I cried. 'You can speak!'

She laughed and nodded. 'Yes. Speak a bit.'

She pushed herself up to her feet, and we both clung tightly to her, laughing and crying all at once.

Then we remembered the really important thing, and we brought out the money that we'd earned.

Mam began to cry, though I think it was happy tears.

'So proud of you . . . both,' she said slowly. 'Enough to . . . see us right through to the spring.'

'Now Mam,' I said firmly. 'I don't want you to fret about money any more. Me and Robbie shall go to work with the herring fleet again next year, and I'm willing to wash and scrub right through the winter, so we'd better start taking in washing again.'

Mam shook her head, smiling through her tears.

'Whatever's got into our Dory?' Alice cried out, amazed at my bossiness. 'I thought you hated all that soap and water.'

'So I did,' I grinned at them. 'But it's all changed. I'm different now. I'm a herring girl . . . I can do anything!'

Acknowledgements

I would like to thank David Pybus for help and advice and kindly sharing his knowledge of the history of alum working and the Whitby area; also Thomas W.V. Roe for information about the Grape Lane riots.

I would also like to thank The Sutcliffe Gallery, 1 Flowergate, Whitby, North Yorkshire for permission to use images from Frank Meadow Sutcliffe's photographs.

'Bread on the waters' by Joe Tomlinson, North Sea fisherman, is a quotation from Dora Walker's book, *Freemen of the Sea*, published by A. Brown & Sons Ltd, 1951.

The Nagars of Runswick Bay by J.S. Johnson, (Runswick Bay Publications) provided useful information on the customs and traditions of a Yorkshire fishing village and an understanding of how the lifeboat might have been launched.

THERESA TOMLINSON spent her childhood on the north-east coast of England and grew to know the area well, travelling round with her mother and her father, who was a vicar, so that her fascination for that part of the world took root early in her life. The original idea for *The Flither Pickers* and *The Herring Girls* came from the photographs of Frank Meadow Sutcliffe on whom she bases the character of the Picture Man; the old life-boat-man is based on Henry Freeman, sole survivor of the 1861 Whitby lifeboat disaster; and Mrs Dryden Smith – Trickey – was a real fisherwoman who lived in Henrietta Street and was well-known for her crafty ways. Mary Linskill was a Victorian Whitby writer.

Over the years Theresa has acquired an outstanding reputation for her novels – she has been twice short-listed for the Carnegie Medal and twice for the Sheffield Book Award.

Recent visits to Turkey have sparked her imagination to research the ancient world of Troy and have resulted in two powerful novels of the Amazon women – *The Moon Riders* and *Voyage of the Snake Lady*.

Married, with three grown-up children, she and her husband have returned to live in Whitby, coastal setting for the three absorbing novels which comprise *Against the Tide*.

THE FORESTWIFE

TRILOGY

THERESA TOMLINSON

A powerful retelling of the ROBIN HOOD STORY

Who will champion the poor against
injustice and cruelty?

When fifteen-year-old Mary flees into the forest to
avoid a fearsome marriage arranged by her uncle, she
little knows what challenges lie in store for her as the
wise and magical Green Lady of the Woods.

In this action-packed and gripping saga,
Theresa Tomlinson breathes new life into the story
of Robin Hood by focusing attention on the women
who live with the outlaws; women who pull a
bowstring and stand up against the cruel laws
of Medieval England.

'A vigorous and powerful story' TES

CORGI
0 552 55034 5

THE
MOON
RIDERS
THERESA TOMLINSON

An epic novel of triumph and tragedy

'At last they emerged from the rising dust. A great party of strong-armed young women, all on horseback, their eyes and body pictures gleaming in the torchlight.'

When young Myrina becomes one of the warrior priestesses known as the Moon Riders, she is well prepared to perform their sacred dances, hunt and fight when necessary. But when the visionary Trojan princess, Cassandra, joins them, events take a tragic turn. Myrina becomes her confidante and the Moon Riders are drawn into the drama of the siege of Troy.

Mysterious tales surround the exotic but little-known Amazon women. Theresa Tomlinson paints a fresh, intriguing background to an ancient story, combining her own drama with existing myths.

'An epic tale, well-researched, imaginative and interesting'
CAROUSEL

'Blends rich characters and strong emotions'
THE BOOKSELLER

CORGI
0 552 54910 X

VOYAGE
OF THE
SNAKE LADY

THERESA TOMLINSON

The dramatic sequel to THE MOON RIDERS

'I have seen them!' cried Cassandra.
'Iphigenia! Myrina and her young daughter!
They are in terrible trouble . . . taken prisoner
on a boat . . .stripped of all weapons.'

Some years have passed since Myrina reassembled the
Moon Riders after the fall of Troy. During that time the
brave warrior women have lived in peace. But now. once
again, Myrina's life is savagely disrupted, this time by
Neoptolemus, avenging son of Achilles.

Slavery, storm, shipwreck and strife plague Myrina, her
fate closely entwined with that of Iphigenia, daughter of
Agamemnon. Can she free them both and fashion their
destiny towards a more peaceful life?

'Thrilling, authentic, imaginative, original – very highly
recommended' *HISTORICAL NOVELS REVIEW*

'Inventive and fast-paced' *TEACHING & LEARNING*

CORGI
0 552 55163 5